Volume Two

Peter Varnicrast

Demon Healer Naberius: Volume Two
Peter Varnicrast

First Published in January, 2021
Cover art and closing illustration by Thanaphon
"Tostantan" Kaewmuangmun
Logo by S. Beltramo

ISBNs:
978-1-7352112-7-5 (EPUB), 978-1-7352112-8-2 (PDF),
978-1-7352112-9-9 (Mobi), 978-1-954588-00-4 (Paperback)

Table of Contents

DEMON ~~MAGE~~ HEALER
NABERIUS

Volume Two

Prologue

Shortly after being summoned to Rullia, Naberius made a list of everything she wanted to try while she was stuck in the mortal realm. From spending a day at the beach to eating every burger on Top 'N' Bottom's menu, the demon had plenty of the experiences she wanted to sample before returning to Hell.

However, there was nothing remotely close to "being surrounded by thugs in the dim office of a mob boss" on her list.

This is terrible… How did we get into this mess?

Naberius—nicknamed Nabby—was quaking in her boots. Despite being a member of Hell's elite Goetia, she came off as nothing more than an anxious young woman, mostly due to her abnormally humanlike appearance. Similarly, her adventuring gear covered her most demonic features, and the way she nervously gripped her white coat was a far cry from the expected viciousness of Hell's residents.

Conversely, her partner Lilibosa was as cool as an ocean breeze. She was a scylla—a humanoid possessing tentacles in lieu of legs—and the fact that she was dressed more for spring break than adventuring made her stand out in the office. Yet she carried herself almost as brusquely as the thugs, and she didn't even bat an eye when they locked the doors.

Hopefully that confidence wasn't just for show. Given the man before them, Nabby was praying Bosa knew a way out of this nightmare.

The mob boss could only be described as massive. He was tall and broad-shouldered, and sitting behind a desk did nothing to ease his intimidating aura. His pressed suit declared authority, unfettered by the red flower pinned to his jacket, and Nabby felt he looked scarier than any of his underlings, though there was no way she was going to say that out loud.

Silence pervaded the room as the boss took a long drag from his cigar, staring right through the demon. A millennium could have passed before he finally spoke.

"So. I hear you two are lookin' for some easy money. This true?"

"Yup," said Bosa.

"Well, y-yeah, b-but our situation isn't actually *that* bad!" Nabby hurriedly added. "W-we just completed a couple jobs, so things should be fine for now. A-and while more money is always nice, I don't think we—"

"Don't waste my time," he growled. "You wouldn't be standin' in my office if you weren't interested in what I've got to offer. You *do* know who I am, yeah?"

"Y...yes, Don Testa."

"And I take it you heard what it is I do in this city?"

"Y-yes."

"Good. Saves me some trouble." He gestured to the chairs in front of his desk. "Take a seat. Let's start our negotiations."

Nabby looked to Bosa, but the songstress simply shrugged before sitting down. The demon took her place on the cushionless chair, feeling the chill of the hardwood creep up her spine.

Don Testa took another puff of his cigar, then put it out in an ashtray. Savoring the smoke, he let out a long, slow exhale before leaning forward.

"You're here cuz of that job postin' I made on Parti, yeah?"

"N-not exactly!" squeaked Nabby. "We heard about the job from a fellow adventurer, so we didn't—"

"We were told you were expecting us."

Nabby cringed. Maybe Bosa thought the don would respect someone who didn't cave under his presence, but wasn't she laying it on a little thick?

Please, please, please—*tell me you know what you're doing...*

"Heh-heh, that's right. You two are here to replace the girls I *wanted* to hire. Sorry about that—runnin' an organization this big can make you lose track of the details."

"Sure," said Bosa. "We heard you wanted a private chat because the job you've got in mind isn't the same as what you advertised."

"Ooo, straight to the point. I like that in a girl."

"Glad to hear it. Care to explain what you've actually got for us then?"

While Bosa wasn't afraid to be flippant, the only thing flipping for Nabby was her stomach. They had agreed to take the job knowing full well the posting wasn't accurate, but after meeting the don in person, Nabby knew that that was a mistake. While he was allegedly running a "non-profit organization", it was clear he had something unpleasant in mind.

She began to search for an escape, careful not to draw attention.

"Don't you worry about that. It's easy work—perfect for a couple ladies," said Don Testa.

"Oh yeah?"

"Yeah. It's real simple and won't take any skills you don't already got. Might be a little tirin', sure, but I think you two'll enjoy it."

"Fantastic. But what if we're not interested?"

Bosa locked eyes with the don, staring defiantly at the much-larger man. The atmosphere somehow took on an even greater weight—only to be toppled by Don Testa's amused chuckles.

"Oh, trust me, this ain't an offer you can refuse. Cuz if you do—"

He reached into his jacket.

And pulled out a switchblade.

"—heads are gonna roll!"

The weapon in question was unusually large—likely to match its owner's stature. With a grin, he pressed on the release and revealed the blade. The concealed knife was just as long as its sheath, and it swung out in a terrifyingly wide arc.

An arc that passed right through Don Testa's neck.

"*Grk…!*"

The don's eyes went wide with shock. He dropped the knife and grasped at his throat.

Knocking his head loose from his shoulders.

Don Testa's head hit the desk with a macabre thud. It rolled forward and gurgled at Nabby as his body went slack in the chair.

The demon's scream would have put the eternally damned to shame.

Sansei-san
Dirt Bike

Job Four — Cardinal Mage

1

A month before Nabby blew out Bosa's eardrums, the scylla was in her home, thinking about how much she hated budgeting.

It was a pain in the ass. Coordinating her projected income and expenses for the coming month was both a chore and a grating reminder of how far she had fallen. Every tap on her phone's calculator added to her aggravation, and it didn't help that the numbers weren't looking good.

I know I'm not pulling in as much cash as before, but… For fuck's sake, I didn't think things had gotten this *bad.*

Granted, she wasn't solely responsible for her dismal situation either.

Seated together at the dining table in their one-bedroom apartment, Bosa and Nabby were sorting through a mountain of receipts. Nabby was smoothing out and organizing the crumpled pieces of paper while Bosa handled the math, and the two barely said a word as they went about their depressing business.

Bosa would have preferred to make Nabby figure out her own finances, but seeing as they shared the bills and the demon was impressively bad with money, it was better for her to manage both their accounts. It made budgeting even more obnoxious, but ensuring they'd still have electricity was worth the effort.

"…Adding a hundred a week for groceries—give or take fifty—along with power, water, internet, my school loan payments, and rent…" muttered Bosa. "Taken out of our combined income, we're…"

Nabby looked at her expectantly.

"…at least three hundred dollars over budget."

"What? How?!"

"Shit, this has gotta be wrong. Read me those receipts again."

Bosa was confident she hadn't made any mistakes, but if they were this fucked, she had to know for certain. She cleared her calculator and started over.

Bosa didn't think her estimates were unreasonable. Working as freelance adventurers through the Parti app meant they'd never be rolling in the dough, but they should have at least had enough to make ends meet.

Yet the numbers were falling short. Bosa would have expected this three weeks ago, when she had to empty her savings to cover not getting paid for *that priest's* bogus job, but she and Nabby had gone on a few gigs since then. Their finances should have stabilized by now.

Bosa finished tapping out her equation again. "Aaand— what the fuck? Now it says we're *four hundred* in the shitter!"

"Huh?! A-are you sure you didn't hit the wrong key?"

"*Nngh*, fuck it!" Bosa tossed her phone on the table and leaned back. "The exact number doesn't matter. Point is, we're screwed if we don't get some cash soon."

"I don't understand… I thought things would be better since Parti promoted me to Rank E…"

"Your rank doesn't mean squat if there aren't any jobs looking for a healer and songstress duo. But we wouldn't be in such a tight spot if you hadn't bought yourself all that shit to celebrate."

"Me?! *You're* the one who blew an entire paycheck on clothes and alcohol!"

"Shut up. You read those receipts—tell me again how many of them were for hamburgers. And if we're gonna start bitching about new clothes…"

One of Bosa's tentacles snaked its way over to Nabby and flipped her skirt up—revealing her official Sansei-san leggings.

"H-hey!" Nabby slapped the tentacle away. "I told you I really wanted a pair, a-and these were only available for a limited time!"

"Yeah, and they were overpriced as hell. Do you really think having that dumb cat's face on your legs warrants an eighty-dollar price tag?"

"*Sansei-san* is an icon of inspiration for people everywhere! Besides, your new top cost almost twice that!"

"My top—" Bosa froze mid-sentence. She wouldn't admit it, but Nabby wasn't wrong. "...Was made with genuine barometz wool?"

"So what?! You've got enough shirts to carpet the floor! You didn't need another one!"

"I needed to replace the one that got fucked up on our last job! Nobody mentioned those slimes were corrosive!"

"If you wore proper adventuring gear, it wouldn't have been a problem!"

"Oh? And I take it your kitty pants are 'proper adventuring gear'?"

"Better than those butt-floss shorts you wear!"

Sheesh. Looks like my lovely little demon is showing her fangs today.

Bosa shook her head. Fighting like this wasn't going to get them anywhere. The last thing they'd need is to be at each other's throats.

"Alright, alright," said Bosa. "I think we *both* messed up. Arguing won't solve anything, so how about a truce?"

Nabby opened her mouth to retort—only to let out a sigh. "Yeah... Truce. I'm sorry for snapping like that."

"Same. Sorry for trying to pin the blame on you."

With that, the situation was disarmed—leaving them free to ponder their financial straits in peace.

It was almost funny how Bosa ended up like this. Only a couple months ago, she was riding high as the internet's favorite adventuring idol. She was swimming in cash thanks to guys donating their paychecks just to see her videos a day early and even bigger suckers lining up for the privilege of joining her on Parti gigs.

Naturally, Bosa's ego inflated from all that easy success. And like a classic fable, a demon came along and sent her tumbling to her downfall.

Nabby's first job as an adventurer had her working with Bosa and her fans, and the demon's unique style of "drain healing" was uniquely irritating to Bosa. Midway through, Bosa pulled Nabby aside to try and force her to quit the job, and one of Bosa's fans quietly recorded the heartless things she said to the fledgling healer. It took only a few hours for that video to go viral, and since someone followed up that exposé by hijacking Bosa's social media accounts and posting all sorts of nasty shit under her name, her life as the Seafoam Diva was over before she knew it.

Not that she held it against Nabby, mind you. That same job saw Bosa nearly end up dinner for a giant tarantula, but even after their 'discussion', Nabby didn't hesitate to come to the scylla's aid. That alone caught Bosa's eye, but their bond was fully cemented when circumstances pushed them to become roommates. Bosa couldn't afford rent without her fans' support and Nabby needed a permanent home. It only made sense for them to become adventuring partners as well, forming a two-woman support cell.

And since that day, Bosa had come to realize just how much she hated pretending to be some airheaded idol for the masses. Adventuring might not be half as cushy, but to a degree, she was almost thankful her idol career got axed.

Because she was now free to be nothing but herself.

…Still miss all that easy money, though.

Bosa didn't completely give up on the internet goldmine, however. A couple weeks ago, she released an apology video in an attempt to win back some of her fans while simultaneously directing them to her new endeavors. She talked about how she wasn't really the bubbly idol she portrayed, why she snapped at Nabby, and what happened with her social media.

It went over about as well as she expected—so like a turd in the punchbowl.

Nobody believed Bosa's side of the story, and all her effort did was reignite her scandal. And considering her "new endeavors" were cam shows and an adult Batreon page, Bosa's former fans laughed at her for being so shameless.

As one of them put it, "she thinks she can just show her tits and erase what she did!"

But Bosa was satisfied with the attempt. Even if her apology video flopped, at least it was honest. She even allowed herself a bit of pride for not getting Nabby involved despite how the masses would have responded better to an appearance from the demon.

Now, if she could be just as satisfied with her cam shows…

Bosa thought being a camgirl in the evening would be an easy way to supplement her income, but she couldn't have been more wrong. The market was beyond brutal, and there were plenty of scylla already filling her niche. Add on the fact that faceless jackasses kept entering her chat just to talk shit and Bosa felt lucky to have two subscribers.

That lackluster success combined with how Nabby didn't do any side work left the two reliant on Parti gigs, and now even that had dried up. Nabby offered to start selling handcrafted clothes to staunch the bleeding, but the plan had to be scrapped since they didn't even have money for materials.

I did suggest selling her underwear instead, but she didn't seem half as keen on that idea.

So, at this rate, the two would either need to find a decent job soon, or Bosa was going to have to swallow her pride and beg her parents for money. And with how badly she wanted to avoid the latter, her standards for 'decent' were getting pretty loose.

"Any ideas for lunch?" Bosa asked, breaking the silence.

"Um... Well, since we cut back on grocery spending, we don't have a lot of...anything," said Nabby. "I think I might be able to make something like a casserole out of those old hot dog buns and the sauce packets, though."

"Are... Are you serious?"

"It's kinda the best I've got."

Bosa was torn between feeling impressed and disgusted. She knew Nabby was a talented cook who could make the most of even the worst ingredients, but there had to be a limit somewhere.

Maybe today they'd find it.

"Sounds delicious..." grumbled Bosa. "I'll comb through Parti again while you get started on that."

"Alright. But, while I know we're in a tight spot, please remember—"

"*Your class might be Mage, but you only want to do healer work*—don't worry, I know. But if I can't find us any gigs because of that, you're gonna join me in groveling at my dad's feet."

Nabby got up from the table and headed into the kitchen, tying on her apron. Bosa picked up her phone again and searched through Parti for the umpteenth time this week.

As expected, she didn't find any job offers waiting for her. Her next move was to scroll through the open gigs, but they lacked the qualifications needed for any of the new listings. Somehow there weren't enough sword-swinging dumbasses in need of a support duo.

But Bosa wasn't going to be so easily dissuaded. She loosened her search filters and dove back in. Worst case scenario, she and Nabby might end up taking separate jobs.

Sure enough, Bosa was finally able to find a gig looking for a songstress. She would have snatched it up in a heartbeat if the work weren't so reminiscent of one of the worst experiences of her life.

"…Hey, Nabby. There's another job looking for a songstress' help in taking down a lionwolf."

Nabby twinged at the prospect. "O-oh. Is that so…"

"Yeah. I'm pretty sure this one's legit, though. The customer says they'll handle all the fighting themselves and that they only need help tracking the lionwolf and putting it to sleep. Their offer is in line with what you'd pay a couple non-combat adventurers too."

"Hm. Is there any more information on the client?"

"Says here he runs an enchantment workshop, but there's also a link to his Parti profile." Bosa clicked through. "…What the fuck is a 'Cardinal Mage'?"

"Cardinal Mage? Is that his class?"

"Apparently. You got any clue what that means?"

"Not at all. But…the 'Cardinal' bit sounds *priesty* to me," Nabby said bitterly.

"Hmm… Information's pretty scarce on the internet too. There's nothing saying the class has any connection to the church, but also nothing saying it doesn't."

"You should just keep looking. I don't want to risk working with a priest again so soon—especially if it supposedly involves a lionwolf."

"I'd like to, but we're running out of options and this job pays enough to get us back on our feet. Besides, they're not looking for a healer, so I'll be going solo."

"What? B-but…"

Nabby frowned at Bosa. The scylla raised an eyebrow in return.

"What's the matter? You afraid I'm gonna find a new partner while I'm out there or something?"

"No, I just don't want you to go alone on what might be a dangerous job. I won't be there if something goes wrong…"

"Aw crap… Don't give me the puppy-dog eyes, Nabs. I did tons of gigs on my own before—it's no big deal. It's cute that you'd worry about me, but I'll be fine."

Seriously, cut it out. You'll make me second-guess myself.

"W-well, how about I go with you instead?"

"Aren't you sweet. You'd be willing to play with another priest for my sake, huh?" Bosa smirked. "But you can't. The customer needs someone who can track monsters, not a healer."

"Um... I might be able to help with that, actually."

"What? You're not bullshitting, are you?"

"Well, to be specific, *I* can't do any tracking. But I have some familiars who can!"

"Really? Why didn't you mention that right off the bat?"

"I never really considered using them to find monsters," said Nabby. "And...I thought you wouldn't like them."

"Who cares how I feel? If they're your ticket into this gig, then bust 'em out. I wanna see what kind of familiars a future Marquis keeps anyway."

"Understood!"

Nabby put the finishing touches on her "casserole" and slid it into the oven. She then pushed the coffee table away from the sofa to make space for a summoning.

Taking a deep breath, Nabby closed her eyes and muttered an incantation. A magic circle appeared on the floor in front of her and began to glow an infernal orange. At the conclusion of her chant, the circle flashed and hot air blew into the apartment, signaling the arrival of Nabby's hellish familiars.

As hellish as three dogs could be, that is.

Bosa stared at them incredulously. Nabby took that as her cue to begin introductions.

"This is Cerulean!" She gestured to the silver wolf that was stoically looking around the apartment with piercing blue eyes. "She's a Valhallan spirit wolf—a deadly hunter that silences her foes without mercy!"

Nabby then moved to her next dog: a massive, rottweiler-esque beast with black spines protruding from its back. It panted dopily as Nabby wrapped her arms around its neck.

"Next is Bergundy, my fearless guardian! He's a purebred hellhound that can trace his lineage back to Lord Lucifer's kennels!"

Bergundy took that opportunity to lick his master's face. Barely holding back a smile, Nabby continued to what appeared to be your average pug with a horn sticking out of its forehead.

"And here we have Rusty!" she declared. "A Dog of War given to me on my sixteenth birthday by the eponymous Horseman of the Apocalypse, he's…really soft and fun to hug!"

The small dog leered up at Nabby with something analogous to a frown. In fact, it looked like the pug had never been happy in his life.

"So, there you have it! Cerulean, Bergundy, and Rusty—the legendary hounds of House Naberius! With them at my side, I'm sure we won't have any trouble tracking down a lionwolf or any other monster!"

"…"

Bosa was at a loss for words. As the dogs began milling around the apartment, the silence became palpable. Nabby was soon hit with embarrassment, and her posturing turned timid as she looked at her friend with uncertainty.

"Um… Bosa?"

"…"

"B-Bosa…?"

"…Why…"

"Huh?"

Bosa glared at the floor in disbelief—before excitedly shooting out of her chair.

"Why did you think for a second that I wouldn't like them?!"

Without warning, she snatched Rusty off the ground and hugged him against her chest. The dog's face continued to look miserable, yet his tail wagged in betrayal.

Nabby was both shocked and relieved. "R-really? You like them?!"

"Of course I do! I love dogs—especially pugs!"

"Um, but Rusty's not a pug. He might be even-tempered, but he really is a Dog of War."

"Nah, he's just a *puggy-wuggy, wittle puppy!*" Bosa gave the small dog a big kiss. "Really though, what made you think I wouldn't like them?"

"I guess I thought you didn't like animals. You never mentioned having or wanting pets, so I assumed they weren't really your thing."

"Nabby, this apartment isn't big enough for pets. Frankly, it's a wonder I was able to fit you in here—especially since you turned down my generous offer to share the bed."

"Th-that wasn't my fault!"

"Though I guess the topic never really came up either. But now that I know you've got dogs on demand, I can get all the puppy love I want without worrying about where to keep them." Bosa paused. "Hey, where do they go when they're not summoned?"

"They live in my home back in Hell. One of my family's servants feeds them and stuff so I know they're being taken care of."

"Huh. But you can't use that summoning spell as a way of going home or talking to your family?"

The only reason Nabby lived with Bosa right now was because the summoning ritual that brought her to Rullia was half-assed, cutting off the demon's return to Hell. Apparently, her only way back now was to wait until a higher-ranked member of the Goetia recalled her, and while Nabby's mother had already petitioned one, it could be a long time before they actually brought her home.

And considering it's already been three months, I get the feeling she's gonna be my roommate for a while.

Nabby shook her head. "No, summoning magic doesn't work that way," she explained. "The spells are tied to the entities they transport, and God has forbidden demons from using them as a means of sending non-emergency messages."

"Well, that blows. Might've been nice to send a letter to your mom back with Rusty."

"Yeah. I hope she and Grandad aren't too worried. But the fact that I called upon my familiars should tell them that I'm still doing okay!"

"True. She'll at least know you haven't eaten shit out here." Bosa put Rusty back down and began running her hand through Cerulean's coat. "So, did you train these guys how to track monsters yourself?"

"Um, actually, they've never done any tracking before. But they're all way smarter than your average dog—Rusty in particular! He's able to understand pretty much everything I say and pass it along to Cerulean and Bergundy, so it won't be a problem."

"Hm. Can you demonstrate?"

"Sure." Nabby squatted next to the Pug of War. "Rusty, if it's not a problem, could I ask you to get Bergy to bring me one of the receipts off the table, please?" She notably refrained from pointing out the objects in question, likely to show just how sharp Rusty's comprehension was.

The little dog scowled at his master and sighed but did as requested. He approached Bergundy and jabbed the hellhound with his horn, yapping as he nodded towards the table. Bergundy then straightened up, plodded over to the receipts, and pulled one from the pile. He dropped the drool-soaked piece of paper in front of Nabby and awaited his praise.

"Thank you very much, Rusty!" she said as she patted Bergundy. The pug huffed in response.

"Well, I'll be damned—he's cute *and* smart. I'll let the client know we'll take the job right now."

Bosa took her phone out and quickly punched in an application. She almost had it back in her pocket before it buzzed with a notification.

Their client had already approved them.

In fact, he wanted to start the job in exactly two hours. *And* he was planning to pick the girls up at their apartment. *Fuck. There goes my confidence in this gig.*

"Hey, Nabs. Looks like the client's already taken our offer," Bosa said dryly.

"What? Didn't you just send it like two seconds ago?"

"Yep. Maybe he's just super eager, but let's stay on our toes. He says he's gonna come here and teleport us straight to the job site himself."

It was awesome that their client knew teleportation magic, but also unusual. Very few adventurers specialized in that school of magic because it had so little combat application, yet this customer had already promised to fight the lionwolf *on his own.*

"Bosa, I don't feel so good about this job anymore…"

"My gut's also saying something's up, but don't worry— the moment things look fishy, we'll bail. I'll also ask a friend to call the cops if they don't hear from me an hour after the job starts, so we'll be fine even if things get super fucked."

Bosa was probably being overly cautious, but after the situation with *that priest*, she wasn't going to take any chances. Even if that incident also proved Nabby was more than capable of protecting them both, Bosa had promised Nabby she'd never have to do so again.

Not after the way it left her feeling.

Thankfully, Nabby seemed satisfied with Bosa's precautions. "Okay. Then I guess it can't hurt to at least meet the client. I hope they're nice."

"Considering how badly we need the cash, I'll settle for 'not a complete asshole'. But between your dogs and my singing, our involvement is gonna be pretty minimal."

"Right. I don't even get to do any healing…"

"I still listed you as a healer on our application, so you'll get credited as such. But, if you like, I'll try and stub a tentacle while we're out there."

"Hey, don't go that far. But I appreciate that you kept my role in mind!"

The oven then dinged, signaling the "casserole" was ready. Seeing as introductions were over and the job wasn't for a couple hours, Nabby unsummoned her dogs before returning to the oven. Likewise, Bosa set the table and prepared her stomach for what could be a miracle or a nightmare.

The anomaly Nabby scooped onto the plates convinced Bosa it was the latter.

"...Nabby. Why does it look like colored cardboard?"

"I-I don't know. It looked a lot more foody before I baked it... It should taste fine, though."

Bosa poked at it with her fork while she waited for Nabby to try a bite of her own cooking. The demon didn't seem to love the taste, but she didn't spit it out either.

Grimacing, Bosa speared a chunk and gave it the slightest nibble.

...Corn flakes and salsa.

That was the best comparison she could make. It wasn't amazing, but it was edible.

Nabby really can make the most of anything...

2

Two hours later, Bosa and Nabby were waiting on the sidewalk near their apartment complex, decked out in adventuring gear and somehow unafflicted with food poisoning.

The weather was clear and the roads were quiet, giving Bosa the rare chance to appreciate how nice the neighborhood was. Despite being only a couple blocks from downtown, the area was mostly apartments, and the few nearby businesses were small and unobtrusive. Local landscapers kept all the greenery pruned and weed-free, giving the street a scenic appeal not found in the busier parts of town.

Which was probably why the rent around here was so fucking expensive.

Then again, every part of Ambarino is overpriced.

Bosa checked her phone. The client had specified their meetup to the minute, and they were about to hit his prescribed time. There wasn't anyone walking along the sidewalk, but considering their client knew teleportation magic, he was presumably going to warp himself nearby.

…Then again, now that Bosa thought about it, wouldn't that just complicate things?

She had only given him the address of their apartment complex, without saying where he could find them. Bosa figured hanging around the front door would work, but their client could have gone to the other entrance on the opposite side of the building. The parking lot was over there too, so—

"Hello."

The adventurers jumped as someone spoke behind them. Whipping around, they found themselves face to face with a tall garuda, still glowing with the residual magic of teleportation. He seemed both unsurprised and unashamed that he startled them.

He had the appearance of a songbird, with some of the red feathers cresting his head graying with age. He wore a long coat decorated with some sort of compass motif, but the tools on his belt and rolled up sleeves suggested he was a craftsman—meaning he was almost assuredly their client.

Bosa was about to chide him for scaring them, but the garuda spoke first, swiftly and without inflection.

"My name is Su Ling, and I can see you were expecting me," he said. "However, in the interest of clarity, I will confirm that I am the client who has hired you to aid him in hunting down a lionwolf. You are unquestionably Mikayla and Naberius, as your appearances match your profiles, and I appreciate that you have offered to lend me your respective abilities as a songstress and a healer, though I acknowledge that Naberius is in fact providing her tracking abilities today, which is likely much more fitting considering I have never seen a demon work as a healer previously. Regardless, your work records assure me that I have nothing to worry about and I am confident we will have no difficulty accomplishing this task. I will now teleport us to the area where the lionwolf was last seen."

"Wait, wha—"

"*Teleport.*"

Before Bosa could wrangle a proper explanation out of the man, he cast his spell.

In the blink of an eye, they went from gray city streets to the beige hills of god-knows-where. But considering the sky was now stained pink with an impending sunset, Bosa could at least deduce they had been zapped to the other side of the continent.

"Huh?! Where are we?!" fretted Nabby as she glanced around their new surroundings.

"An unclaimed zone sixty-three miles outside of the city of New Llork on the eastern coast of the Stately Union of Glanerica," Ling answered. And just as curtly, he began walking up a nearby hill. "Naberius, please begin searching for the lionwolf. I will see if I can spot any tracks from an elevated position."

"Hey... Hey, hold on! I wanna ask you a few questions first!"

Bosa ran after Ling, with Nabby right behind her. It would seem their client was in a hurry, but that didn't justify such a cold opening. Bosa was already unsure about this job—she was primed to hit the eject button now.

"What's the rush?" Bosa asked as she slid alongside the garuda. "You got a hot date after this or something?"

"No, but there is no reason to delay. Please begin tracking the lionwolf." Ling didn't even turn to look at them.

"C-can you at least tell us why you're hunting the monster? I'd feel a little more comfortable if I knew why you hired us," Nabby tried.

"No need. That information will not help you fulfill your responsibilities."

"Well, that's true, but... Then can you tell us more about your class—the Cardinal Mage? We've never heard of it before and—"

"Irrelevant. My abilities will not affect your work."

"Oh, *come the fuck on!*"

Bosa hit her boiling point. She grabbed Ling's arm, spun him around, and forced him to meet her furious eyes.

"You just pop in and drag us out to the middle of nowhere with barely more than a hello—I oughta knock you on your ass right now. But I'm gonna give you *one chance* to stop being a shithead before Nabby and I tell you to go fuck yourself. *Got it?*"

Bosa really hoped it wouldn't come to that—that would leave them stuck in the wilderness after all—but she couldn't let things continue like this. As loathe as she was to intimidate the guy who'd sign her paycheck, something had to give. She did all she could to make her threat feel legitimate as she glared at the taller man.

Ling looked back down at her—and let out a heavy sigh as his shoulders slumped.

"I-I-I'm sorry…" Like his body language, his tone crumpled from impassive to despondent. "Aw man, I'm really, *really* sorry! I-I know what I was doing was rude, but I… No, you've got every right to be mad. I'm so ashamed— I can't believe I just did all that to a couple young women to boot! Oh god, the fact that I just took you to some unpopulated area with barely any explanation must look terrible!"

"Huh…?"

Under other circumstances, Bosa would have thought she had accidentally grabbed Ling's timid twin brother. The sudden shift in his attitude threw her for a loop, and she fumbled to maintain her pressure.

"Uhh… I mean, y-yeah—you pissed us off," said Bosa. "You were being a huge asshole just a second ago and all…"

"I know—I'm really sorry for that! That side of me just gets so focused on the job that I forget about being considerate and… Augh—I'm just making excuses again! Please, I'm truly sorry about what I did!"

Ling suddenly plopped onto the ground, causing Bosa to let go of his arm. His head drooped with shame as he halfheartedly fiddled with the grass he sat on.

"Man… I'm such a big, fat jerk…" he muttered.

Bosa exchanged confused looks with Nabby. Neither one had a clue as to what was happening, but Nabby's soft heart couldn't ignore Ling's gloom. Her face wrinkled with concern as she knelt next to the old bird.

"H-hey, it's okay," she said. "Sure, you might have been acting rude a moment ago, but it's fine now. You don't need to keep beating yourself up about it."

"No, it's not fine. What I did was awful—unforgivable!"

"Um… Then maybe you'd feel better if you made up for it instead? We were hoping to ask you a few questions, so if you answer those, we can call it square. Right, Bosa?"

"Sure, I guess. I'd like to hear what a Cardinal Mage is at least."

Ling let out another sigh. "No, I don't deserve to be forgiven, and any explanation I give right now will be worthless. I knew that side of myself would make things difficult, but I still went with it because I didn't feel like walking to your apartment complex. This will only cement how pathetic I am, but the best way for me to apologize would be to let Dragon handle it."

"'Dragon'? What dragon?"

Ling didn't answer. Instead, he just rotated himself ninety degrees to the left.

Causing his demeanor to shift once again.

"Hahaha!" he laughed, suddenly grinning from ear to ear. "What a mess I got myself into! Aw well, nothing I can't handle! A man oughta be able to fix any problem he creates, right?"

"*What the fuck…*"

3

Bosa had no idea what was going on, but Ling was acting like a different person again. Instead of being machinelike or self-abasing, he now guffawed like a jolly father.

Shit. I really should have listened to my gut...

"Sorry for the fuss, girls. I can tell you're beyond confused, but don't worry—I'll answer all your questions now. Telling you what a Cardinal Mage is should clear up most of them anyhow, so let's start there."

"No, forget that," countered Bosa. "Why the hell does your personality keep changing?"

"We'll get to that. I know it's my fault we're all befuddled, but it's best if I do things in order."

"Seriously?"

"Serious as a heart attack. Just let me tell you two about my class and it'll all make sense."

"Then please do. I'm having trouble keeping up with all this..." said Nabby.

"Understandable. I can't imagine I'm the easiest guy to deal with when I'm spinning through personas like that." Ling moved into a cross-legged position, planting his fists on his knees. "Well, plainly put, a Cardinal Mage is a jack-of-all-trades that can use different schools of magic based on what direction they're facing. North, south, east, west—what I can do changes with where I'm looking."

"Oh, so that's where the 'Cardinal' bit comes from. I was afraid it had something to do with *priests*." Nabby made sure to end her statement with sufficient venom.

"Well, I *can* use holy magic, but not out of any affiliation with the church. I'm just spiritual enough to draw on Heaven's mana."

"So, you're a holy mage then?" Bosa asked.

"One-quarter correct! I can also use black, druidic, and arcane magic."

"No shit? I thought most people don't try to learn more than two schools of magic because managing all the formulas gets too hard."

"It normally is, but that's where the power of directional energy comes in," grinned Ling. "I underwent special training that lets me 'reset' my mind and change my magic by focusing on a certain direction. Thanks to that, I can do almost every role for a party—at the same time!"

"Hmph. Sounds handy. What's the catch?"

"You've already seen it. All that mind-resetting eventually messes with your head and makes your persona shift with your direction as well. Because of that, my whole attitude changes with my abilities, leading to stuff like me pulling you out here with barely a 'how do you do'. Some Cardinal Mages actually work with eight styles of magic, but I figured four personas was already pushing it. My wife's got her hands full enough as it is!"

Ling let out a hearty laugh, slapping his knee to emphasize just how funny he thought he was. Bosa was glad he had shifted into a more amicable persona, though it was now obvious why information on Ling's class was so scarce.

Who in their right mind—or minds, I guess—would train in a class that intentionally fucks with your head?

Being able to attack, heal, teleport, and god knows what else was undeniably useful, but the tradeoff almost made Bosa and Nabby drop his gig. Kudos to Ling's wife for marrying that level of nonsense.

"You might wanna include all that in the job description next time you make a Parti posting. We didn't have any idea what we were getting into because there's barely any information about Cardinal Mages on the internet," Bosa said, massaging her temples. "At least tell your stiff-ass persona to explain things before he runs off."

"Ah, you don't need to worry about that. I call them personas because they're simply different parts of me. My

Phoenix side will remember this just as well as the rest of me."

"Oh, that's right. Your timid persona called you 'Dragon' too. Do those names mean anything?" Nabby asked.

"Not particularly. They're just nicknames I have for my directional personas. The quick rundown is North is the Phoenix of utility magic, South is a defensive Tortoise, East is a healing Dragon, and West is an offensive Tiger."

"Wow! If you've got all those skills, why did you need to hire us?"

"Well, while I might be a one-man party, that doesn't mean I can do everything," he said. "I don't have a clue on how to use song magic or track monsters to any real degree, and since I need a lionwolf's pelt for a commission, it seemed like hiring some young blood was in order."

"Right, you mentioned that you run an enchantment shop in your posting," said Bosa.

"Exactly. I make the gear as well as enchant it, and since my next shipment of furs isn't due for a while, I figured I'd get one myself. Though, to be frank, I also just enjoy heading out into the field on occasion. Reminds me of my old adventuring days, and it's fun seeing the younger generations at work." Ling climbed to his feet and straightened his coat. "There—I think that answers all your questions. I'll apologize again for my earlier rudeness, but if we're all on the same page now, how about we finish this hunt before nightfall?"

He smiled at them enthusiastically. Bosa and Nabby side-eyed one another.

"Uhh… Give us a sec?"

Without waiting for an answer, Bosa put an arm around Nabby's shoulders and pulled her into a huddle.

"What's your read on him?" whispered Bosa.

"Well, he's weird, but I don't think he's a bad person."

"Yeah, his persona shit is wack as hell, but not enough that I'd say we should bail. You okay with riding this out?"

"Yeah, I'm fine. I kind of wanna hear more about his four-sided style too."

"Sounds good. I'll leave chatting up Mr. Weathercock to you then."

They turned and faced the garuda again. He tilted his head slightly, but otherwise seemed just as eager as before.

"Alright, we're good to go. Sorry for making you play twenty questions," said Bosa.

"Nah, you don't need to apologize. I hired you, but that doesn't give me free reign to be discourteous."

Thank god this side of him is easy to work with. Hopefully the lionwolf is somewhere in the east.

Confident their client was bizarre but benign, Bosa explained how they were going to track down the monster while Nabby summoned her familiars. Strangely, Weathercock stiffened a little as she spoke, but he made no protest.

Once all three dogs were back on Rullia, Nabby crouched down next to Rusty. The little pug seemed as unhappy as ever as he listened to his master's request.

"Rusty, would you be all right with asking Bergy and Cercer to look for the trail of a lionwolf, please? Our client needs its fur, and I promised him you'd be able to help..."

He stared at her a moment longer before rolling his eyes and turning to the other familiars. The larger dogs snapped to attention when Rusty barked, and after some shorter yaps, Cerulean and Bergundy began sniffing around the field.

It didn't take long for them to pick up the scent. Cerulean seemed to find something, and she silently looked back at Rusty before continuing her prowl. The pug let out another bark, apparently an order to Bergundy, and they began tailing the spirit wolf.

"O-okay, I think they've got the scent," said Nabby.

"Man, Rusty is so cool," gushed Bosa. "What kind of treats does he like?"

"Um, I don't know. He's never really gotten excited over a treat."

"Huh. Maybe he likes cheeseburgers, like his master."

"I hope not. I don't wanna share…"

The adventurers then followed the dogs as they ascended a hill. The larger familiars took point in their formation, with Rusty lingering behind like an overseer.

After enough awkwardness, they were finally on their way to hunt down the lionwolf. Bosa was now free to relax, take in the scenery, and look forward to the easy paycheck she'd get for singing a lullaby.

Or she would have if she weren't so distracted by how Weathercock was walking backwards.

"…Hey, boss?"

"What's up, Mikayla?"

"Well, two things. First, call me Bosa. Mikayla makes me sound like a little kid."

"Alright."

"Second, why the fuck are you walking like that?"

Weathercock chuckled sheepishly. "W-well, I don't really have a choice right now, seeing as we're headed west. My Phoenix and Tortoise sides can't stand dogs, so moving sideways isn't an option either."

"Why not switch to your west persona? Will you still dislike dogs like that?" asked Nabby.

"Tiger loves them, actually. But I get a little, uh, *fired up* when I'm facing west. It's best if I keep that part of me tucked away until I'm ready to fight."

"What a pain in the ass."

"More importantly, that's not safe," added Nabby. "Would you like to hold my hand? You're less likely to trip that way."

"What a considerate young lady you are! I'll gladly take that offer—much appreciated!"

Frankly, it looked like walking backwards over uneven terrain wasn't giving Weathercock any trouble, but having someone ready to catch him must have been reassuring for the aging man. And if it also kept his persona shenanigans at bay, Bosa was all for a little handholding.

Nabby's familiars continued to follow the scent of their target. Given how the hillsides only bore solitary trees and bushes, spotting the lionwolf would be easy once they got close enough, but hopefully the beast wasn't too far. Lionwolves were nocturnal, and Bosa had no desire to tangle with one after the sun had set.

"Mr. Ling?" Nabby asked over her shoulder. "Would it be alright if I asked why you decided to become a Cardinal Mage? Did you know about the, um, side-effects?"

"No problem at all. I actually wanted to be a rogue when I was young, but my school's tests showed I had a knack for magic. I went with the Cardinal style since I liked the breadth of its abilities and thought I could resist the personality fracturing."

"Oh. Are some people able to do that?"

"Not that I've ever heard of. But it's not as bad as it seems. Heck, it's not even noticeable when I'm working at my shop since my personas seem to only get really distinct while I'm adventuring. Of course, I fully understand why the style never caught on."

"Is that why you moved to crafting gear instead?"

"Nah, that was just part of getting old. I'm sixty-four, you know—can't be running around fighting monsters like I used to," laughed Weathercock. "Going out for an odd job like this is nice, but needlework is where my heart is at these days."

"Aw man, I love handcrafts too! Not to brag, but I made almost all of my adventuring gear myself!"

"You don't say! You must be quite the talented young lady to have sewn a nice coat like that!"

"Oh, that's actually the one piece I didn't make. This coat was given to me by my hero, a healing Alchemist named Reese."

"Ah, I see. But... Hm. I'm not sensing any enchantments. If you like, I can put a little magic in it—make it enhance your spells or offer better protection."

"No, I'm okay. I've gotta return it to her one day so I don't wanna mess with it."

"Yeah, Nabs isn't gonna do anything less than reverential to her savior," Bosa chimed in. "She'll need to have Reese's Pieces' signed permission before she'll let you touch that coat."

"Hey, she really helped me out after I got stuck in Rullia! I didn't even have any clothes back then, but she rented out an inn room for me and gave me a whole bunch of money! I'd have to be a real jerk to mess with her coat after that!"

"Ah, it's sure nice to know there's still good people out there," said Weathercock. "Am I right to assume this Reese girl is why you've become a healer, Naberius?"

"Yessir! Reese told me she can't use any magic because she has 'Locked Mana Syndrome', but she still became an awesome healer despite that. It's my dream to be just like her. Even if demons can't use normal healing magic, I'm gonna prove to the world that we can be healers too!"

"A fine goal indeed. On that note, how *do* you heal?"

"I use a modified form of *Drain* to heal party members with vitality taken from monsters, and I can transfer ailments back into the baddies that caused them with my custom *Contaminate!* And I already knew *Dark Return* for resurrecting people!" Nabby proudly explained.

"Mm. But that means you're dealing with the caveat that you need a monster around to do any healing. Maybe I'm overstepping here, but I can feel you've got a lot of dark power in you—more than I've ever seen, in fact. Wouldn't it be better if you stuck with offense?"

"Oh... Um..."

"Or you could try causing ailments yourself if you just don't like attacking directly. Either way, isn't forcing yourself to be a healer rather counterintuitive?"

"W-well, I—"

"That's just not what she's into, boss."

Knowing all too well where this conversation could lead, Bosa cut in.

"Nabby promised Reese she'd become a healer too. Even if it's not the easy path, there's nothing wrong with trying to live up to those you admire, right?"

Of course, that was only half the story. Nabby wouldn't have latched onto the concept of healing so strongly if it weren't for the fears dwelling in her heart.

Fears so fucked up she can't even feel good about protecting someone.

Because of an incident in her childhood, Nabby did everything she could to avoid using her magic offensively. Even hurting soulless monsters didn't always sit well with her—she only did so because her healing magic necessitated it.

As Nabby loved to say, her dream was to "heal, not harm". Bosa had no intention of letting anyone force her friend to explain why those words were so important to her.

Even a resident of Hell should be allowed some peace from her inner demons.

Thankfully, Weathercock was able to read the atmosphere. He paused for a moment before nodding.

"Fair enough. Then I'll root for your success, Naberius."

Nabby gawked a moment, as though she were already prepared to dredge up her most painful memories. But once she realized there was no need, she smiled at Bosa with eyes full of gratitude.

The scylla winked back.

4

"But, if I may," Weathercock continued, "I *am* a master of four schools of magic, and I've picked up a few things in my years. I've got some advice that might help you improve your healing, if you'd like to hear it."

Nabby shook her head. "That's a nice offer, sir, but I don't think I'd like having my personality shift like that…"

"Ha! No, I'm not talking about that. How about this: have you ever considered *your mindset* when using a spell?"

"Um…hm. No, I guess I haven't."

"Have you ever had any trouble getting one of your custom spells to work?"

"Yeah, actually! I've been trying to get *Internal Decay* to target only pathogens, but I keep accidentally rotting the host too."

Bosa narrowed her eyes. She made a mental note to ask Nabby when and where she'd been practicing that.

"Well, being someone who uses several varieties of magic, I'm familiar with the nuances of manipulating mana," said Weathercock. "A lesser-known fact is that the way you *think about* your spells can have a decent impact on their effectiveness. Correct me if I'm wrong, but you still consider your healing spells reworked combat magic, yes?"

Nabby gasped. "Wow, now that I think about it, I really do!"

"Then my advice is to start thinking of them as proper healing spells. Your mind has a huge influence on your magic, so you need to make sure the way you see your spells lines up with how you're using them to make sure they flow smoothly. Doing so will improve your efficiency, control, and power. It'll probably make retooling the rest of your dark magic easier too."

"Really? It can help that much?"

"Think of it like a myrmidon becoming a knight. He might still be swinging a sword around, but now he's gotta focus on blocking hits instead of dishing them out. The way you wield your magic is just as important."

"Yeah, I think I read something similar online once," Bosa concurred. "It's not widely known since most people don't have the skills to rework spell formulas. Guess it's only a problem for stubborn dreamers."

"Hmmm..." Nabby pondered the advice. "I'll definitely have to consider that, Mr. Ling—especially next time I run into a roadblock. Thank you very much!"

"My pleasure. Feel free to come visit me at the shop if you'd like to hear more."

Bosa put a finger on her chin. "You know, that gives me an idea of my own on how we can improve your healing. Could be something to try on our next job."

"Really? What do you—*Ow!*"

Rusty had turned around and jabbed Nabby's shin with his horn, stopping her in her tracks. Unfortunately, Weathercock's momentum caused him to bump into the demon's back, pushing her further into the Pug of War's prod.

"Ow ow ow...!" Face tight with pain, Nabby gripped her miserable leg. "Rusty, please be careful with your horn. It really hurts when you poke me with it!"

"I think he just wanted your attention, Nabs. Looks like the other two found something."

Bergundy and Cerulean had stopped near the top of a nearby hill, seemingly cautious of going any further. Bosa had a pretty good idea what that meant, and she moved just far enough past the dogs to confirm her suspicions.

They had found the lionwolf.

It was sleeping in the branches of a large tree sitting atop the hill. Despite its name—a dumbass joke left behind by the monstrologist who discovered the species—the monster looked like a cross between a bear and an owl. It was massive, easily as large as a truck, and its absurdly tough hide was why the beasts were normally dispatched by full parties.

Bosa hurried back to the group. Weathercock still had his back towards the hill, so she and Nabby circled around him to discuss their approach.

"Looks like your lionwolf is already asleep in a tree, just over the hill," Bosa told the garuda. "How do you wanna handle this?"

"Seeing as he'll wake up the moment I start preparing my attack, I'm thinking we should open with your lullaby. A magical sleep is much heavier than a natural one, so once he's out for good, I'll go all Tiger and blast him to bits."

"You're really gonna fight it on your own?" asked Nabby.

"Yep. I'll open with my strongest stuff, but he's almost certain to survive and counterattack. So, before then, I'd like you two to get a safe distance away."

"Are you sure? But then if you get hurt, I might not be able to heal you in time or—"

"Don't worry about me. Not sure if you read my profile, but I hit Rank A on Parti during the two years I actively worked for them—so I'm not all talk. Besides, it'd break my heart to see you girls get tore up over a fur coat."

"Let it go, Nabby. If the boss is that confident, I say let him do his thing." Bosa then gave Weathercock a dry sneer. "But that doesn't mean you're free to eat shit, old man. You've still gotta bring us home—no fucking way am I walking to New Llork."

Weathercock put a hand over his beak, barely suppressing his laughter. "You've got my word, Bosa. I'll make sure you're back before supper."

With that settled, Bosa led the garuda man up the hill while Nabby spoke to her familiars. She took a moment to thank and pet each of them before sending them back to Hell.

"Alright, I'll first switch to Phoenix and give myself some defensive enhancements. Once Tiger comes out—and you'll know when that happens—start singing your lullaby, please."

"Sounds good. Just do me a favor and don't attack until you know it's under the effect of my song, alright?"

Weathercock didn't answer. He had already turned northward and was now quietly chanting. His hands periodically flashed as he cast spells on himself.

Great. He's already an asshole again.

Not that there was any helping it. Since he was going alone, he'd need protection. But that didn't mean she had to abide by his persona's dickishness.

Bosa glanced over her shoulder. Nabby was hanging back, likely in preparation of their retreat. She still seemed anxious about leaving everything to Weathercock, but Bosa's gut told her she could trust his boasting.

Probably.

"Yeah, you better not be full of hot air, old man," muttered Bosa.

"Relax, sea-bitch. I didn't survive this long *pretending* I'm hot shit—I've been murderizing monsters since before you were born. Anyways, you ready to start singing? I got my defenses set, so how about we stop fucking around and kill this shithead?"

Bosa's jaw dropped as she turned towards Weathercock. But instead of facing her, he was glaring at the lionwolf with his arms crossed. No longer an antisocial stiff, he now presented himself as a foul-mouthed wildman.

"Sea-bitch", huh? Never heard that one before. No wonder he didn't want to show this side of himself earlier.

"So, this is Tiger…" She sighed. "Yeah, alright. Let's get this over with."

"Agreed. Walking all this way was a pain in the ass. I shouldn't be putting my joints through this shit—and for a fucking fur coat too. I didn't even get to enjoy those dogs because my Phoenix side screwed up the intros!"

"You're upset over that?"

"Damn straight I am! When the fuck else am I gonna get a chance to play with a purebred hellhound like that?"

"Maybe in a few minutes, after this lionwolf sends your feathered ass to the Underworld."

Before Weathercock could peck back, Bosa began her lullaby. Unlike her other songs, she didn't slip on her headphones and sing along to a melody. She simply didn't need one. The lullaby was her mother's favorite, and its tune was ingrained in Bosa's heart.

Slow and affectionate, the song echoed across the hills. Weathercock was unaffected, thanks to his protective spells, but the lionwolf certainly wasn't.

Despite its resistance to magical attacks, it had no defense against the gentle touch of a lullaby. The monster was roused by the sudden commotion, but it just as quickly wobbled with languor. It tried to dig its claws back into the branch, but the lionwolf was asleep before it could resecure itself.

It fell in a heap next to the tree, a peaceful look on its unconscious face.

"Stupid shithead can't even resist a little tune like this? Tch—fucker's as good as skinned!" bragged Weathercock. "Alright, now get your ass back. I'm gonna blow this bastard to hell in just a second."

Bosa finished her song and nodded. "Sounds good. Be sure to send us home before you bleed out." She then turned around. "Okay, Nabs, let's go find a tree to hide…behind…"

Bosa froze in place. It took only one look for her to know that Nabby hadn't heard a word she said.

She was too busy sleeping face first in the grass.

Bosa grit her teeth in exasperation. She completely forgot to warn Nabby, or at least loan the demon her noise-canceling headphones. Then again, Nabby should have realized she didn't have any protection against the lullaby and said something!

Now the dumbass was dead asleep—and set to be just plain dead with how close she was to the impending battle.

"*Gahahaha!* Aw *shit*, this is gonna be a big one!" Weathercock roared as he readied his attack. "Hey—you assholes aren't nearly far enough away! Unless you wanna get caught in the blast, go find a hole or something!"

"Gimme a second! Nabby got knocked asleep too!"

"Well, I can't stop now! Better grab her and run!"

"Motherfucker…!"

Bosa ran to Nabby, flipped her over, and dragged the demon away as fast as she could. Unfortunately, the demon was heavier than she looked.

"Dammit, Nabby…! How many hamburgers…have you been eating…?!"

She barely managed to get them to the base of the hill before something exploded behind them. Bosa looked back and saw magic incinerate the lionwolf's tree—*and* the hillside behind it.

"Oh, *fuck yeah!*" hollered Weathercock. "Big spells like that always feel great! And you're still alive—just like I hoped! Now we can have some *real* fun!"

Bosa shook her head. She continued dragging Nabby until they were both behind a tree of their own, hopefully safe from the chaos on the hill.

Nabby didn't show any signs of waking up. Even after Bosa slapped her cheeks, she remained peacefully asleep. The songstress would have felt pride in how effective her lullaby was if the timing weren't so shitty. She could only sigh instead.

Looks like you still have a lot to learn, my friend.

But at least they had done their part. Now Weathercock could handle the rest.

Another explosion cracked through the air, prompting a rain of dirt and pebbles. Bosa shielded Nabby with her arm, but the demon didn't stir one bit. In fact, she was smiling now, probably lost in some pleasant dream.

Bosa was beyond jealous.

5

About half an hour later, the duo was back in their apartment, with Bosa brewing a pot of instant coffee while her partner snoozed on the sofa. Now that the job was over, Nap-erius was free to sleep as long as she liked.

Though… Maybe I'll practice my death metal if she doesn't wake up soon.

To Bosa's relief, Weathercock's battle with the lionwolf didn't last more than a few minutes. After it was slain, she climbed back up the hill to check out the aftermath while the old man took a breather. Despite all the explosions, the lionwolf's fur was nearly undamaged—proof of its incredible defenses. It's corpse practically seemed out of place amidst the burning craters.

Then, once he caught his second wind, Weathercock switched to his Phoenix persona and teleported Bosa and Nabby back home, stating there was no reason for him to keep them any longer. Were it his Dragon side, Bosa might have offered to stick around and watch his back while he collected the pelt, but as things were, she decided she'd rather give Nabby a better place to sleep than on the ground.

Besides, the guy had just single-handedly killed a lionwolf. Every monster in the area would have already scattered so they wouldn't have to face ol' Weathercock.

Bosa was debating between taking a shower and plugging a microphone into her sound system when Nabby yawned from the couch. The healer rubbed at her eyes as she sat upright.

"Oh man, what a nice nap. I haven't slept that well in a while."

"Welcome back, Sleeping Beauty."

"Oh, hey, Bosa. You're not gonna believe this weird dream I had. You and I were on this job to hunt down a lionwolf, and our customer was this garuda guy who came with us. But he had this weird quirk were his personality was different every time he changed the direction he was facing and—"

"That wasn't a dream," Bosa said flatly. "You got knocked unconscious by my lullaby and I had to drag your ass home. You literally fell asleep on the job."

"Wh-what?! You're kidding me!"

"Nope. Why the hell didn't you say something before I started singing? It's not my job to make sure you don't get zonked in the crossfire."

"I-it slipped my mind?"

"Dumbass. You're lucky Weathercock didn't care. He thought it was kind of cute—and that was his Phoenix side talking."

"Aw man… B-but what about my review…?"

"Hmph. Five stars." Bosa pulled up their scores on her phone and presented it to Nabby. "We both did the jobs we were hired for, so he decided your impromptu nap wasn't worth bitching over. But he did say he wants you to come by his shop so he can see your dogs again."

Nabby nearly deflated with relief. "I'll definitely do that. I'm kinda bummed I didn't get to see Ling take down the lionwolf though."

"Shit was crazy too. Once I'd gotten you away from the battle, I watched what I could from our hiding spot. Dude was practically spinning as he threw out spells of every kind. He wasn't kidding when he said he could handle it alone— damn thing couldn't even touch him."

"Wow… That sounds incredible!"

"It was, but his Tiger persona kinda ruined it. Here."

Bosa handed Nabby a cup of coffee and sat on the sofa next to her. The demon looked positively ecstatic at the kindness.

"My goodness—thank you, Bosa! You're being really nice today!"

"I'm always nice. I just figured you'd need something to perk you back up after your sweet dreams."

"It really was a good nap too. I didn't realize how effective your lullaby is."

"Me neither. I should use that next time I feel like fucking someone in my own bed."

"H-hey!"

Bosa smiled mischievously as she took a sip of her coffee. "By the way, do you remember what our client told you about changing your perspective on your spells?"

"I do, but... Do you think that will actually help?"

"No clue. Weathercock certainly seemed to think so, and considering dark magic really wasn't built for healing or support skills, I don't think it'd hurt to try. Worst case scenario, you'll learn how to *not* improve your spells."

Nabby nodded. "True. I'd love to have more options for healing, so I guess it's worth a shot. Who knows—it might be the key to getting *Internal Decay* to work!"

"That reminds me; when the hell have you been practicing that?"

"We had some old cheese in the fridge that had gone bad. I tried destroying only the mold, but I ended up rotting the whole block."

"*That's* what that smell was?"

"Oops... I thought you didn't notice."

"How the fuck wouldn't I?!"

"I threw it away right after!"

"That doesn't make the smell go away, dumbass!" Bosa sighed. "Whatever. What I was gonna say is that I came up with a plan to help you get your perspective in order. I've got a theory on why you're still treating your spells like combat magic, so we'll put it to the test in our next gig."

"Sounds fun! What kind of plan is it?"

"That's my secret for now. The important part is that, while you were asleep, I found us another job. Next week, you're playing healer for a dungeon-clearing party."

Nabby's eyes widened with excitement. "Ooo, I haven't gotten to go to a dungeon yet! Are those jobs different from our usual work?"

"Sort of. They take longer and sometimes involve more than just slaying monsters, but they pay really well so who gives a shit."

"Right. We could certainly use the extra money."

"Today's job made sure we won't get evicted, but we're not out of the woods yet. As impressive as your eldritch casserole was, we're gonna need to dip back into the red and burn some cash on groceries. Make sure you're on your best behavior during our dungeon crawl, okay?"

"Nothing to worry about! I'm feeling zappy about getting to be a proper healer again, and I'm even more excited to see what kind of plan you have for me!" said Nabby. "I really appreciate you thinking of ways to help me improve, by the way."

"Heh, I'm sure it'll be a good time for everyone. And one way or another, I know my little test will make you a better healer."

"Do I get a prize for passing it?"

"Why not. You'll probably get a few attempts, but I'll buy you a burger if you clear it even once."

"Deal! Oh man, now I'm triple fired up!"

"Oh yeah? Think you're gonna ace it?"

"You bet your sweet bippy I will! You'll wish you made it more difficult!"

"Nice—roll with that confidence. I'll be cheering from the sidelines."

The two of them continued to banter on the sofa as they enjoyed their cheap coffee. But while Nabby shifted to discussing the dinner she could make from their insipid pantry, Bosa's mind lingered on the test she had planned for Nabby.

A test the demon was certainly going to fail.

Sorry, Nabs. Hate to get your hopes up—especially with a burger on the line—but what I've got in store for you isn't nearly as straightforward as you'll assume. I really do hope you'll succeed, but…

Well, sometimes tough love is the best love, right?

Sansei-san
Mirror

Job Five — Halfling Trio

1

The day had finally arrived.

Barely able to contain her excitement, Nabby got up early to prepare for her very first dungeon gig. She was showered, dressed, and had breakfast on the table before the sun had even risen. She accidentally woke Bosa up with all the commotion, but seeing as their job was set for ten o'clock, she wouldn't mind starting a little ahead of schedule, right?

I wish. Ms. Grumpy Butt definitely minded...

The two were now walking down the sidewalk, en route to the dungeon. Bosa had made them stop at a coffee shop so she could get a "cup of the strong shit", but they were still on track for a punctual arrival. Nabby felt energized enough that she could have sprinted to the job, but since it wouldn't look good for her to show up without her partner, she redirected her enthusiasm towards teasing out Bosa's plan.

"Sooo... What kind of test is it? Do I need to demonstrate my healing skills? Or is it more like a multiple-choice quiz?" prodded Nabby.

"Like I said, you'll find out later." Bosa's coffee clearly hadn't kicked in yet.

"I know, but... Is it more physical or mental?"

"Can't say."

"Then maybe it's a spiritual test—like meditating under a waterfall!"

"*Nabby.*"

"C'mon, a little hint won't hurt! I'm already excited about going into a dungeon, but knowing you've got a secret training plan for me is driving me bonkers!"

"Then how about you tell me something first: do you know a damn thing about dungeons?"

"…U-um…"

Nabby did not.

"Figures. In the interest of making sure you don't embarrass us, I'll tell you the basics. So shut up and listen." Bosa popped a stiff joint in her neck. "For starters, dungeons are pocket dimensions filled with monsters that periodically appear in cities. They're assumed to be caused by the Source of All Monsters, but they can't be kept away by anything less than top-class wards."

"They also come from the Source? But if no one's ever found it, how do they know?"

"Could have sworn I told you to shut up. It's *assumed* they're connected because everything involving monsters traces back to the Source. I think there's also something about mana samples in dungeons matching the shit found in Monstralia, but I don't remember the details."

The piqued Nabby's interest. Reese was currently adventuring in Monstralia, with the grand goal of tracking down the Source of All Monsters with her party. Knowing that dungeons had some sort of link to Monstralia made Nabby smile.

It was like she was getting a little closer to her hero.

"Anyway, your average dungeon is about the size of a two-story house and can pop up just about anywhere," Bosa continued. "Most cities see at least one 'emergency-level' dungeon a year, though, and those can start off as big as an office complex."

"'Start off'? Can they get bigger?"

"Yup. Once they appear, dungeons start absorbing nearby mana. They grow new rooms, the monsters inside get tougher, et cetera. Most dungeons aren't found for a few weeks, so it's rare to get one while it's small. It's also thought that the mana a dungeon absorbs affects its interior, but considering I once helped remove one that looked like a strip club from the TV section of a department store, your guess is as good as mine on how that works."

"Weird. So how do you clear them? Do we have to defeat all the monsters inside or something?"

"Thank god no. Each dungeon has a 'boss monster' at its heart, and killing that asshole causes the whole thing to fall apart. Once it's dead, the dungeon fades away after twenty-four hours, without a trace it was ever there."

"That sounds like something you'd see in a video game."

"Well, duh. Where do you think game developers got the idea?"

Good point. It wouldn't make any sense if it were the other way around—that video games had somehow inspired the way dungeons function.

That'd just be silly.

"…Wait, what happens if you're inside a dungeon when it fades away?" asked Nabby.

"No idea. There was a monstrologist who decided to stay inside one and find out, but no one ever heard from her again."

"Spooky…"

"I heard some criminals use that to dispose of dead bodies. Which is probably half the reason the city pays well for timely dungeon removal," said Bosa. "That reminds me: we're free to keep any treasure we find in there. It's usually just mimic gold or condensed mana crystals, and we'll have to share with the rest of the party, but be sure to call out if you see something shiny. Any extra cash we can scrounge up is worth it."

"Got it. Is there anything in particular I should keep in mind about today's party or the dungeon?"

"Nah. The dungeon looked about two weeks old when I signed us up, so it'll probably be around the size of a grocery store with monsters that aren't complete pushovers. But that won't matter since the combat half of our party is composed of B Rank adventurers. They're all halflings, though, so watch your step."

"Why'd it take so long for someone to find the dungeon?"

"How often do *you* wander into abandoned car washes?"

"That's where it is?"

"Nabby, I'm gonna spank you next time you forget to read the job details. We're almost at the fucking place—how the hell did you not know where we were going?"

"I-I knew *where* we were going! I just didn't know *what* was at the address!"

"Whatever. Just let me do the talking when we get there. Explaining our training plan thing was already gonna raise some eyebrows, so try not to say anything else that'll tell our new friends you're as green as my ass."

"Isn't the saying 'as green as grass'?"

"For most people, sure." They rounded a corner. "Be honest—you sure you're ready for this?"

"Absolutely! I'm right as rain and ready to *Drain!*"

"*Pfft...* Alright, Captain Clog Remover. Just keep in mind that things could be harder than I'm expecting—maybe hard enough that we'll have to shelve your test. I doubt we'll run into anything the halflings can't handle, but stranger things have happened."

"Gotcha. Either way, I'll give this job everything I've got!"

"Then I'll balance things out and half-ass it."

The two then made their last turn, putting the abandoned car wash in sight.

The business was composed of several washing ports and a small building. The property wasn't decrepit, but it was obvious that it hadn't been open in years. A "For Sale" sign had been posted on the building's window, and miscreants had graffitied an uncomfortably artistic phallus over the lease information.

They couldn't find their party members anywhere outside, so Bosa figured they were waiting inside, near the dungeon entrance. The front door was unlocked, so the two went in to check.

"—so it's not my fault Kafei got banned! Look for yourself—my butt's way more covered than Tousen's! If any of us drove him over the edge, it was her!"

They found three halflings inside, with one of them sticking out her leather-clad rear for the others' assessment.

2

"I-it's an honor to work with you, Miss Lilibosa!"

One of the halflings—the one that was showing off her butt when Bosa and Nabby entered—stepped forward and greeted them. She even bowed at the waist, making her diminutive form look even smaller.

Bosa frowned. "Thanks, but it's just Bosa now. I dropped the whole 'Seafoam Diva' thing."

"Oh, I-I know! But I'm still a big fan of yours! I knew that video didn't tell us the whole story, and the fact that you've been working with Naberius tells me I was right!"

"You sure about that? For all you know, I'm just sticking near her in the hopes that someone will notice and spread the word of what a good little girl I am."

Now Nabby had to frown. She knew Bosa was just being facetious, but she still hated hearing her friend say nasty things about herself—especially as a means of introduction.

Bosa was only as imperfect as anyone else. She didn't have to wear her mistakes on her sleeve.

But, to Nabby's chagrin, there wasn't much she could do. Bosa was a self-admitted "prideful asshole"—she even turned down Nabby's offer to appear in her apology video just because she wanted to stand on her own. Speaking up would just annoy her.

Still… I wish she'd stop trying to cast herself in a bad light.

"N-no, I know you're not that kind of person," insisted the halfling. "Even if you're not really a bubbly idol, you kept adventuring long after you wanted to quit because you didn't want to make your fans sad. A-a-and you tried to explain things even though you knew people would ridicule you!"

"Hmph. Nah, I did all that cuz I liked the money. But thanks for believing in me, I guess."

"I still believe in you! The Seafoam Diva's videos helped me during some tough times—I wouldn't be who I am today without your music!"

"Huh? Really?"

Bosa looked genuinely surprised. Nabby couldn't help but smile as she watched her friend sheepishly pull at one of her long ears.

"Of course! And it's exciting to see you enter the cam show business too! I moonlight as a dominatrix myself, so I know how hard working in the adult entertainment industry can be. I don't really watch those kinds of things, but I made sure to subscribe to help you out!"

And that endearment left Nabby just as swiftly.

Bosa, however, was impressed. "Wow, that was nice of you. It's cool that you're not afraid to talk about that kind of stuff either."

"Of course! My sisters and I were trained to be unabashed! If anything, I'm proud to declare my support!"

"Right, and on that note, how about we get some intros going? You clearly know who we are, but I can only guess which one of you is which."

"Oh, right. Sorry about that. I got a little too excited and... R-right—introductions!"

The halfling stepped back to her sisters, and the three of them assumed a formation, facing away from Bosa and Nabby. They then suddenly turned around, each of them striking a pose as they gave their name.

"Middle sister, Sera the Toned!"

"Youngest sister, Tousen the Ox!"

"And eldest sister, Mina the Dope."

""""Three of Kinki Shikozaki's Lurid Blades, masters in the art of love, we are the infamous sisters known as the Trio of Titillation!"""" they finished in tandem.

They then relaxed into normalcy, as though that were even close to a normal introduction.

The... "Trio of Titillation"?

They definitely looked like sisters, but that was all they had in common appearance-wise. Sera wore an all-leather outfit that pronounced her bust, Tousen was dressed like a professional wrestler, and Mina's robes looked like they had been sized for a human. Likewise, they all kept their platinum hair in different styles: Sera wore hers in twintails, Tousen had a boy cut, and Mina's appeared to have never been cut in her life.

Still, they couldn't be anything but a matched set. People didn't pose together like that unless they were close, and none of them were a step out of beat.

Nabby was filled with consternation. On one hand, the way the Trio moved in unison and announced themselves was beyond cool. But on the other, she had a terrible feeling on why they were called "Lurid Blades" and "the Trio of Titillation"—especially after Sera described her *other job*.

"Well. That was a thing," said Bosa. "Can't say I've ever heard of Kinki Shikozaki or his Lurid Blades, but it sounds like you three aren't run-of-the-mill adventurers."

"Nope! Master Shikozaki was one of only nine people to hit Parti's Master rank," Tousen said enthusiastically. "After he retired, he then trained one thousand students in the art of 'sensual combat'."

"'The path to enlightenment is not one of purity or temperance, but the act of embracing our most raw desires.' He loved that phrase so much he had bumper stickers made," added Sera.

Nabby wasn't liking where this was going. She was used to working with Bosa, a known pervert, but how was she supposed to handle three more of her kind?

No—this was *worse*. Bosa just had a dirty mind. These three were *elite* perverts.

Aw man… Something weird is gonna happen today, isn't it…

"Kinki trained his last dozen students more intensively and dubbed them the Lurid Blades. My sisters and I are among them," Mina dozily explained. "Though, to be fair… None of us have ever met any of Kinki's other nine hundred and eighty-eight students. And he was known to lie. *A lot.*"

"Where are the other nine Lurid Blades?" asked Bosa.

"No idea," said Sera. "We work with them on occasion, but everyone went their separate ways after graduation. We did team up with a fourth Blade for our last few jobs, but he's, uh...*unavailable* now."

Tousen guffawed loudly. "What are you saying, Sera? We were just talking about how Kafei got banned from Parti!"

A lump formed in Nabby's throat. "Banned? Did he break the rules or something?"

"Yeah. Our fourth was a goblin named Kafei the Fiend that worked as a Paladin and our healer," said Mina. "His problem was that he kept using *Lay on Hands* as an excuse to try and grope his party members. He went off on some job without us, then called the next day to let us know he got slapped with a sexual harassment lawsuit."

"Gross..."

Nabby couldn't believe someone like that worked the same role as her. Healers were supposed to be better than that.

"I'm guessing that's why you hired Nabby. And you took me because...?"

"Oh, I...just saw you applied and really wanted to meet you, Miss Bosa," admitted Sera, fiddling with her hands like a shy child. "This dungeon's been sitting here for a while too, so I figured it wouldn't hurt to have some extra help."

"Fair enough. Then I just need to ask what each of your roles are so I know who to stand behind."

"Sure thing. I'm a Whipmaster, so I'm our main fighter. I'm skilled at binding foes and beating them into submission. I'll render our foes helpless, remind them of the pathetic dogs they are, and punish them for misbehaving!"

Sera's cheeks flushed and she began to pant with excitement. In fact, she looked like she could start drooling at any moment.

Nabby's shoulders slumped as she realized her worst fears were coming true.

"Well, I guess I'm best described as an offensive mage," Mina said with a yawn. "My class, Somnambulist, specializes in dream magic, and I'm particularly good at giving monsters fulfilling dreams."

Thank goodness Mina wasn't so gutter-minded. Nabby wasn't sure what a "fulfilling dream" might entail, but at least the halfling could explain her class without getting aroused.

"And I'm our tank!" declared Tousen. "I'm a Grappler by class, so I protect my sisters by pinning down our enemies. And since I'm built like a brick shithouse, I can take more than a few hits!"

"Damn. That's impressive, given your size," said Bosa.

"Ha! I don't have any trouble taking on monsters bigger than me! I'll have you know I once suplexed a haunted train, in fact!" She pounded her fists together. "To me, nothing's better than working up a sweat while you wrestle a beasty. Blood pumping, muscles tensing, feeling your bodies twist and grab one another... Shit, just thinking about it makes me wanna tackle White Coat!"

"Eep!"

Sensing danger, Nabby ducked behind Bosa. The scylla wasn't pleased to be used as a shield, but Tousen just laughed instead of making good on her desires.

"All five of us make a well-rounded party together so I doubt we'll run into anything we can't handle," said Sera. "I made sure my sisters know what you're capable of, Miss Bosa, but I have to admit I don't understand what Naberius does."

"Call her Nabby. She uses an unconventional style for healing, but her track record should show she isn't a quack."

"True. The only bad review she had was for some slime job, right?"

"Th-that one wasn't fair though! I healed everyone just fine—the client didn't mention she expected me to know a protective spell!"

"Yeah, they were super pissed when I had to spend the rest of the job topless," Bosa nodded. "But while we're on the topic of Nabby, can I ask you three a favor?"

"Of course. What's up?"

"This is Nabby's first dungeon, and I was hoping to try something to help her improve as a healer. I promise it won't get in the way of the gig, but I can't explain more until we find a monster."

The halflings exchanged glances. None of them seemed even a little hesitant, and they came to agreement without a word.

"Nope, that's fine with us."

"Yeah, could be fun to watch," said Tousen.

"Awesome—thanks a ton."

"Yes, thank you very much!" Nabby bowed her head.

She hadn't thought about it, but they were incredibly lucky to have teamed up with experienced adventurers like the Trio. To them, having a neophyte train on the job likely came off as more of a novelty than anything. Lower-ranked adventurers would have been uncomfortable and denied Bosa's request immediately.

Yeah, I guess they're cool. F-for perverts, that is.

On that note, being busy with Bosa's trial would also help Nabby ignore her teammate's inevitable debauchery. While she was unlikely to get through the job unscathed, she now had something much more pleasant to focus on.

"So, where's the dungeon door?" asked Bosa.

"Right behind you." Mina pointed with her staff.

Nabby turned around. Sure enough, there was a steel door sitting next to the building's glass one. It was completely mismatched, looking more like something you'd see in an underground bunker, but Nabby was more perplexed by its location.

The building's wall wasn't even a foot thick, and the steel door certainly didn't go through to the other side. Bosa mentioned that dungeons were pocket dimensions, but

Nabby didn't realize that meant their entrances functioned more like portals than real doors.

"A metal door, huh? Hope that doesn't mean we're gonna get stuck fighting automatons. Does *Drain* even work on mechanical monsters?" asked Bosa.

"I…haven't had a chance to find out."

"Good thing you've got those potions in your pockets then." The scylla turned back to the Trio. "Well, we're good to go. You guys need any more time to prepare?"

"Nope, we're set. Let's head on in."

Tousen flung open the steel door, and the room filled with the scent of chlorine. She went in first, followed by her sisters, then Bosa and Nabby. The demon clenched a fist as she passed through the portal.

Here we go! Time to take on the dungeon—and Bosa's test!

3

The interior was not what Nabby expected. When she thought of dungeons, she imagined dank passageways lined with traps and lit with torches. However, Bosa's theory about automatons left her assuming they'd find something like a sci-fi laboratory instead.

Yet neither proved to be correct. Instead, the dungeon's interior was akin to the lower decks of a freighting ship. The walls were made of steel and the pipes along the ceiling dripped water at irregular intervals. There were fluorescent lights in lieu of torches, circular windows that offered a view into a murky, blue abyss, and a chill that nipped at Nabby's nose.

All this managed to fit inside the car wash's wall, huh?

"Oh, neat. It's actually kinda aquatic-themed," noted Bosa. She turned to Nabby. "That means the boss is probably some kind of sea monster, but there could be all sorts of baddies crawling around. Stay on your toes."

"Got it."

"Hmm, no enemies in the entryway. Guess they haven't gotten too aggressive yet," said Tousen. "Alright, gang, where to? I'm seeing three hallways and a flight of stairs, but I vote we save the second floor for later."

"Agreed. Wanna try the left hall first?" suggested Mina.

"Sounds good to me. Forward march!"

The group's footsteps clanged on the steel floor as they walked, the sole exception being Bosa's slithering tentacles. Nabby would have been concerned about alerting monsters, but her companions' casual banter convinced her she had nothing to fear, leaving the demon free to take in her surroundings.

It was hard for Nabby to believe that a phenomenon created by the Source of All Monsters could look so man-made. That mysterious entity was rumored to be the cause behind monster appearances throughout the world, but considering it was allegedly responsible for dimensional spaces like this as well, it was no wonder Reese and her friends wanted to find it.

Hopefully Nabby would be able to help them with that goal one day.

Mina grunted behind her. The halfling seemed to be having trouble with her pack, and she shifted it around in an effort to find her balance. Carrying her oversized staff at the same time made the process difficult, however, causing her to lag behind.

Nabby wasn't about to leave her be. She slowed her pace and offered Mina a hand.

"Here, let me carry some of that for you."

"Hm? Oh no, I'm okay," Mina said with a tired smile. "There are people of every size out there, so being on the lower end of the spectrum is sure to come with some problems, right? I'm used to it anyway."

"That's awful! You shouldn't have to get accustomed to such things! Don't they make adventuring gear in halfling sizes?"

"They do, but it's really expensive. Clothes are one thing, but packs, weapons, and stuff are another."

"I know how you feel. Bras in my size are super overpriced…"

Mina's smile twitched slightly. "Ahaha. Yep, we're definitely two peas in a pod here."

"Are you sure you don't want any help?"

"Well, I guess it'd be rude to turn you down twice. Would you mind carrying my pack for a bit?"

"Not at all!"

"Maybe my staff too? And how about my item satchel while we're at it?"

"O-oh, sure!"

Nabby reached down and took the items off Mina's hands. She was a good deal more encumbered by the extra gear but seeing the relief on her ally's face was worth it.

"*Phew*… Thanks, Nabby."

"Happy to help!"

"You dumbass." Bosa looked back and scoffed at her partner. "You're not thinking things through at all, are you? Shit like this is exactly why you need training."

"Huh? I don't see what this has to do with your test. Aren't party members supposed to help one another?"

"Just remember your role, my auspicious apprentice."

With those cryptic words, Bosa waved off any further discussion. Nabby looked at Mina, but the halfling just shrugged.

They found a door at the end of the hallway, but the room beyond it was just as monster-free as the dungeon's entrance. It did contain a metal box filled with shining coins—"mimic gold", according to Bosa—but they agreed to leave it for now. They'd come back for it after they dealt with the boss.

The group then doubled back and moved clockwise to the next hall, which immediately turned a corner into a dead-end. Fortunately, the last hallway led to another door, and cracking it open revealed what Nabby had been waiting for: the first monster of the dungeon.

It was finally time for Bosa to reveal her test.

Oh man, I wonder what it's gonna be? Does she want me to describe what techniques I should use against it, or is it gonna be a quiz on the best way to Drain *it? Maybe she even wants me to try* Internal Decay *on it!*

The party convened for a quick discussion before they challenged the beast. All eyes were on Bosa, curious to hear what she had in mind.

"Looks like there's only a single okiagari in there. Is that okay for your trial?" asked Sera.

"Yeah, should be perfect," Bosa nodded. "So, here's the plan. We'll all enter the room together, but then I want Nabby to—"

The demon held her breath.

"—demonstrate how she should confront that monster."

And nearly choked.

She was completely flummoxed by Bosa's request. She assumed it was going to be some test of her unique healing style, but she wanted *that?!*

How the heck is fighting a monster supposed to make me a better healer?! And especially if I'm doing it solo?!

"I don't understand! Why do you want me to *attack* the monster?!"

"Don't worry—you don't have to kill it or anything. I know you don't like fighting, so I just want you to show me what you're supposed to do against that monster. If it's what I'm hoping to see, you win a burger. Easy as that."

Tousen raised an eyebrow. "You sure that's safe? Nabby here doesn't seem helpless, but she's still our healer."

"We can all jump in if things start to go south. I'm not expecting her to solo the dungeon—I just want her to prove she knows what to do."

"Hmmm... Oh. *Ohhh*. So *that's* what you meant by 'unconventional style'." Mina pointed at Nabby. "You're using reworked dark magic, aren't you?"

"Y-yeah, that's right."

Nabby confirmed Mina's suspicions, but she didn't understand why that was relevant. Or how the halfling had figured out her method of healing.

Mina began muttering to herself. "Interesting way to get around her limitations as a demon. Gotta be some problems with the mana flow, though—which must be why Bosa is..."

"Mana flow?" Sera cocked her head. "...Ah! I get it! You think Nabby's—"

Bosa cut her off immediately. "Do me a favor and keep the spoilers to yourself. There's no point to the test if she hears the answer."

Tousen laughed. "Well, *I* don't get it, but that doesn't matter shit to me anyways. You guys ready to rock?"

"All set over here. How about you, Nabs?"

Nabby bit her lip. It still didn't make any sense for Bosa to ask her to attack a monster, but Sera and Mina seemed to understand the plan. With that in mind, Nabby could assume fighting monsters would help her become a better healer…somehow.

I'll just figure it out as I go. I'll beat Bosa's trial and win that beefy goodness!

"I'm ready. Let's go!"

After Nabby passed Mina's gear back to her, the party pushed through the door and confronted the monster—with their healer stepping forward to challenge it.

That was when Nabby realized she had no idea what her opponent even was.

Sera called it an "okiagari", but Nabby had never heard of it before. It was about the size of a human, with a body shaped like a fuzzy bowling pin. Its arms and legs were short and thick, and its face would have looked cartoonish if it weren't for the sharp fangs lining its wide mouth.

Nabby's heart pounded in her chest. She had never faced a monster alone like this, and she could feel it staring right at her. The okiagari seemed to be deciding if it should focus on Nabby or the larger group, but that hesitation wouldn't last forever.

She needed to figure out her plan of attack *now*.

Judging from Bosa and Mina's words, it sounded like the test had something to do with Nabby's custom dark magic and a problem with its mana flow. Su Ling the Cardinal Mage mentioned something similar as well, so she could assume there was a hint there.

But attacking the monster meant she couldn't think of her spells as healing magic during the fight, so following Ling's advice and shifting her perspective was out of the question. Nabby also didn't carry a weapon, so there was no way Bosa wanted her to demonstrate her physical strength. But if she was supposed to attack with consideration to issues in the mana flow of her dark magic, then what was she—

Wait—that's gotta be it!

Bosa wants me to show how I'd take down the monster without using my dark magic!

Nabby could barely keep her smugness to herself. Bosa had intentionally kept things ambiguous, but now it was all too obvious what she had planned.

If Nabby was going to treat her dark magic like healing spells, she'd naturally need a new way to defend herself! Bosa wanted to put her in a tight spot so she'd have to use her magic offensively, with the trick being that Nabby would fail if she used *Dark Blast* or *Hellfire!*

Too bad Nabby was cleverer than that. The demon could already taste her victory.

Because even if she couldn't attack the monster, there was nothing saying she couldn't bring in some friends to do it for her!

Nabby quickly gathered mana and chanted her spell. Magic glyphs appeared and flashed in front of her, bringing sulfur-tinged heat into the dungeon.

"Come forth, my loyal familiars!"

Cerulean, Bergundy, and Rusty were summoned before their master. The dogs were happy to see her, but they immediately raised their hackles and growled once they caught the scent of the nearby monster. Bergundy put himself between Nabby and the okiagari while Cerulean and Rusty stood ready at her sides.

Nabby thrust a finger at the monster. "Alright, guys, let's take this monster down! But be sure to back off if things get scary, okay?"

Nabby and her dogs rushed the okiagari. Once they were close enough, Rusty zipped away and barked at the monster, drawing its attention away from Cerulean and Bergundy. The larger dogs then leapt onto the okiagari's back and tore into it.

Nabby's familiars soon had their target lying motionless on the dungeon floor. Her dogs had taken it down effortlessly, and she rewarded them with all the affectionate petting her arms could muster.

Which was quite a lot, considering how happy she was to have completed the test on her first try.

"So, how did I do?" she asked Bosa with a grin.

"Dunno. Is that your final answer?"

"Why shouldn't it be?"

"Because all you've done is piss it off."

"Huh?"

Nabby whipped around—and saw the okiagari climbing back onto its feet.

4

The okiagari rose, completely unfazed by its wounds. It began to plod towards the healer once again.

Nabby grimaced. She shouldn't have assumed a dungeon monster would go down so easily. Her familiars stopped attacking because they thought the okiagari was dead, and it was their master's fault for not knowing better.

Nabby had no intention of repeating such a rookie mistake.

"One more time, guys! Let's make sure it stays down!"

The dogs shot away from Nabby and struck once more. The okiagari managed to put up something resembling a defense this time, but it was still no match for the canines. It toppled over, and Cerulean went for its throat to ensure the beast was defeated.

Which it was—for a moment. Before Nabby's familiars could return to her, the okiagari was standing yet again.

"Wh-what the heck…? What's with this thing?!"

"Haven't you ever seen an okiagari before?" Sera asked from the sidelines.

"No, I haven't!"

"It's a special kind of monster that grows stronger every time it gets back up. You can't beat it with just brute force; you have to make sure it can't move before you go for the lethal blow."

"*Nngh*… Got it—thanks!"

Nabby's dogs resumed their attack, though they now had to contend with the okiagari's improved speed. Once the monster was on the floor again, Cerulean and Bergundy pinned it down and sank their fangs into its hide.

But that still wasn't enough—the okiagari found new strength and threw the dogs off. The familiars' counterattack temporarily downed it yet again, but the effort left them panting.

They were fatigued, yet the okiagari had more vigor than ever.

The monster began to shuffle towards Nabby. Bergundy held an unsteady guard while his fellows tried to catch their breath.

This isn't good…

If her dogs couldn't keep the okiagari down, then there wasn't anything Nabby could do to win. Bringing in dark magic would fail the test, but her familiars were already exhausted.

Her mind raced to find the answer she needed.

"Alright, I've seen enough. Time to pull back, Nabs."

Bosa's voice snapped Nabby out of her fluster.

"Let's leave this one to the professionals before things get even more out of hand. Do you mind, Sera?"

"Not at all. I was hoping I'd get to punish this jerk for bullying our healer!"

Sera eagerly hopped onto the battlefield, brandishing her whip at the okiagari. She was grinning widely as her face grew flush with color.

Conversely, Nabby and her familiars pulled back to the main group. She wasn't happy to retreat like this, but if Bosa said it was over, then it was over.

"I'm really sorry I put you guys through that," Nabby said, kneeling next to her dogs. "I'll send you home now, so please, get some rest. I'll get you some treats later."

She gave each dog a sympathetic pet before unsummoning them. Once they were safely back in Hell, Nabby stood to ask Bosa what she did wrong.

However, the songstress spoke first. "We'll talk more once Sera's done. But I'll tell you right now that you didn't pass."

"…"

Failure was always a bitter pill to swallow, but Nabby was especially frustrated by how unclear her objective was. Bosa insisted that Nabby demonstrate how she'd handle the okiagari, so it was disheartening to hear that having her dogs attack wasn't the solution.

I can appreciate not making the answer obvious, but this is pushing it.

But they'd clear that up soon enough. For now, Nabby may as well watch Sera clean up her mess.

The okiagari was waddling at Sera, and she simply stood and waited for it. She cracked her whip rhythmically, more to warm herself up than intimidate her opponent.

As soon as the monster was only a few strides away, Sera snapped into action. Quick as lightning and loud as thunder, her whip tore through the air and wrapped around the okiagari's legs. The monster fell onto its face, and Sera didn't waste a second before jumping on it.

Seated on the okiagari's back, she quickly wound her whip around its limbs and hogtied it. Despite being able to throw off two large dogs a moment ago, the monster's struggles were futile against a leather whip.

Sera then climbed off the okiagari and licked her lips at its helpless form. She stepped on it with a sharp-heeled boot, took out a riding crop, and viciously beat upon its hide.

"Naughty, *naughty!* Picking on poor Nabby like that… It's about time someone taught you some manners!"

The okiagari squealed as it fought against its bindings, but between the whip and Sera's boot, it could do little more than squirm. She continued to rain blows upon it, her face red with exertion and excitement. But as the okiagari could not rise again, its strength only waned as Sera exacted her punishment.

Before long, the okiagari arched its back and let out a disturbing groan before going limp. Sera then took her foot off the monster, confident it was truly down for the count.

"Another satisfied customer," she panted.

The halfling collected her whip and walked back to the party. Tousen and Mina gave her some pats on the back, but Nabby didn't have the heart to join in. Even though she was fully aware of the differences in their abilities, seeing Sera take down the same monster she had to retreat from left Nabby feeling embarrassed.

So, rather than dwell in her shame, Nabby turned to Bosa for her assessment.

"Do you know why you failed?" asked the scylla.

"Because I didn't know enough about the monster, I attacked it the wrong way," Nabby said glumly. "That gave the okiagari a chance to grow too strong for my familiars to handle."

"Nope. Not even close."

"What…? Then what did you want me to do?!"

"I can't tell you. That's why it's a test."

"C'mon, that's not fair! I need more information than that!"

"Okay, then here's a hint: you shouldn't have offered to carry Mina's stuff for her."

Bosa shot a stink-eye at the halfling. Mina looked shocked for a moment, but when it became clear Bosa's glare wasn't going to let up, she shifted into a snide mien.

"Well, crap. What gave me away?"

"I spent years putting up a front as an idol—I could tell from the get-go you weren't some dopey chick. Didn't think you were enough of a bitch to take advantage of Nabby like that, though."

"Hey, it's not my fault she took pity on me. If she's willing to take a load of my back, why shouldn't I let her?"

"Whatever. Just keep your laziness to yourself from now on."

Nabby scowled. "Wait, are you saying Mina didn't actually need help carrying her stuff?"

"Nope. That ass tricked you into playing mule."

"*Nngh…*" Her cheeks burned even hotter. "But how was I supposed to know?"

"Nabby, she's a high rank adventurer. Do you really think someone that experienced would use oversized gear without a good reason?" Bosa looked exasperated. "More importantly, *your job is to heal*—not carry someone else's shit. It's one thing if it's treasure or equipment for the gig, but if someone's bringing more gear than they can handle, that's on them."

"She's right," said Mina. "It's good to be a team player, but you gotta be smart about it. At the end of the day, your party members aren't the ones signing your paycheck."

Nabby glared at Sera and Tousen. "And you two are okay with her tricking people?!"

"Actually, I normally call Mina out when she does this kind of stuff," said Sera. "But Bosa stopped me before I could say anything."

"I figured it'd fit into our lesson plan," shrugged Bosa. "So there—that's your hint. Think hard on it and maybe you'll realize what you need to do."

And that was that. Bosa and the Trio refocused on the job and headed towards the next room of the dungeon. Nabby wallowed in her frustration a moment longer, then hurried after them.

5

The next room contained a group of undines, and the party took them down as a team. Since Bosa only wanted to test Nabby against solo monsters, there was no reason for the halflings to stand back. The fight was quick, easy, and even gave Nabby an opportunity to demonstrate her healing techniques to the Trio.

Unfortunately, not even showing off her drain healing could put her in a better mood.

Nabby continued to mull over what Bosa had said. There was apparently something wrong with her doing anything that didn't explicitly support her role as a healer, but how was that supposed to help her when she was told to fight monsters?

Some hint that was...

The party passed through a couple empty hallways before they came upon another solo monster. It was a cat-sized lizard covered in mirrorlike scales, and it failed to notice the adventurers before they ducked back around the corner.

"Alright, here's your next chance, Nabby," said Bosa. "Just show me what you're supposed to do against this guy."

Nabby furrowed her brow. "...Hey. Can you at least tell me if I'm allowed to use dark magic or not?"

"If that's how you wanna handle this, sure. I never said you couldn't."

True, but with how vague Bosa's instructions were, Nabby had to figure out where the lines were drawn herself.

But, regardless, knowing she had her full repertoire available to her was a relief. And if those options were open, then maybe Nabby wasn't half as restricted as she had assumed.

"Can I also ask about the monster? I've never seen that one before."

"Absolutely." Bosa smirked. "Look at you—taking your mistakes in stride and learning from them. I'm so proud I could cry."

"Ha ha. I'm glad this is so funny to you."

"Hey, I'm being serious…mostly. I'm genuinely happy to see you treating this like a real test."

"…Really? You really mean that?"

"Of course. And I know it sucks to feel like you're in an unfair situation, but I promise it'll all pay off in the end. Just trust me and keep at it, okay?"

"O…okay. Thank you, Bosa!"

Nabby could feel the anger leave her. That's right—even if she messed up and made herself look dumb, Bosa's whole plan was made with the intent of helping her improve. She was even given multiple attempts, meaning Bosa accounted for her failing at least once. And considering the Trio were fully aware she wasn't the most experienced adventurer, Nabby shouldn't be ashamed to slip up in front of them either.

Yeah—I let my ego get the better of me. Of course, I want to look my best in front of everyone, but I shouldn't have thought I'd do everything flawlessly.

Like Grandad always said, "Failure is the first step to success"!

Filled with renewed vigor, Nabby prepared to consult her party members—only for Mina to tug on her coat.

"Hey. I've got the scoop on that monster if you wanna hear it," she said.

"Um… I don't—"

"C'mon—consider it my way of making up for tricking you earlier. I'm gonna be the one who steps in and kills it if things get dicey anyway, so you can trust me."

"Don't worry; I'll let you know if she's lying," Sera assured. "While we might call her 'Mean-a' on occasion, my sister's not the type to put anyone in real danger."

"Tch. Whose side are you on?"

"Alright then. What should I know about that monster?" asked Nabby.

"It's called a *reflection*, and it's a kind of shapeshifter," Mina explained. "Once it looks at you, it'll start copying your body, abilities, and every move you make while simultaneously sapping your vitality. It can't act on its own in that state, but keep in mind that everything you do to it will be sent right back at you."

"Is there anything it can't mimic?"

"Everything that has to do with your soul—so basically your personality and mana. It's only a reflection, not the real deal."

"Got it. Anything else I should be wary of?"

"Nope. If you've got a way to abuse its lack of a soul, it'll be a piece of cake."

Nabby looked at Sera. She gave a thumbs up, confirming the info was good. Nabby nodded back as her mind began working out how to best the monster.

"Understood. Thank you, Mina."

"No problem. But, hey, if you're really feeling thankful, maybe you'd be willing to carry my stuff again?"

"No."

"Damn. Well, good luck."

As Sera went to chew her sister out, Nabby stepped around the corner. Bosa and Tousen tossed her some encouraging words as she approached the reflection.

The lizard perked up and immediately locked its eyes on Nabby. Its scales then flashed, and as promised, it transformed.

The demon was now facing a perfect copy of herself.

She waved at the monster, and it waved back. She struck a few poses and was ecstatic to see them mirrored before her. She even got close and used the reflection as a reference for adjusting the bow in her hair, watching as it realigned its own ribbon.

""Wow… This is kind of cool!""

Nabby was taken aback by the sound. The reflection even copied her voice, echoing her every word.

But she knew better than to play around too long. The effect was subtle, but she could feel the monster was feeding off her vitality. It was high time she took it down and cleared Bosa's test.

Nabby began chanting, as did her doppelganger. As soon as they finished, the two unleashed their spells on one another.

""*Drain!*""

Of course, Nabby wasn't using her healing version of the spell. Instead, she cast the traditional one—with the intent of stealing the reflection's mana.

If it runs out of mana, then it won't be able to send my own spells back at me! And since it can't copy my bigger reserves, I just need to wait until its mana goes dry!

She could feel the reflection was doing the same to her, but that was to be expected. It had no choice but to copy her actions and submit itself to an inevitable defeat. The process might be tiring for Nabby, but she was determined to endure it.

It was a battle of attrition, but one she'd never lose.

…

……

………

Ten minutes later, Nabby was still locked in a *Drain* contest with the reflection. Sweat was dripping from her brow, but she pushed on. No matter how tough the monster was, she was going to be tougher!

…But I didn't think it had this much mana. I thought for sure it'd have run out by now.

Unfortunately, the test proctor's patience *did* run out.

"Okay, I've had enough of this shit." Bosa walked behind Nabby and put a hand on her shoulder. "I got a good laugh out of it, but now this is just sad."

""No, I've got it on the ropes! Just a little longer and—
""

"The only thing you've got on the ropes are my nerves. You're done—c'mon."

Nabby opened her mouth to protest, but Bosa's humorless expression told her she wasn't hearing any of it. Reluctantly, Nabby dropped her spell and slinked back to the main group.

"Guess that means I'm up," Mina groused. "Nice effort, Nabby."

"Thanks…"

Mina then took her place in front of the reflection. With another flash, the beast took on the halfling's shape, staring back at her with equally sleepy eyes.

"Any idea what you did wrong this time?" Bosa asked Nabby.

"Um… I used the wrong attack?"

"I guess, sure. What the fuck were you trying to do anyway?"

"I was draining its mana so it wouldn't be able to cast spells back at me."

"You know it was draining your mana too, right? I mean, yeah, maintaining the spell meant it was gonna run out before you, but that's like defrosting something by waiting for your freezer to break down." The scylla sighed. "Whatever. Point is, you made your mistake before that."

"Before that?"

"How about this: I'll give you one more shot. If you still don't figure it out by then, I'll just tell you the answer. But if that happens, you forfeit your burger—okay?"

"Aww…"

Nabby didn't like that. Sure, getting another chance was nice, but knowing she was one step from failure made her nervous—especially because she still didn't understand what she was doing wrong.

I messed up before I even attacked... But doesn't that make even less sense? Bosa confirmed it was okay for me to use my dark magic and ask about the reflection, so where did I make my mistake?

Nabby knew there was no point in asking the tight-lipped scylla. She'd have to settle on the next best thing.

She reapproached the reflection to observe how Mina dealt with it.

"Do you mind if I watch?"

""Nope."" As expected, her voice was now echoed by the reflection. ""But if you want me to explain what I'm about to do, you'll have to carry my backpack for me afterwards.""

"...Fine."

""Smart girl. Watch and learn.""

Mina and the reflection then began casting a spell. But unlike Nabby's attempt, they unleashed the magic on *themselves.*

""*Sleep.*""

Nabby was confused as to why Mina would put herself to sleep, but she remembered halfling's class before she spoke up. A somnambulist utilized the power of dreams, so, naturally, someone would need to be asleep.

Eyes shut but still standing, Mina began her explanation. ""There. I am now able to use my magic."" Her voice was now slow and lacked inflection, a shift in personality reminiscent of Su Ling. ""Through my *Lucidity* and *Sleep Talk* abilities, I may seem as though I am still conscious, but I assure you that I am asleep.""

"That's pretty interesting. But how does that help you against the reflection?"

""In this state, it is vulnerable to my specialty skill, *Midnight Delight.* Allow me to demonstrate.""

She conjured a fresh spell and, just like before, cast it on herself. But this time, there was a clear difference in the effect it had on Mina and the reflection.

The fake Mina began to waver like a desert mirage, with glimpses of the reflection's lizard form slipping through. It continued to mimic Mina's stance and remained unmoving, but its illusion was coming apart at the seams. It was like watching an old lightbulb burn out.

"*Midnight Delight* is a spell created by Kinki Shikozaki that brings out a target's most libidinous dreams," said Mina. Apparently, the reflection had lost the ability to copy her speech. "While they lack souls, monsters still have reproductive instincts. Taking advantage of that allows me to overwhelm its mind and disable its ability to copy others."

As if to illustrate her point, the monster's mimicry finally gave out. It fell onto the dungeon floor, splayed on its back with its legs twitching in the air.

"...I see," Nabby said with distaste. "But doesn't that spell affect you too?"

"No. As you can see, my mental training affords me protection from the effects. I am able to suppress my sexual urges and resist the dream."

So she claimed, but Nabby could see Mina's face was a deep red. She was even squirming as her legs pressed together.

"Thus concludes my demonstration. I will now finish off the reflection and reawaken."

Mina then fired an *Arrow of Reverie* at the reflection—a simple magic bolt. The spell pierced the lizard's hide and slew it in a single strike. She then followed up with *Rouse* and returned to her snarky self, making sure to remind Nabby of their agreement as they walked back to the party.

Right. Hopefully Bosa won't get mad at me for carrying Mina's backpack again…

Especially since Nabby didn't gain anything from watching the halfling.

Beyond lacking techniques suited to fighting the okiagari and the reflection, she still had no idea what she was doing wrong. Her only clues were that it had something to do with her role as a healer and that she made her mistake before she attacked, but those hints were pointless given that Nabby's only instructions were to fight the monsters.

Was she expected to buff herself before attacking? Did Bosa want her to request a song first? Or was Nabby supposed to ensure her party members didn't need healing before she went into combat?

...No. None of that feels right.

The answer continued to evade Nabby as the party continued their quest.

6

"Yeah, that's a big frigging door. I'll bet you dollars to donuts the boss is in there."

Tousen rapped her knuckles on the massive steel bulkhead. Its frame towered over them, exuding an air of finality.

Mina laid a palm on the door. "…Yeah, I can feel this is where the dungeon's mana is centered. I'm ninety-nine percent sure the boss is the only monster in there too."

"Sweet. Sounds like a perfect way to close out Nabby's test."

Nabby's jaw dropped at Bosa's suggestion.

The group had finished clearing out the base floor of the dungeon and since moved up the stairs. Like the entryway, several halls branched off from a central room, but the first one they went down ended almost immediately in the boss' door.

Nabby assumed they'd come back to it later, so hearing that she'd have to fight the boss—the strongest monster in the dungeon—alone, here and now, made her head spin.

"A-a-are you serious…?"

"Yeah? The other monsters weren't that tough. I doubt even the boss is anything to worry about."

You weren't the one who had to fight them! "Weren't that tough" my butt!

"I guess, but… W-wouldn't it be better if we looked for another solo monster instead?"

"Nah, this is fine. In fact, I think confronting the boss will help push you towards the answer you need."

"I don't know…"

"You don't have anything to worry about, Nabby," said Sera. "We'll still be right there with you, and if the boss turns out to be something really dangerous, we'll take care of it."

Tousen pounded her fists together. "Yeah, I'm ready to tackle any beasty! I'll gladly do my part and save your ass!"

Knowing the Trio had her back was reassuring, but Nabby still wasn't sold on the idea of going solo into her first boss encounter. She looked at Bosa apprehensively.

"You can do it, Nabby," said the songstress. "Don't think of it as your last chance—think of it as the time you'll succeed. I believe in you."

Motivation and hesitation collided in Nabby's heart. She wanted to rehash how daunting the idea was, but having her companions encourage her left the demon feeling like she couldn't disappoint them. Her mouth twisted as she tried to decide, waiting for one of her desires to trump the other.

Ultimately, her determination won out.

"...Alright. I'll give it a shot."

"Damn—you must really want that burger." Bosa grinned. "Good girl, Nabs. I knew you wouldn't back down."

"Just promise me you'll explain everything if I screw up again."

"I will, but don't take that as an excuse to do less than your best. I know you have what it takes to ace this dumb test of mine."

With that small consolation, Nabby girded herself for the coming battle. Tousen made sure the group was ready, then pushed the bulkhead open.

The room inside felt different from the rest of the dungeon. Half of it was an empty space covered in puddles while the rest was dominated by a deep, dark swimming pool. A large window stretched along the distant wall, granting a disquieting view into the blue abyss, and the lights above were swaying gently.

The party moved slowly into the room. The boss evidently wasn't waiting to greet them, and Nabby could only guess where it was hiding. Her eyes darted around, trying to catch sight of her next opponent, but even after Mina thumped her staff on the ground, it remained unseen.

Sera figured it was likely lurking in the depths of the pool, but Bosa wasn't willing to dive in and find out. After some discussion, they settled on approaching the pool's edge as a group while they determined how to draw the monster out.

That problem quickly solved itself. Once the party got within a few strides of the pool, something huge launched out from the deep end, erupting water into air as it splatted onto the dungeon floor.

The boss had revealed itself at last. Nabby's final challenge would be against a fearsome sea monster—the infamous kraken.

Her blood turned to ice as she looked upon its slimy form.

It was the largest monster Nabby had ever faced. Its body was mottled blue and purple, with yellow eyes gleaming in nasty contrast. Tentacles slithered beneath its big head as it leered at the party.

"Oh shit, it's a kraken!" Tousen said excitedly. "It's been *forever* since I've gotten to tussle with one of those! Yo, I call dibs if Nabby doesn't kill it!"

"Go for it. My whip won't be very good against it anyway," said Sera.

"Ditto. All yours, sis," said Mina. "And seeing as the boss isn't worth a damn, I'm gonna go have a snack. Let me know when you guys are done." She then plodded off, yawning.

If only Nabby could be so carefree.

She had no idea how to deal with such a big monster, especially if attacking in general was out of the question. Even if the Trio didn't consider it a threat, Nabby still had to take it down somehow. She went to ask Sera for advice—but froze before she could utter a word.

For whatever reason, the kraken was staring right at Nabby.

She locked eyes with the beast and felt a fresh wave of fear crawl up her spine. Her legs instinctively twitched.

The kraken noticed—and immediately charged at her.

The rest of the party made no effort to stop it. Likewise, the kraken slid past them in favor of singling the healer out.

Of course, Nabby didn't even try to hold her ground. She turned heel and ran as fast she could, wailing as the kraken slapped wetly across the floor behind her.

"*Nooo!* This isn't fair! Why'd it have to be a kraken?!" she cried. "For God's sake, why'd it have to be something with *tentacles?!* Hasn't Bosa antagonized me enough?!"

While Nabby zigzagged in hopes of losing the kraken, Sera and Tousen looked at Bosa curiously.

"That was *one* night, drama queen! And you left before I actually did anything!" the scylla called back, evidently more concerned with her image than the awful situation she had put her friend in.

Nabby's mind was a maelstrom of desperation. Despite Bosa's assumption, facing the boss alone didn't help her one bit. She couldn't go on the offense—doing so would make her fail *and* put her in reach of the kraken. Running wasn't helping either, but until she figured out whatever the answer was, it was her only option.

She jumped over one of the pool's corners, and the kraken hopped back into the water to head her off. Its arms shot out from the depths, trying to grab Nabby as she ran a lap around the pool. She hoped that luring it back into the water would make it stay there, but it resumed its land-based pursuit as soon as she ran for the other side of the room.

Why me?! Why'd it go for meeee?!

The kraken continued to sling its tentacles at Nabby. She kept dodging, but after narrowly avoiding them for what felt like the hundredth time, Nabby came to the sudden conclusion that she didn't want to do this anymore.

She was perfectly fine with losing if it would put an end to this nightmare.

"Bosa—please! Just tell me what I'm supposed to do!" she begged.

"Can't do that, Nabs. C'mon, you've haven't failed yet—just think a little harder."

"No, I can't do it! I just don't know what you want!"

"Then here's another hint: *it's one of the main things you're supposed to do as a healer.*"

"Y-you want me to heal the kraken?!"

"Only if you want me to call you a dumbass."

Then what was that supposed to mean?! Fighting wasn't one of the things healers were meant to handle, but that was all she was being tested on! And clearly running away wasn't right either, so what could Bosa possibly want?!

Trying to unravel such a riddle only distracted Nabby. She slipped on a puddle and skidded across the ground.

The kraken was all too happy for this chance to close in on its prey.

Its wild eyes leered at her even more intensely. Slowly, its arms crept towards Nabby, and she could only squeak in terror.

"Okay! That's my cue!"

Tousen flew in from the side, barreling into the kraken with a dynamic drop kick. The monster was knocked away, and Nabby didn't hesitate to get back on her feet and escape.

She ran straight to Bosa and fell to her knees, wrapping her arms around the scylla's waist as she cried with relief. Nabby knew all too well that she had failed, but she'd worry about that later.

Right now, she just needed someone to comfort her.

Bosa patted Nabby's head. "Well, I hate to say, but you didn't pass."

"I know… I'm sorry…" Nabby blubbered. "I'm just too stupid to figure out what it is I'm supposed to do…"

"No, you're not stupid at all. This whole thing was meant to help you realize one of your problems, but I didn't realize how ingrained it was. You're a champ for putting up with this shit."

"Seriously, Nabby, you were super brave to go against all those monsters!" said Sera. "You did your best and that's what matters, right?"

"Mm-hm…"

Nabby stood up and wiped her face. She appreciated Sera's kind words, but knowing she gave a good effort didn't make her feel better. She looked back towards the battle, even as her thoughts lingered on the hamburger she had lost forever.

Farewell, my charbroiled prize...

Despite the immense difference in their sizes, Tousen was holding her own against the kraken. It repeatedly entwined her in its arms, but she kept slipping out and grabbing the monster back, countering with a series of powerful slams as she raucously laughed.

Strangely enough, though, the kraken seemed to be enjoying itself too—like it wasn't genuinely trying to win. Maybe it was just Nabby's imagination—probably because she had spent all day with the Trio of Titillation—but she swore it kept grabbing at Tousen's hips and chest as they wrestled. It had more than a few opportunities to restrain her head or arms, but the monster continued to favor the halfling's curves.

Thank goodness that's not me.

...Wait. Was that why it singled Nabby out of the group? Did it hope to grab her like that?

N-no, that's not possible. A monster couldn't think like that...could it?

The thought was too terrifying to consider. Nabby found an even greater admiration for the Trio's grappler.

"Alright, that's enough playing around," Tousen said after landing a spinning piledriver on the beast. "Time to tie up loose ends!"

That was evidently a pun as she then seized two of the kraken's tentacles and tied them together. While the monster struggled to free its limbs, she bound another pair, and soon it was little more than a ball of knotted arms.

Helpless as it was, Tousen then took hold of the kraken and chucked it straight up. It hit the ceiling and bounced back at the halfling, and she finished it off with a well-timed punt.

The kraken slammed against the distant wall with a resounding clang, sliding slowly onto the floor like spilled gelatin.

Nabby didn't even need to ask if it was dead. The air in the dungeon jittered like a stopped heart. It just as quickly returned to cold placidity, but the message was clear.

The dungeon's boss had been defeated.

7

Tousen roared with fresh laughter. "Shit, it's been a while since I've had that much fun! Squishing up against that bastard was just what I needed!" She unwedged her singlet out of her butt and snapped it back into place. She then shook like a dog, flinging water and slime all around, before jogging back to the party. "So, who's up for checking out the rest of the dungeon? I'm not even close to tired."

"Why not," said Mina, stretching her back. "We haven't found enough treasure to make this worth my time, so we might as well keep looking."

Bosa nodded in agreement. "Good idea. It'll also give Nabby a chance to put what I'm about to tell her to use. And on that note…"

She then faced Nabby, with the Trio watching behind her. The demon felt too embarrassed to meet any of their eyes.

"Now, across all three of your attempts and with everything I told you, why do you think none of your answers were correct?" asked Bosa.

Nabby bit her lip. "Well, at first I thought I wasn't supposed to use my dark magic and instead called my familiars, but that turned out to be wrong. Defending myself at all apparently wasn't right, and neither was running away. You kept saying it was something I'm supposed to do as a healer and made it sound like I could already do it, but that didn't make any sense to me considering I had to fight the monsters. So, it's like I know *how* I failed, but not *why*."

"Good—you really thought it through. You're absolutely right; fighting and running away weren't correct, and the right choice *is* something you know how to do. In fact, you did it during our first job together."

"I…I did?"

"Yup. What you were supposed to do," said Bosa, "was stand back and let your party members deal with each monster. You should have immediately pointed out that you're our healer and let someone else handle it."

"*What?!*"

Nabby was outraged. Bosa kept telling her she had to demonstrate how she'd deal with each monster by herself—clearly excluding her party members. Finding out the test had been rigged from the start was infuriating.

"That's not fair, Bosa! You said I had to show you how *I'd* fight each monster!"

Bosa shook her head. "Wrong. I told you to show me what you're *supposed to do* against those monsters. You had to face them, but I never said you had to do it alone or even attack. You decided all that yourself. And that's exactly what I'm trying to fix."

Nabby's mouth hung agape. She dug through her memory, trying to cite the exact moment Bosa instructed her to attack.

But nothing came to her.

All Nabby had were a series of ambiguous requests that she misconstrued as instructions to fight monsters without any help.

Now Bosa's clues made sense. Being reminded of her role, her mistake being made before attacking, the answer being one her duties as a healer—it all obliquely implied that standing down and leaving combat to the team's fighters was the right answer.

But while learning what she should have done was illuminating, it was the realization that came soon after that truly shocked the demon.

Even though she called herself a healer, Nabby's first thought was *to fight.*

"It's not a bad thing that you thought about how to defend yourself. It's just that nobody expects a healer to do any fighting," said Sera. "Adventurers focus on their respective roles so that they can excel in their responsibilities. That's why my sisters and I didn't have any trouble defeating the monsters, for example. It can be good to have skills beyond your role, but for you, healing should always be foremost in your mind."

"Couldn't have said it better myself," concurred Bosa. "Trying to do more than what you're hired for will just make you look like a jackass. That's why I don't know how to fight—there's simply no reason I should."

Nabby was pretty sure Bosa didn't know how to fight because she was too lazy to learn, but she kept that comment to herself. Ignoring the anecdote, Bosa still had a point.

"But... How did you know I wasn't thinking like a healer?"

"When Weathercock brought up his spell perspective stuff, it reminded me of how you mentioned demon kids are encouraged to beat the crap out of each other. Between that and how your spells were originally made for offense, I got the feeling that a healer's perspective wouldn't come naturally to you."

Mina tilted her head. "'Weathercock'?"

"She's referring to a Cardinal Mage we met during our last job. His real name is Su Ling," said Nabby.

"Ohhh, I know Su. He's the asshole that made my staff and assured me it couldn't be any shorter without diminishing its enchantment," the somnambulist said with vexation. "But yeah—that old bird knows his magic. Any advice he gave you is worth listening to."

"He told me that I could improve my spells if I started thinking of them as proper healing magic. Doing so would help my efficiency and control and maybe even make it easier to rework more spells in the future."

"Yeah, that sounds about right. Your workaround for demonkind's inability to use traditional healing spells was clever but tweaking dark magic like that is kinda extreme. I figured there must have been something wrong with your mana flow when Bosa explained her test, but I didn't realize it was your mindset that was screwy."

"Is it really that important to think of your spells in a way that matches the way you use them?"

"Magic is an inexact science. Your emotional state can have a huge impact on how your spell comes out. You're pretty lucky to have a friend who wanted to help you straighten out your perspective."

"Trust me, when you live with someone who won't shut up about becoming the *world's greatest demon healer*, it gets hard to not think of shit like this. Last thing I'd need is for my partner to plateau and get depressed," Bosa sassed. She then looked at Nabby. "There you have it. That's why I couldn't give you clear-cut instructions. I know you hate fighting, so I'm sorry that's what you assumed you were supposed to do, but I figured making that mistake would help you see where you needed to improve. Try to forgive me?"

Bosa winked as she put her hands together for an exaggerated apology. However, Nabby was too stunned to appreciate seeing her snarky friend act so servile.

She did all this...just to help me achieve my dream?

Nabby wasn't about to pretend the whole experience was suddenly fun and games. Fighting all those monsters was terrifying.

But to find out it all happened because Bosa could see she had hit a developmental roadblock was... Well, it almost made it all feel worthwhile.

More than anything, it filled Nabby with gratitude.

"*...Sniff.*"

"Shit, I thought this might happen. C'mon—no more waterworks, Nabs."

"I know, it's just... I can't believe you thought of all that for me," she said through her tears. "I...I really appreciate it!"

"Don't. I only did it to make my own life easier. The better you get, the higher rank you'll reach, which leads to more money and less stress for me."

"W-well, sure, but—"

"You guys are too dang cute, you know that? Here."

Sera offered Nabby a handkerchief. She accepted and blew her nose, but the tenderness in her heart wasn't ready to subside.

"Thank you," she sniveled. "Bosa's super cool, isn't she?"

"Definitely! I was kinda nervous about working with her, but she's just as nice of a person as I thought!"

"Tch. You're both a couple of saps," Bosa said dryly. "Anyway, Nabby, you need to double-down on working on how you see your magic moving forward. Remember that you're using *healing* spells, not reworked attack crap. Do that, and I'm sure you'll catch up to Reese's Pieces."

"Got it! I won't let today's lessons go to waste! A-and I'm sorry I wasn't able to figure it out on my own!"

"Christ—you're fine. There's nothing to apologize for."

"Right... S-sorry..."

"Wow, you're kind of a milquetoast for a demon, aren't you?" Tousen laughed. Sera shot her a reprimanding glare.

"She is, but that's what I like about her. That and her cooking," said Bosa. "By the way, thanks again for putting up with this, you three."

"Eh, I got Nabby to carry my stuff, so no thanks needed. Seeing a demon heal was interesting enough, anyway," shrugged Mina.

"Still, thank you." Nabby bowed deeply. "Um... So now that the boss has been defeated, what do we do next?"

"Scour the rest of the dungeon and grab all the treasure. Much as I'd like to go home and take a nap, I'm not leaving until I'm paid what I'm worth."

"I could certainly use some extra money too. I'm gonna have to buy my own hamburger now..."

Bosa smirked. "Still stuck on that, huh. Tell you what— if you can be a good healer until the job's over, we can still get burgers for dinner."

"R-really?!"

"However, if even one of our halfling friends complains, then I get ownership of Rusty instead. No ifs, ands, or buts."

"What?! No! You can't do that to Cer-cer and Bergy! The three of them are a team!"

"Too bad—those are the rules. Though I'll let it slide if it's just Mina whining about you not carrying her share of the loot."

"Feh. Bitch."

Nabby wasn't sure she could take such a risk. Rusty seemed to like Bosa, sure, but the thought of breaking apart the Hounds of House Naberius was inconceivable. Doing so over a hamburger was even more absurd.

But…backing down would basically be the same as admitting she hadn't learned a thing.

This was about more than just beefy goodness. Nabby's pride was on the line, and she was done looking like a fool.

…*I'll just make sure Rusty never hears about this.*

"Okay, you're on!" Nabby said with fiery determination. "I'll be the best dang healer you've ever seen! I'll stand back and not fight like a pro!"

"Atta girl, Nabs. Then what say we stop fucking around and go get our full paycheck?"

The party gave a round of agreement. They gathered their things and headed for the boss room's door, eager to find whatever treasures still awaited them.

But before the group passed through the bulkhead, Nabby took one last look around. Her encounter with the kraken was obscenely unpleasant, yet the experience of her first dungeon was invaluable. She felt a little sad that this room and everything around it wasn't going to exist by tomorrow.

But at least she'd always have her memories—and the best friend she made them with.

Nabby smiled and faced forward again. She followed alongside her party as they traveled through the final halls of the dungeon.

8

Sometime in the afternoon, the party stepped out of the dungeon's entrance and back into the dingy building of the abandoned car wash.

With the exception of Tousen, they were all exhausted. There ended up being an inordinate amount of loot in the final rooms, leaving them overburdened with mana crystals and mimic gold. They might have made out like bandits because of that but having to carry it all out of the dungeon left Nabby questioning if it was worth it.

There were also a lot more monsters in those last rooms too. What a backwards layout… Who the heck puts the boss before the underlings?

The tired adventurers were now busy counting coins while Tousen dug a can of spray paint out of Mina's backpack. She then tagged *"BOSS DEAD"* on the dungeon's door, followed by today's date and a doodle of what looked like a peach with a sword run through it.

"That's the symbol of Kinki Shikozaki's Lurid Blades," said Sera. "It's good manners to mark a cleared dungeon, but we also like to advertise ourselves while we're at it."

That sounded reasonable to Nabby. Maybe she'd come up with a symbol for her and Bosa next time they got a dungeon job.

Aside from the back-breaking labor, the rest of the gig went smoothly. Nabby was completely focused on her role as a healer, staying back and avoiding combat as much as possible. All the fighting gave her plenty of opportunities to consider her perspective as well, and she did her best to think healy thoughts every time she used *Drain* or *Contaminate*.

While doing so appeared to help, Nabby couldn't tell if that was just confirmation bias. Her magic felt *smoother*, but since Mina said her emotions could affect her spells, maybe it just seemed easier because she was in a good mood. It was hard to say at this point, so Nabby concluded she'd just have to monitor herself next time she tried reworking *Internal Decay.*

She also made a mental note to give her custom version a less sinister name.

More importantly, none of the Trio had anything bad to say about her healing. In fact, Mina seemed quite taken with it now that she understood what was going on. She was less thrilled when Nabby refused to play pack mule again, but Bosa had thankfully foreseen as much. As they sorted through the crystals and gold, the scylla proudly confirmed that Nabby had successfully secured her burger. And Rusty.

Once they were done, each member of the party was handed their respective share of the loot. The halflings' portions were almost as big as them, but Tousen didn't have any trouble carrying all three shares. The group then left the empty building and prepared to go their separate ways, stopping in the parking lot to say farewell.

"Guess this is goodbye," said Bosa. "Thanks again. It was good working with you."

Tousen grinned wide. "Same—I had a blast! Not having to deal with Kafei trying to grab my ass after every fight was great too!"

"Can't argue with that. Nabby's healing might be weird, but I'll take that over having her cop a feel."

Nabby couldn't quite tell if Mina was complimenting her. She put on a smile regardless.

"True. And there's a decent chance we can work together again sometime in the future," said Sera. "Without Kafei, we'll be relying on freelance healers for the foreseeable future. We normally handle more intensive jobs than this, but I hope you two will be willing to team up with us again sometime."

"Of course! To be honest, I thought you guys would be hard to work with because of all the pervy stuff, but I actually had a lot of fun!" enthused Nabby.

...Though it would be nice if you cut down on the pervy stuff.

Mina scoffed at her sister. "Hey, Sera, why don't you stop beating around the bush and just ask them? I know you've been looking for replacements after Tousen and I dropped out of that job in Purpurrot."

"H-hey! I was gonna ask them! I just wanted to make sure they'd be up for it first!"

Bosa raised an eyebrow. "Purpurrot? Isn't that a few states over?"

"Yeah, it was some wack-ass gig where the client only wanted to hire women," said Tousen. "It didn't involve any fighting, so I wasn't interested. Mina's busy that week too."

"They're only hiring women? That sounds pretty sketchy."

"That's what I thought too, but hear me out," Sera implored. "The job is from a man called Don Giacomo Testa, head of the Testa Family, and he personally contacted us in hopes of hiring the Trio of Titillation. The gig description cites standard monster-slaying work, but the don told me it's actually for help with a private matter. He promised that it was low-impact and offered to pay for teleportation and lodgings, but he can't tell us what the job really entails unless we meet with him in person."

"Okay. Now it sounds *sketchy as fuck*."

"W-wait, I'm not done yet! Sure, I know it seems weird, but he was practically begging for our help! He also already hired two groups before us, a-and they said the work wasn't anything to worry about. They wouldn't disclose what he asked them to do, but it's obviously nothing illegal."

"Hm. And what makes you think he'll be okay with taking me and Nabby instead of your sisters?"

"My guess is that the don is hiring female adventurers for something like a photo op, so I don't think he'd mind getting the Seafoam Diva on board. I doubt he'd turn away a figure like Nabby's either."

Nabby blushed and pulled her coat closed. Bosa seemed intrigued.

"Alright. I wouldn't mind playing up my old moniker for some easy cash." She turned to Nabby. "How about you? Interested at all?"

"...Not really. If it's not real adventuring work, there's not much reason I should take it."

"True. We did just spend the day reinforcing your mindset as a healer." Bosa took out her phone and searched the internet. "Hmm... This Don Testa seems like an interesting guy though. He's apparently a community figure for Purpurrot. Maybe he's looking to have us act like role models for little girls who wanna become adventurers?"

"Oh, I didn't think of that!" said Sera. "The Testa Family is a nonprofit organization that runs a lot of public events, so it'd make sense for them to do some sort of career fair. Maybe he doesn't want anyone talking about it so he can keep it a surprise?"

That completely flipped Nabby's switch. Doing simple work that didn't involve healing normally wouldn't appeal to her, but she was way more interested if the job meant she could teach children the joys of adventuring.

She always loved her grandad's stories. This could be her chance to pass that love onto the next generation!

"Ugh, but if that turns out to be true, I don't wanna go without Nabby," said Bosa. "I can't stand kids, so—"

"Um! I changed my mind!" Nabby blurted out.

"Really? You wanna babysit that badly?"

"I loved hearing about adventurers when I was little! Being able to show kids how cool it is to be one would be awesome—no, it'd be an honor! Not to mention that I could prove to them that demons *can* be healers while I'm at it!"

I'll bring down that old stereotype by making sure those kids know better from the start!

"Huh. Well, okay then." Bosa faced Sera and shrugged. "Looks like you're getting both of us after all. Pass me your phone and I'll give you my number."

"R-r-really?! I get to have Lilibosa's phone number?! Oh man, this is like a dream come true!"

"Text me too much and I'll block you."

"Understood—thank you!" Sera trembled as Bosa handed her phone back. "I'll tell Don Testa I found some replacements and let you know what he says!"

"Sounds good. Guess we'll see you in a couple weeks then."

"Yup! Take care!"

Sera and her sisters waved as they walked away, with Mina chiding her sibling for being so submissive to a washed-up idol. Nabby waved back before following Bosa in the opposite direction.

"So, where do we take our treasure?" Nabby asked as she adjusted her pack.

"There's a potion shop in that mall we passed on our way here. We can stop in and sell this shit before picking up dinner."

"Awesome! I can't wait to see how much this is all worth!"

"Don't get your hopes up. Natural mana crystals aren't any better than manufactured ones, and mimic gold is made of the same stuff as monsters, so it's basically worthless outside of alchemy. We'll be lucky if this covers more than a week of groceries."

"What…?"

No wonder Mina said the job wasn't worth it until they had found this much. Thank goodness the gig itself paid much better.

"At least we'll get the cash on the spot. Let's hit up somewhere nice for dinner so I can get a drink while we're at it," said Bosa.

"You don't feel like going to Stummelschwanz?"

"Nah, too early. Besides, they don't serve burgers there."

"Oh, good point." Nabby paused. "You know, we don't actually have to get burgers. I appreciate that you gave me another shot, but I don't feel like I really earned it…"

"Carrot and stick, Nabs. You got the stick earlier, now it's time for carrots."

"*Bleck*… Who puts carrots on a burger?"

"Lagomorphs, probably. But in all seriousness, take your prize and be happy. It's just a fucking hamburger after all."

"You wouldn't say that if you grew up in Hell. There's nothing even close to beef there. That succulent meat is proof of the love God has for His children on Rullia." Nabby's mouth was already watering at the thought.

"Someone should tell Top 'N' Bottom to open a franchise in the Underworld. They'd probably make a killing."

"Hopefully Lord Lucifer would allow it." Nabby then shifted topics. "Do you really think we'll get to be role models for children during our next job?"

"I hope not. Even if the job pays well, I don't wanna deal with a bunch of brats. Too many of them have never seen a scylla and try playing with my tentacles."

"I think it'd be fun. Kids are always so full of hopes and dreams, it would be really cool to talk to them and help them discover how incredible being an adventurer can be."

"You only say that because you still think like a kid. You do remember that there's no proof we'll be playing career fair at all, right?" A wicked smile then crossed Bosa's face. "On that note, what are you gonna do if it turns out the don has something salacious in store for us? He wanted to hire the Trio of Titillation after all."

"I thought Sera said the other adventurers confirmed it was nothing illegal."

"So what? Doesn't mean Mr. Testa isn't looking for some eye candy. He's probably got some epicurean tastes, considering he's been blowing through girls like there's no tomorrow."

"Then I guess I'll have to turn him down. That's not the sort of thing you should hire adventurers for."

"You sure? Who's to say he doesn't have a giant python he'd like you to *Drain?*"

"Gross! I'll let *you* handle that!"

Bosa tutted. "For shame, Nabby. Running away and leaving me with the dirty work—are you sure you're actually my partner?"

"I could ask you the same thing!"

They bickered over which possibility was more troublesome a while longer. Nabby wanted to be a role model, Bosa was fine with engaging in debauchery, and neither reality would satisfy them both. Eventually, they agreed to cross that bridge when they came to it.

I'm still not gonna help with any "pythons" though.

"For real, it'd be nice if Don Testa wasn't planning anything shady," Bosa said to get them back on track. "He seems like a man with some influence, so I'll be pissed if he tries to strong-arm us into some unsavory shit."

"We should approach this the same way we did Su Ling's job and quit if things start to look bad."

"Agreed. Big shots tend to have blurry morals, and I'd really like to keep my nose clean. One chat with the police was enough for me."

"And two was more than plenty for me. Anymore and I'm worried they'll start remembering my name…"

It was a genuine concern for Nabby. She had to go to the police station to undergo the citizenship process after she got stuck on Rullia, and again after the incident with *that priest.* Going there a third time would be embarrassing—yet Bosa just laughed.

"Let's hope Don Testa's got his head on straight then."

Sansei-san
Sunny Day

Job Six — Dullahan Youth

1

Unlike the rest of her, Nabby's scream was utterly hellish. Bosa winced as it shrilled through her ears.

God damn… For such a big office, these acoustics are terrible.

The sight before them deserved a scream, however. After being led into Don Testa's office, his goons locked the door—for "privacy", apparently. Bosa was irritated by all the secrecy but getting funneled into a dark room by a bunch of burly men left Nabby as strung out as a violin.

Then their dumbass client pulled out a switchblade and took off his own head, inciting Nabby's outburst. Don Testa's noggin was now lying sideways on his desk while his body sat slack in his chair, looking like a scene straight out of a B-list horror flick.

What a fucking idiot. Who the hell starts negotiations like this?

Bosa glowered at the don's head. His tongue continued to hang out of his contorted face—before suddenly retracting for a chuckle.

"Heh-heh. Kids love that bit. Always gets a few laughs and—"

"*Dark Return!*"

Having found her composure again, Nabby snapped into healer mode and attempted to resurrect the seemingly dead don.

"Whoa, whoa—hold the magic! I ain't really dead!"

"Eek! H-he can talk?! How did he turn into a zombie already?!"

"I ain't undead neither! Calm yourself, girlie!"

Don Testa's headless body gesticulated frantically as he tried to assure Nabby he was still among the living. He wasn't gaining much ground, however, so Bosa interjected.

"Chill out, Nabby—he didn't actually cut his head off. And unless you're hiding a lich under your skirt, there's no way he turned into a zombie."

"What?! Th-then how is he talking—a-and moving like that?!"

"You've gotta be kidding me. Haven't you ever heard of a dullahan?"

"...He's a dullahan?"

"That's it—you're getting a spanking later. I told you to read up on our jobs ahead of time, but it looks like the lesson isn't gonna take without some reinforcement." Bosa rubbed her forehead. "You at least know that dullahan are a race whose heads aren't connected to their bodies, right? He couldn't have cut his head off because it's never been attached."

"B-but he looks just like a human!"

"You're one to talk. Take a peep at his neck—humans don't have blue fire coming out of their throats, do they?"

Nabby looked at the unnatural flame rising from Don Testa's body. "...No, they don't." She timidly returned to her seat. "Um... S-sorry, sir. I...didn't know..."

"Ain't a problem. Kinda hurts to see my best joke fall flat, but that's on me for assumin' you knew what I am. Never occurred to me that a little decapitation would freak out a demon, though." Don Testa set his head back on his shoulders. "Well, looks like havin' fun is out of the question. How's about we get down to business instead?"

"Sounds terrific. And how about you get us something to drink while you're at it? Preferably with more flavor than water," said Bosa. Nabby quietly nodded as well.

"Sure thing. Hey—Vinny! Get these ladies some coffee, alright?"

The goon standing next to the door grunted in affirmation and left the room. Barely two minutes passed before he returned, placing a couple steaming mugs in front of Bosa and Nabby. The scylla said a quick thanks before taking a sip.

Dark and full-bodied. Not bad at all.

"Now then, the name's Giacomo Testa, head of the Testa Family business. People like to call me the don, feel free to join 'em."

"Like Nabby said, we know who you are. We need to know *why* you hired us. As delighted as I am that you're willing to take us instead of Sera's sisters, I'm not relaxing until I know what I've signed up for." Bosa looked around the room. "On that note, where *is* Sera? I thought she was supposed to meet us here."

"You mean Ms. Sullivan, yeah? I already spoke to her. She agreed to the job, so she's waitin' in the breakroom. I wanted to explain everythin' to you myself, so I asked her to go elsewhere."

"What's with all this cloak-and-dagger bullshit anyway?"

"This whole mess is…a personal matter. It ain't somethin' I can post on Parti, and I ain't proud to be askin' for help with it anyways. So I appreciate you two takin' the time to hear me out." Don Testa took a deep breath. "What do you know about the Testa Family?"

"Um, I heard it was a non-profit organization?" said Nabby.

"And that it was formerly a full-blown crime syndicate," Bosa finished.

Nabby glanced at her partner nervously. Of course, the demon probably had no idea, considering she didn't even know their client was a dullahan until a few minutes ago. She already freaked out when the don locked them in his office— it must have put her back on edge to hear she was in the heart of a criminal headquarters.

You can relax, princess. These assholes used *to be mafia.*

"Bingo. Nowadays, we work to support the community, mostly by clearin' monsters out of low-income areas pro bono, but my family's got a nasty history. Drug rings, smugglin', assassination—there's a reason word on the street used to be 'don't test Don Testa'."

"*Pfft.*" Bosa couldn't help but laugh. "What changed?"

"My father got tired of skirtin' the law and decided we oughta go legit—mostly cuz it was too fuckin' hard to keep dodgin' the IRS. He managed to convince the city we turned over a new leaf, though the family almost went bankrupt in the process. But thanks to him, we get to do fundraisers and anti-litter campaigns instead of scams and extortion. We live and die on donations now, but I'll take that over fleecin' people, ya know?"

"W-wow! That's really cool!" Nabby seemed genuinely impressed, completely forgetting her anxiety. "I bet your community is really happy to have you!"

"Ain't you sweet. But yeah, you can rest assured that you'll be workin' for decent people."

Bosa wasn't half as awestruck. "That's nice to hear and all, but that still doesn't tell us shit about the job."

"Hold your horses, I'm gettin' to that. A rabbit and an ice queen—you two make a helluva duo." Don Testa relit his cigar and took a drag. "As you can guess, this ain't traditional adventurin' shit. You might see some monsters, but I'm bettin' you won't need to raise a finger. Maybe some support work at most."

"That sounds exactly like what we normally do. What's the catch?"

"Catch is that it ain't all you're gonna be doin'. Full disclosure: I'm payin' you out of my own pocket since it ain't right for me to use donation funds for my own agenda. So, regardless if you agree to help me or not, I'm gonna need your word that you'll keep this to yourselves before I go any further."

Bosa and Nabby looked at one another. Nabby seemed much more on board now that Don Testa had explained his company's operations. Likewise, Bosa was curious enough about the job that she wouldn't mind pretending to be trustworthy.

It's not like she'd feel bad about lying to a guy who thought feigning decapitation was a good way to start a meeting.

"Alright, we promise. We won't say a thing."

"Appreciate it."

Don Testa puffed on his cigar again. He then leaned back and rested his hands on his belly, his eyes darkening with seriousness.

"I want you two to try and seduce my son."

2

Nabby nearly spat out her coffee. "Y-y-you want us to do *what?!*"

"Sure. So long as he's an adult, I don't mind hitting on your kid," Bosa said indifferently. "But I'm not gonna fuck him unless he's funny or cute."

"...You don't gotta go that far, Ms. MacNamara," said the don.

"And why exactly do you want us to seduce him?"

"My boy's twenty years old now, but he ain't never been on a date. He don't seem to have any trouble talkin' to the ladies, but he never gets serious with 'em either. Even though I've seen plenty of girls practically throw themselves at him, he's turned 'em all down. As his father, I can't help but worry about him."

"What, you afraid he's into dudes?"

"Nah, it don't matter to me what he's into. I'm afraid he might be actin' like somethin' he ain't for my sake."

"What do you mean?" asked Nabby.

"The Testa Family business has been passed down for generations, so we take pride in our family line. I'm worried his confidence might just be an act, or that he feels like he can't be with the girl he actually likes cuz she won't be good enough for the family." Don Testa paused. "...I figure there's also the chance he's just into somethin' *unorthodox* and feels he can't be open about it out of embarrassment."

"'U-unorthodox'...?"

"Yeah. Maybe he's into races you don't see much around here—like mermaids or dragonfolk, ya know?"

Bosa could understand that. Scylla were rare outside of coastal areas, so it wasn't uncommon for her to be the first one someone had seen in person. It was entirely possible the don's son simply had a fetish for a certain race and didn't care for anything else.

Hm. And if he's into scylla, I might be able to reel in a new subscriber.
Bosa finished off her coffee. "I guess I can see where you're coming from. But isn't hiring women to flirt with him kinda extreme? Wouldn't it be easier to just, I don't know, *talk to him?*"

"I tried, but my boy turtled up. I even chatted up his pals, but they ain't got a clue what's goin' on either. Trust me—I wouldn't be doin' this if I had a better option. I'm hopin' one of you ladies will catch his eye and get him talkin'."

"The first two groups couldn't get him to open up?"

"Nope. He kept things strictly professional. Here's hopin' third times the charm."

"That's a lot of cash you're throwing at a non-issue. Are your son's romantic interests really that important to you?"

"Nah, they ain't. But I want my boy to be happy, capisce? If all this crap just ends up tellin' me he's content as he is, then I'll be satisfied."

"You must really care about your son," Nabby said, clearly moved. "But, um, why did you want to hire the Trio of Titillation? They're all halflings after all."

"I figured their skills with the 'sensual arts' might help. I was hesitant when only Sera signed up, since my boy don't strike me as bein' into BDSM, but I think gettin' you two instead is gonna work out even better."

"Really now. Then I take it you know who the Seafoam Diva was?"

Bosa wasn't trying to flaunt her former fame—the opposite if anything. If Papa Guacamole was serious about helping his son, then she wanted him to be fully aware of her reputation.

"Yeah, I read about what you did. Nasty stuff. I was gonna turn you away, but then Ms. Sullivan filled me in on what happened afterwards. You apologized and now you're best pals with Ms. Naberius—so I'm guessin' you ain't the bitch in that video anymore."

"Hmm."

Not bad. Maybe the don wasn't a complete dumbass.

"Knowing you were an idol might appeal to my boy too," he continued. "That's not to say that's all you got, though. That sassy attitude, your college girl look, the fact that you're a scylla—you're coverin' a lot of interests, Ms. MacNamara."

"You've got a weird way of flattering girls. I can see why you'd hire me, but what do you like about Nabby besides her boobs?"

"Bosa!"

"She seems like a sweetheart—the kind of girl guys wanna protect. I would've liked someone who looks more demonic, but eh—she's got pretty eyes. I also hear she's innovatin' some new form of healin', so maybe that'll pique my boy's interest."

Nabby was already red from Bosa's comment but hearing Guacamole's assessment left her a steaming pile of bashfulness. Bosa smiled at the sight.

Yeah, I can see what you mean.

"Alright, then I guess you know what you're getting into," she said. "Do you have some kind of plan on how we're supposed to approach your kid?"

"He's part of our monster-clearin' division, and I've been…makin' misjudgments in our personnel distribution that have necessitated hirin' adventurers to fill in on our patrols. Tomorrow, you and Ms. Sullivan are gonna join my boy while he sweeps a local neighborhood. He'll be able to handle any monsters you run into but support him if you gotta."

"Got it. And you want us to hit on him while we're out there."

"Exactly. Chat him up, cheer for him, whatever you think will turn him on. I ain't askin' you to make him fall in love with you, just see if you can't figure out what he likes."

"Um… Is it okay if I *don't* flirt with him?" asked Nabby. "I don't mind tagging along to provide healing, but I'm not really into *that* kind of work. I don't have much experience with dating either…"

"She's still a pure maiden," Bosa quipped.

"Sure, that's fine by me. Might be better to balance things out against Ms. MacNamara's forwardness anyhow."

"*Phew*… Thank you."

"For the record," said Bosa, "if I do end up fucking your son, I'm not gonna stick around and become his girlfriend. I'm always up for a good time, but I'm not looking for anything long-term."

"Okay, well, uh… Yeah, that's fine. I'm just lookin' for information." Guacamole scratched at his receding hair. "So, am I right in assumin' you two are gonna help me?"

"Yup. If all I have to do is tease your son a bit, then I'll gladly take your money."

Nabby's mouth twisted. "Well, since I can still treat this mostly like a normal healing job… Yes, I guess I'm in as well."

"Wonderful—you have my gratitude. You'll be workin' with my boy in the morning, so feel free to take the rest of today off." The don put his cigar out once again. "You got any other questions? I got a board meetin' in fifteen."

"Yeah, we were promised accommodations," said Bosa. "Did you want us to invoice you a hotel or…?"

"No need. We got a room prepared for you and Ms. Sullivan on the second floor, and we serve breakfast and lunch in the breakroom. While you're here, you're welcome to everythin' the Testa Family offers its staff. Vinny'll give you the tour once we're done here."

"Nice. Then I think we're good to go."

Bosa looked at Nabby, and she nodded back in affirmation. Guacamole grinned, apparently pleased he managed to hire two more women for his asinine scheme. He stood up and shook their hands.

"Thanks again, Ms. MacNamara, Ms. Naberius. I look forward to hearin' from you tomorrow."

The don escorted them to the exit and passed them off to Vinny. The goon then led the duo along the scenic route to the breakroom.

The Testa Family estate was pretty swanky. The architecture had a classic, refined aesthetic—a testament to its history with Guacamole's family—and the whole place was lovingly maintained. The floors were waxed, the plants were trimmed, and the central fountain bubbled with clean water. There were even pieces of art spread along the halls, marked with placards listing their artists and acquisition dates.

But despite looking like a bourgeoisie mansion, the first floor was dedicated to business. Employees milled about with their work while visitors came and went in the lobby. Vinny extolled their businesses operations as they passed by the offices, but it all went in one ear and out the other for Bosa.

Yeah, yeah—your job's great and you wanna ride the don's dick. We're here for the tour, not a sales pitch.

The goon's ramblings finally came to an end when they reached their destination. He concluded with instructions on where the adventurers could find their sleeping arrangements before opening the door to the breakroom. Nabby thanked him as she and her partner stepped inside to look for Sera.

The "breakroom" ended up being more like a cafeteria, or maybe a dining hall. It was filled with mass-produced tables and chairs and stretched about as long as the entire mansion. Some employees were taking their breaks within, but there was only one halfling jumping up and down on her seat.

"Hey! You guys made it!" Sera called as she waved them over. "Did you already talk to the don?"

"Yup. We probably should have agreed to meet up before coming here, but we've heard what he wants us to do," said Bosa.

"I wanted to wait but Don Testa said he felt bad about me sitting alone in the lobby. I don't really get how that was any worse than sitting alone in the breakroom, but whatever."

"He's definitely a strange one."

"I'll say. I can't believe he thought pretending to cut his own head off was a good way to clear the air…" groused Nabby.

"He did that for you guys too? Man, that had me rolling on the floor! How'd you like his 'where's Ichabod Crane' bit?"

"We didn't get that far. We had to skip straight to business cuz Nabby pissed herself and screamed."

"I did *not* pee myself! And you'd have done the same if you didn't know he was a dullahan!"

"Remind me again which of us actually takes the time to read about her jobs."

"Well, I'm really excited for this job! Getting to tease some guy while hanging out with Lilibosa? Yes, please!" Growing up with siblings must have taught Sera how to derail petty squabbles. "Hey—you wanna place bets on why the don's son is avoiding relationships?"

"Sure. Ten bucks says he's got a weird kink."

"My money's on him being gay. How about you, Nabby?"

"I'm betting that I'd like to finish this job as soon as possible…"

After some more grab-assing, the three decided to seek out their room before it got too late. Following the goon's instructions, they found it near the end of what appeared to be the mansion's employee-only wing. There was a note stating the room was reserved, and the door was unlocked.

The inside looked like some sort of nap room, but it was surprisingly luxurious. While two sets of bunk beds dominated a wall, the presence of a television, sofa, and attached bathroom made it feel closer to an inn suite. Someone had even brought their luggage here.

Good service in this joint.

Sera dove onto one of the lower beds. "*Ahhh… This is gonna be so much fun!* I almost never get to travel without my sisters. It's weird not having them around, but also kinda refreshing, if that makes any sense."

"You won't be thinking that soon enough. Nabby snores like a drunk minotaur."

"I do not!"

"That's okay—I packed ear plugs!"

"I said I don't snore!"

"Dibs on top bunk." Without waiting for a response, Bosa tossed her bag onto her desired bed.

"Fine by me. Everyone knows the bottom bunk is better anyway," Nabby said petulantly.

"Oh yeah? Are you sure you wouldn't prefer the sofa, your highness Marquis Naberius VIII?"

"I'm certain, Miss Mikayla Lilliana MacNamara du Bosa Nova."

Sera laughed. "You two are just like Mina and Tousen. Maybe this isn't so weird after all."

"I'm about to make it weird. Nabby, I've had enough of your backtalk. It's time for your spanking."

"Huh?" The demon froze in the middle of unloading her suitcase. "W-wait, you aren't serious, are you?"

"You'd better believe I am. I promised you a spanking for not reading about our client and it's high time I made good on my word. Now, we can do this the easy way or the hard way—it doesn't matter to me. I *will* get my hands on that ass."

"You're crazy! Stay away from me!"

"I figured as much. Sera, don't let her escape."

"With pleasure!"

Like rambunctious children, the three of them ran circles in the room, undoubtedly creating a racket for everyone on the first floor. Bosa expected the don's men to come bursting through the door at any moment, yet somehow their horseplay went uninterrupted.

Credit where it's due, Nabby proved to be a slippery target. She managed to avoid capture, though it was mostly because Sera refrained from using the tools of her trade. Recognizing a stalemate, Bosa decided to let Nabby off the hook this once, allowing her to rest easy with an unscathed bottom.

But next time, I'm not gonna say anything. Forget to research your job again and that booty is mine.

The rest of their evening consisted of getting some takeout before watching television and exchanging theories about the don's son in their borrowed room. Soon enough, the clock chimed for midnight, and in the interest of being well-rested for their gig, the three agreed it was time for bed.

Bosa could hardly believe it had already gotten so late. Despite being on one of the weirdest jobs she'd ever taken, she was having fun, and sharing a room with Nabby and Sera made it feel more like a vacation than work.

It almost made Bosa forget she didn't like being an adventurer.

3

It was unexpectedly easy for the girls to complete their morning routines without bumping elbows. Bosa and Nabby were already used to sharing a bathroom, but Sera turned out to be an early riser. She was already dressed in her leathers by the time Bosa woke up, leaving the scylla free to savor her time in their room's wonderfully spacious shower.

Once they were all presentable, they headed to the breakroom for some breakfast. They were far from the only ones looking for food, but the Testa Family had a team of line cooks preparing everything from fruit salad to full breakfast platters.

There were also a few scraggly individuals picking up meals as well, and it didn't take a genius to figure out they were vagrants, likely invited here as part of the Testa Family's public aid. However, the cooks regarded them the same as employees, earning a bit of respect from Bosa.

Glad to see they're not all talk.

After waiting their turn in the line, the adventurers sat at a table to enjoy their meals. Sera had gone for a simple plate of eggs and toast while Nabby had piled on as much meat as they'd allow. Bosa just took a muffin, mostly because she was more interested in getting another cup of the coffee they served here.

It was good stuff. And it was free.

Midway through Bosa's second cup, one of the don's men approached and stated that Guacamole's son was waiting for them. A glance at the clock told Bosa it was almost nine, so she could concede it was about time they got to work. She pushed Nabby to scarf down the rest of her unbalanced breakfast before heading for the lobby.

They found a headless body loitering by the receptionist's desk. His head was nowhere to be seen, but as their client was the only other dullahan she'd seen in the mansion, Bosa was confident this was the aromantic son she'd been hired to hit on.

Like his father, the son was huge. The casual suit he wore expressed an air of thuggery, further complemented by the sledgehammer holstered on his back. The only part of his appearance that didn't suggest "ruffian" was the white flower pinned to his jacket.

But unlike Guacamole, this dullahan didn't have a fatherly belly—he was just shredded as fuck. His clothes were well-fitted, and Bosa could see firm muscles peeking out of the top of his shirt. The son's body was even shadowboxing while he waited, as if to declare how serious he took his fitness.

Nabby walked up to the body, her head tilting as she tried to figure out where to look. "Um, hello? Are you Don Testa's son?" she asked.

"Yeah, that's me."

The voice came from behind the group. The don's son had left his head on a nearby chair, assumedly so he could observe himself throwing punches.

And what a head it was.

For an older guy, Guacamole wasn't bad looking, but his son blew him out of the water. He had all the graceful masculinity of a teen movie heartthrob, and his bleached-blonde hair was stylishly slicked back. Bosa could immediately understand why girls were falling for him.

Damn... I might actually make good on my offer to sleep with him.

The son's body walked over and collected his head. He placed it back on his neck, further emphasizing the young man's impressive stature.

"Giacomo Testa Jr.," he said. "I take it you three are the girls my old man's saddlin' me with today?"

"Indeed we are," purred Sera. She wasn't going to waste a minute before laying on the seduction. "You can call me Sera. It's a pleasure to meet you."

She reached for his hand, but the sheer difference in their heights left her awkwardly reaching for his fingertips. After a few more failed attempts, she rerouted to stroking the side of Giacomo's leg, eliciting a look of annoyance from the dullahan.

"Jesus—another shit-for-brains adventurer. Don't know how my old man keeps fuckin' up our staffin' assignments like this." He sighed. "Whatever. Pleased to make your acquaintances and all that. You wanna get started or do I gotta explain the job too?"

...Oh.

Now Bosa could see why the don was concerned. Guacamole had some bizarre notions of what was acceptable for a business meeting, but at least he was cordial. Guac Jr., on the other hand, barely said hello before proving he was a jackass.

Double damn. Nothing but a pretty face, huh?

"All we know is that we're following you on patrol. You can blame your father for that as well," said Bosa. She didn't bother sounding flirtatious.

"That's half of it. We're only goin' on patrol cuz the anti-monster wards in the suburbs need to be updated. I wanna make sure nothin' sneaks in while they're down, and since there've been rumors of a cockatrice wandering around, my old man ain't gonna let me handle things on my own."

Nabby turned to Bosa. "Cockatrice? Is that a dangerous monster?"

"Yeah. They're nothing special *physically*, but you'll die instantly if you lock eyes with it. Makes them a pain in the ass to fight."

"Wait, aren't basilisks the ones you can't look in the eye?"

"No, those just turn you to stone."

"Really? I thought only gorgons could do that."

"They can do that too, but gorgons are people—not monsters."

"Don't you mean lamia?"

"What the hell are you talking about? Lamia don't have special eyes."

"Aren't they the snaky people, with serpents for hair and stuff?"

"Oh my fucking god, Nabby—we'll get your species sorted later. Just don't look the big rooster in the eye, alright?"

"Okay. Sheesh…"

"I really gotta talk to the old man about his hirin' standards…" muttered Guac Jr. "Alright, in case the shit hits the fan, what do you three do?"

"Allow me to go first, cutie." Sera took center stage and struck the same pose she used when introducing herself alongside her sisters. "They call me Sera the Toned, Whipmaster Extraordinaire! One of Kinki Shikozaki's Lurid Blades and the middle sister of the Trio of—"

"Whipmaster—got it. Don't care about the rest."

"H-hey! I wasn't done yet…"

He ignored Sera's mewling and turned to Nabby. "And you?"

"U-um… My name's Nabby, a-and I'm a Mage. But I, er, specialize in healing…"

"Hm. That so?"

"Eep! I-I-I know that sounds weird since I'm a demon and all, but I use custom magic to work around that! Oh, b-but I know I also don't really look like a demon so maybe that's…not what…you were…asking…"

Nabby crumbled under his intimidating presence. But, to Bosa's surprise, Guac Jr. didn't lose his patience.

"Relax. I don't care if you're an oddball. You wouldn't be here if my dad didn't think you'd get the job done."

"O-oh, um… Thank you?"

He then narrowed his eyes at Bosa. "…I feel like I've seen you before."

"You have. I'm the Songstress formerly known as Lilibosa, the Seafoam Diva."

"Ah, yeah. Now I remember. Ain't you supposed to be a huge cunt?"

"Don't worry—I won't disappoint."

"Lookin' forward to it." Guac Jr. gestured to the sledge on his back. "As for me, I ain't an adventurer, but I fight like a Warrior. My old man trained me too, so I ain't full of shit when I say I can handle myself."

"Don Testa trained you? He didn't mention anything about being a Warrior," said Nabby.

"No shit? Normally he takes every opportunity he can to talk about his glory days. He was a real hotshot—crawlin' all over Monstralia, tryin' to find the Source of All Monsters. He only retired cuz my grandfather died and he needed take over the business."

"Oh. I'm sorry for your loss."

"Don't be. That all happened before I was born. You can hit up my old man if you want the details."

"You got any magic or special skills?" asked Bosa.

"No magic, but I taught myself how to fight with my head separated."

"Why the hell did you do that? If your head gets knocked off, I doubt it's gonna end up somewhere that lets you see what your body's doing."

"I got tired of checkin' my form in the mirror, so I started practicin' with my head off to the side. Fightin' in the third person ain't easy but I figured I might as well take advantage of what I can do as a dullahan."

"I guess that makes sense."

Though I don't get why you'd fuss over your form. You fight with a fucking sledgehammer, dude.

"Since none of you seem all that durable, I'll take point if we run into anythin'," said Guac Jr. "That good with you?"

"No complaints here. It'd be pretty sad if a guy your size needed a bunch of girls to protect him."

"Yeah, no shit. Now, how's about we stop fuckin' around and head out? I got a car waitin' outside."

"Aw, you think of everything, Giacomo!" Sera clung onto his leg again in another attempt at wooing him. "You're so strong and handsome too… Say, what's your favorite food? I'd love to cook for you sometime."

"Get the fuck off me. The last two groups had bitches just like you and it pissed me off. I'll tell it to you straight: I ain't interested in whatever you're sellin', *capisce?*"

Sera was in a state of shock as Guac Jr. brushed her off. He walked away, stuffing his hands in his pockets as he told the receptionist they were starting their patrol.

Bosa put a sympathetic hand on Sera's shoulder. The halfling looked up, her eyes bordering on tears.

"That… That's never happened before. I've never had a guy reject me so…bluntly," she said glumly. "No wonder his dad's worried."

"Yeah, I get the feeling flirting with him isn't even worth trying. Thanks for taking one for the team."

"I guess I should have prepared for that. The don did say he turned down every girl before us. Maybe he really is gay."

"We'll see. C'mon—let's go take a ride with the headless lady's man."

Following Guac Jr. out of the lobby, they found a sedan parked along the nearby street. One of the don's men was smoking as he leaned on the vehicle, but he put out his cigarette and opened the passenger doors as soon as he saw the group.

Bosa called shotgun, but Guac Jr. ignored the sacred law and took the passenger seat anyway. She then had to join her friends in the back, but the lack of a third seat belt meant Sera would have to sit on someone's lap. After a quick game of rock-paper-scissors, Nabby was volunteered and Sera got to enjoy using the demon's tits as a headrest.

It ended up being a short drive—barely five minutes—before the vehicle pulled over. The sky was overcast, so the driver offered each of them an umbrella. Guac Jr. and Nabby accepted, but Sera had to decline as using a human-sized parasol risked getting her blown over by a strong wind.

And as for Bosa—

"Don't need one. I like getting wet."

Which was true—scylla thrived in water. In fact, they needed far more hydration than terrestrial races in order to live on land. Most of them circumvented this by wearing enchanted jewelry—like Bosa's navel piercing, for example— but that didn't mean she couldn't appreciate a little rain as well.

Guac Jr. looked at Bosa like she was crazy but didn't press the matter. He just tucked his umbrella under his arm and started walking.

The suburbs appeared to be a low-income area. A lot of the houses looked old and the road was in need of repair, yet there were no signs of vandalism or other petty crimes. If anything, the neighborhood felt welcoming.

More surprising was the fact that everyone they passed was happy to see Guac Jr. Some of them—a few housewives, to be specific—even ran out of their homes just to say hello. He addressed each of them by name as he politely returned their greetings, utterly lacking the hostility he showed the adventurers.

Tch… You know, we might be hired help, but that doesn't mean we don't deserve your good side too, asshole.

Then again, Bosa could just mention that discrepancy when she reported back to Papa Guacamole. He did hire her to expose his son's behavioral quirks after all.

"Um, Giacomo? Where are we going?" Nabby asked as they marched along the sidewalk.

"Nowhere. Whole point of a patrol is to sweep the area. Just keep your eyes peeled for monsters."

"How long are we patrolling for?"

"About ten hours."

"""*Ten hours?!*"""

The girls were unanimously stunned by the premise. They were all used to hiking through forests and over hills, but never for half a day and rarely with a storm on the horizon. Bosa wasn't even sure her tentacles would last that long.

"Y…you're kidding, right?" said the scylla.

"Do I sound like I'm jokin'?"

"No, but… C'mon—ten hours is insane!"

"Jesus. You three seriously can't handle *walkin*?"

"Well, excuse us for being reasonable! Do you not see the fucking fact that I don't have legs? There's no goddamn way you're making me walk that much!"

"Fine. You can take a couple breaks."

"Were you…not planning to give us any breaks?" Sera said as the color left her face.

"I also know a place where we can get some lunch. But you're buyin' your own shit, capisce?"

"Wow. What a gentleman."

Bosa was definitely going to tattle on his ass now. The don was paying them well, but not *ten hours of fucking foot patrols*-well. She'd make sure he saw the receipt for her lunch too.

4

The party shuffled along in silence. Despite it being their job, nobody wanted to chat up Guac Jr. Between his sharp tongue and brutal fitness standards, hitting on him was just asking for a bad time.

All that hotness spoiled by a cold personality. What a frigging shame.

After a couple blocks, Nabby began to show her discomfort with the situation. She leaned over and whispered to her partner.

"Hey, Bosa? Shouldn't you try flirting with Giacomo—at least a little bit? Only Sera's tried so far."

"With his attitude, I'm not gonna waste my breath. He's clearly suspicious about why he keeps getting stuck with random women too, so I'd rather rethink our strategy before I risk getting bitched out."

"Are you sure…?"

"Feel free to hit on him yourself if you'd like."

"N-no, thank you! But… I think we should do *something.*"

"Why don't you try talking to him? Normally, I mean. He seems to like you the most."

"Really? Okay—I'll give it a shot."

Nabby pulled away from Bosa and moved alongside Guac Jr. He continued to face forward, not even acknowledging Nabby's presence.

"U-um, Giacomo? Would it be okay if I asked you something?"

"Hmph." He looked like he wanted to blow her off, but Nabby's sincerity managed to win him over. "…Yeah, go ahead. Ain't like I got a better way to pass the time."

"Thank you! I was wondering what you think about the Testa Family organization, since it's your dad's business and all. Do you like working there?"

A bland question, but that was ideal. Guac Jr. would be hard-pressed to snap back at that, and if he did, that could hint at some sort of friction with his family—maybe even imply he remained single because he felt he couldn't find anyone who'd match his father's standards.

However, the dullahan neither answered plainly nor expressed annoyance. After hearing Nabby's question, his reaction was beyond anything Bosa could have imagined.

He smiled.

"You kiddin' me? Workin' for the Family's the best part of my life," he said, bordering on enthusiasm. "I heard all about how we used to be a bunch of mafiosi, so I'm damn proud my grandpa turned it all around. I can hold my head up high knowin' I'm helpin' make Purpurrot a better place."

Nabby was stunned by the positive reaction, and she looked back at Bosa for direction. The songstress vehemently signaled for her to keep going.

"Y-yeah! And from this neighborhood's reaction, it looks like the townsfolk appreciate what you guys do too!"

"You noticed, huh? This area's one of my main beats, so I guess everyone here recognizes me by now. We do a lot of charity shit, but I like gettin' out on the streets and personally showin' people that we're here to keep 'em safe."

"It's really cool! Do you think you're gonna take over the business some day?"

"I hope so. But I got a lot to learn before then. It'd be real nice to give my old man a chance to put his feet up, since he's always worried about somethin' or another. That's probably why he's makin' all these staffin' fuckups, now that I think about it."

"I'm sure he'd really appreciate that. Then you could look forward to when your own child does the same for you!"

Suddenly, Guac Jr.'s smile left him. "...Yeah, I guess so. But like I said, that's all a long ways off. And, I mean, who's to say that's even gonna happen? Be nice to pass the business down, but..."

He trailed off drearily. Meanwhile, Bosa was already dissecting the results of Nabby's probing.

So, he's proud of his family…yet unsure he'll continue the legacy? Very interesting.

Guac Jr. clearly wasn't lacking in potential partners, so why did he feel there was a decent chance he'd never have kids? Bosa could understand *not wanting* to be a parent, but the dullahan's tone made it sound like he might not even have the option.

This demanded further investigation. Bosa met eyes with Sera, silently transmitting her instructions. The halfling nodded, subtly but affirmatively.

"I get what you mean," Sera said as she schmoozed into the conversation. "My mom gives my sisters and I crap all the time for not having any kids. But it's like, *come on*—I'm only twenty-five! Let me enjoy my life a little before I start cranking out babies!"

"Y…yeah. I'm barely outta high school, so there ain't much reason I should be thinkin' about kids anyways, right?" said Guac Jr.

"Definitely! You've gotta enjoy your youth while you're young after all. I bet your dad's gonna be just fine running things until you're ready."

"Of course he will. It'd take a team of giants and a bulldozer to unseat that workaholic. I can probably help him best by just doin' my patrols for now."

"There you go! No need to worry about inheritance or stuff like that—just do what makes you happy!" Sera then paused in faux thought. "Say, speaking of happiness, have you ever been in love, Giacomo?"

"…What's that go to do with anythin'?"

Guac Jr.'s flat response was a bad sign. Sera got greedy, and now the dullahan was liable to clam up. She hedged for a way to remedy the situation, but all her hem-hawing did was convince Bosa she needed to step in.

Guess it's time for the Seafoam Diva to take the stage.

"She's just making conversation," Bosa said, sliding between Sera and Guac Jr. "There's nothing wrong with never having been in love, sourpuss."

"Oh yeah? Where'd you hear that?" he sneered.

"Nowhere—I figured it out myself. I've been with plenty of guys and gals but wouldn't say I was ever in love with any of them."

"R-really?" Nabby peered from the other side of Guac Jr., looking at Bosa with pity. It would appear the thought of her friend going through so many relationships without finding true love made her sad.

But the don's son wasn't half as sympathetic. "That so. Sounds to me like you're just a cold bitch."

"Maybe. But word on the grapevine is you're not much of a Casanova yourself. Does that mean you're also a 'cold bitch'?"

"Who told you…" Guac Jr.'s mouth tightened as he realized the corner he put himself in. "…Tch. Fine. Guess it ain't that weird to skip out on romantic crap."

"Agreed," smirked Bosa. "You've got people you care about, but just not in *that way*."

"Yeah, that's right. Just haven't felt anythin' special yet. That satisfy your curiosity?"

"For the most part."

"Good. Now do me a favor and keep that to yourself. I ain't the kind of guy who wants—"

"But do you ever get all hot 'n' bothered looking at any of your friends?"

Oh, ye foolish youth. Has no one warned you about straying into the clutches of a scylla?

Guac Jr.'s face reddened. "I… I ain't answerin' that!"

"What are you so embarrassed about? You're a virile young man—nothing wrong with popping a few boners. We're all adults here anyway."

"Really, it's nothing to be ashamed of," Sera added. "None of us are gonna mind if you want to talk about your fantasies."

"H-hold on, *I* mind!"

"Then cover your ears, Nabby. I wanna hear what gets our boy-toy's juices flowing."

"I ain't sayin' shit to you! I told you I ain't never been in love—ain't that enough?!" stammered Guac Jr.

"Nope. Just because you're not in love with someone doesn't mean you can't be sexually attracted to them. If you're dodging the question because you actually like dudes, don't worry—we do too."

"The fuck is wrong with you?"

Bosa swapped to a seductive tone. "But you know... If you're just not sure what you like, you and I could head back to your mansion and discuss some business of our own. I'm sure we could...*come* to an arrangement."

A couple of her tentacles snaked along Guac Jr.'s legs, causing him to jump with surprise. His face turned a deeper shade of red, but he kept his mouth shut.

"I mean, your personality is shit, but you're cute enough while you're quiet," she continued with a giggle. "I've never slept with a dullahan before either, so I'm sure there are some fun things we can try. And I can't deny I'd like to see if the hammer in your trousers can match the one on your back."

"..."

"Aw, what's the matter? Cephalopod got your tongue?"

"..."

"I see—how about if we pull back a bit then? Just tell me what kind of boobs you like."

"...Not small ones like yours."

Now it was Bosa's turn to get mad.

"Excuse me?" she growled. "I fucking *dare* you to repeat that."

"I ain't into itty-bitties like you!"

Bosa would put up with a lot of things while money was on the line. That usually meant the people she'd have to work with, but there were plenty of other irritants she'd ignore for the sake of a paycheck.

Letting some arrogant himbo insult her chest was not among them.

"Hey, asshole, I might not be as jiggly as Naberi-tits, but these are C-cups! You fucking blind or something?"

"'N-Naberi-tits'?!" gasped Nabby.

"You think I'm lying? Come give 'em a feel!" Bosa cupped her breasts and bounced them at Guac Jr. "What's the matter? Scared? Don't have the balls to touch a *cold bitch's* chest?"

"...Jesus. I heard you were a cunt, but *goddamn*."

"Yeah? And I had you pegged for a shithead the moment I saw you. I don't care if you're the don's son—*no one talks to me like that*."

"Forget it. I ain't playin' your game."

Guac Jr. quickened his pace and separated himself from the girls, trying to play it off like he could ignore them. Bosa had every intent of proving he couldn't.

She slid alongside him, glaring at the taller man. "You're a real dumbfuck, you know that? Do you know how many guys would have killed for the chance to feel me up—let alone sleep with me?"

"Shut up already, itty-bitty."

"Fuck off. We were just asking you some fun little questions, but *nooo*—you had to get all pissy. You're so frigging uppity—I bet you've never fallen in love because you think no one's good enough for you, huh?"

The dullahan threw her a nasty look—a clear invitation for Bosa to press harder.

"Yeah, that's gotta be it. Hell, you're probably in love *with yourself*. I wouldn't be surprised if you get off exclusively by sucking your own dick. No point in getting a girl involved when you can just pop your head off and bust a nut in your own mouth, right?"

Suddenly, Guac Jr. stopped walking.

He didn't look at Bosa, but the anger he was radiating put a pit in her stomach. Nabby and Sera looked at the scene in terror as Bosa finally realized she was viciously mocking the young man she was hired to flirt with.

...Shit. I might've gone too far.

Guac Jr. didn't seem cruel. He was an asshole, but not necessarily a bad guy.

But that didn't mean he wouldn't make Bosa pay—most likely by telling his father about everything she just said to him. Guacamole wouldn't be happy to hear she didn't do the job he'd hired her for, but when he found out she had insulted his son instead...

Heads might actually roll.

Seconds ticked by in that pregnant silence. Bosa did her best to stand firm, but she could feel a bead of sweat roll down her neck. Her friends seemed hesitant to jump to her aid and instead braced for the dullahan's response.

And, to everyone's surprise, he just started walking again.

Red-faced and silent, Guac Jr. resumed his patrol like he hadn't just been trash-talked by a scylla half his size.

"Wh... What...?"

Bosa had no idea how to react. She had prepared for the worst, expecting he'd at least blow up on her. To get nothing was *absurd*.

His rough disposition implied he was used to hurling insults back and forth, but it was like Guac Jr. couldn't even manage a response. People usually only froze up like that when you hit them a little too close to home, but that didn't...seem...

...Hold the goddamn phone.

"Wait—*seriously?!* Are you actually not seeing anyone because you're in love with yourself?!"

That would make sense but—n-no, the idea was crazy! Guac Jr. was a prideful guy, but there's no way he was such an extreme narcissist!

But… On the off chance he was…

"H-hey, say something, will you?" Bosa said uncomfortably. "I mean, if that's what you're into, more power to you! Honestly, I wouldn't mind hearing more. I think?"

"M-me too!" Sera hurried to the scylla's side. "That sounds really…u-unique!"

"…"

Guac Jr. kept his eyes forward. His cheeks burned as bright as ever, but he kept his fluster to himself.

Bosa tried again. "C'mon, man. My brain's gonna fill in the blanks at this rate. Just tell if I'm right or wrong and—"

"Bosa! Stop already!"

Nabby was even redder than the dullahan as she pleaded to her friend. She looked to be on the verge of tears from secondhand embarrassment alone.

"Hold on—just let me try a little more!" said Bosa. "I know it's awkward, but we need to hear this!"

"Haven't you said enough?! Look at the poor guy! I know you're just teasing him, but this is going too far!"

"I'm not teasing him! Nabby, I think he might—"

Unfortunately, Nabby got her wish. Bosa's serendipitous line of inquiry was irreversibly derailed—though not from the demon's intervention.

A woman's scream cut off any hope of continuing their discussion.

Guac Jr. snapped to attention. "Shit—that was a couple blocks away, probably at the park. C'mon!"

He ran off without another word. As much as Bosa wanted to press him further, she knew his work took precedence—as did part of hers.

The adventurers shelved the covert side of their job and hurried after Guac Jr.

5

As Guac Jr. suspected, they found an elderly woman at the neighborhood's park. She had fallen over, which wouldn't have been that big of a concern if it weren't for the massive rooster staring her down.

Just to make their job as obnoxious as possible, the cockatrice proved to be more than a rumor.

The park should have been the last place they'd find a monster. It was just an open field surrounded by suburban streets, and the impending weather left it deserted—mostly. Bosa couldn't begin to figure out why some old fart decided today was a good day for a stroll, but she'd ponder that after they saved her ass.

The issue was that the elder in question was a centaur. Getting knocked down sucked for anyone, but it was especially hard on an equestrian body. Add on her age and the fact that she had to shield her eyes from the encroaching monster and it was obvious why the old woman was screaming for help instead of running.

The cockatrice continued to terrorize its victim as it closed in on her. The beast was whipping its scaly tail from side to side as it spread its wings, all the while staring instant death at the centaur.

Guac Jr. wasn't intimidated at all, however. He planted himself between the woman and the monster, drawing his hammer in the process.

"Don't forget you can't look it in the eye," he barked at the adventurers. "Sera—back me up. You two help Dolly."

"Got it!"

Bosa and Nabby ran to the centaur—assumedly Dolly—while Guac Jr. took a few swings at the cockatrice to drive it back. Thankfully, the old woman wasn't injured and only needed a couple firm shoulders to get her back on her feet. Dolly thanked her saviors and cheered for Guac Jr. to "beat that oversized chicken's ass" before scurrying away.

The support duo then rejoined their companions in facing the cockatrice. Sera kept the beast at bay with her whip, but seeing as they couldn't look directly at it, they'd need a better strategy to actually take it down.

"Alright, boss, you got a plan for this?" Bosa asked Guac Jr.

He paused for a moment, then reached into his jacket. "I got a mirror. Think we can make it look itself in the eye?"

"Sorry, but that's just a myth," Sera said as she cracked her whip again. "You can't actually kill a cockatrice by making it see its own reflection."

"Figures. Then I guess we do it the hard way. You got any songs for preventin' instant death?"

"I got a ballad that'll boost your resistance. It won't prevent it, but it'll make sure you don't die from a passing glance."

"Good enough. Be sure to sing loudly so we can draw the bird's attention. You, me, and Sera'll first circle around the bird before we start our attack."

Bosa narrowed her eyes. "Why do we need to move? And why are you excluding Nabby?"

"Cuz she's gonna stay right here and make sure I don't gotta worry about lookin' the fucker in the eye at all."

Without any warning, Guac Jr. took his head off his shoulders and tossed it to Nabby.

She barely managed to catch him. Once she stopped fumbling the dullahan's head, she looked at him with great apprehension.

"W-w-wait! Why do you need me to hold you?!"

"Cuz you're not a fighter. And I feel like *you* won't fuck with me. Keepin' my head separated like this lets me do that third-person fightin' crap I told you about so I can smash the bird without gettin' killed in the process."

"I...I understand. But this is kinda awkward for me. It feels like I'm holding a severed head..."

"Get over it. And point me at my body. I gotta be able to see what the rest of me's doin'."

Nabby looked at Bosa with uncertainty, but the scylla could only shrug back. While Guac Jr.'s plan was obtuse, it did present a uniquely safe way for them to fight the cockatrice. Bosa would have offered to hold him instead, but between her part in drawing the monster's attention and Guac Jr.'s distaste for her and Sera, Nabby was the only option.

With that settled, Bosa, Sera, and Guac Jr.'s body started strafing around the cockatrice, moving until they were perpendicular with Nabby. Leaving their healer singled out was risky, but Sera's whipping kept the monster focused on the attack team.

I'm not really that keen on being so close to the fight, but two groups of two wouldn't work as well. Hopefully our headless friend isn't bullshitting about his skills.

Once they were in position, Bosa slipped on her headphones and pulled up the ballad's melody on her phone. It was a sluggish song that wasn't particularly fun to sing, but the effect was undeniable. And as requested, she belted out the tune as loud as she could.

Guac Jr.'s body then charged forward. With surprising accuracy, he swung right at the beast's skull.

The cockatrice managed to evade, but it was utterly perplexed by its attacker. The incompatibility between its instinct to look its prey in the eye and the reality of a faceless opponent left it stupefied. Not enough to get it killed, but enough that the cockatrice was put on the defensive.

Meanwhile, Sera continued to whip away—to mixed results. She had closed her eyes in her own effort to avoid instant death, but that just made her lashings wild and unpredictable. A couple strikes ended up hitting Guac Jr., and Bosa could see him shouting angrily from Nabby's arms.

Sera then opened her eyes halfway and began attacking with acceptable accuracy. She managed to snatch one of the cockatrice's legs out from under it, giving Guac Jr. a chance to close in.

He raised his sledge for a crushing blow—and was clawed in the stomach.

The bird wasn't as dumb as it looked. Rather than flounder back onto its feet immediately, it used its seeming vulnerability to kick the dullahan in the gut. He countered with a stomp but had to back off to avoid further laceration.

Guac Jr.'s injuries didn't look too severe, but Bosa knew that was misleading. His muscles were hard enough to minimize damage, but a cockatrice's death stare wasn't its only weapon. Its spurs were venomous, and while the ballad would slow the effect, Guac Jr. was going to be in real trouble soon.

Shit. Nabby's literally got her hands full too.

But that didn't faze Guac Jr. He informed Nabby of his predicament and convinced her to heal him while juggling his head. The demon then tucked him under her arm as she chanted her spell, and the sight of Guac Jr.'s displeasure as he was inadvertently squished against Nabby's boobs nearly made Bosa drop her song with laughter.

Nabby then executed her spells in quick succession. First her custom *Contaminate* to transfer the venom out of Guac Jr. and back into the cockatrice, then *Drain* to heal him with vitality stolen from the monster.

The magic blindsided the bird. Being sapped of its energy and suffused with its own toxins didn't do much to slow the cockatrice, but the effects still caught its attention. It cocked its head in search of the caster—and quickly found her.

It then rushed towards the unguarded healer.

Nabby screamed and closed her eyes. Guac Jr. was yelling at her, but she was already panicked. Her terror egged the cockatrice on and drew it in.

But only to its own demise.

Because if the monster was focused on Nabby, it wasn't paying attention to the fighters.

Unfettered by caution, Sera could now look at her target freely. She masterfully lashed her whip around the cockatrice's legs, and it slammed beak-first into the dirt. A couple follow-up pulls kept the beast grounded, giving Guac Jr. all the opportunity he needed.

He drove his sledge right between the cockatrice's wings. Bosa's headphones thankfully drowned out the noise, but she was sure its back was broken. It continued to struggle, but another swing of the hammer put an end to that.

The cockatrice went limp, bringing the battle to an end.

Guac Jr. still gave the dead bird an extra kick. From the way he was holding his shirt, he was probably pissed about it ruining his outfit.

Bosa removed her headphones as the party regrouped. Not needing a moment to catch his breath, Guac Jr. addressed the group from Nabby's arms.

"Nice work, ladies. Guess you ain't as incompetent as you act."

Bosa rolled her eyes. "Look who's talking. From what I saw, only the headless prick on our team got a bellyful of spurs."

"Shut up. I'm our only frontliner. If anyone was gettin' hurt, it was gonna be me."

"It was really impressive seeing you fight with your body separated!" said Nabby. "Do you really not have any trouble fighting like that?"

"Heh. Like I said, I've practiced a lot. Watchin' myself train shows me all the openings in my form, so I'm always workin' to seal 'em up. I used to have this habit of exposin' my back durin' the follow-through of my swing, but settin' my head aside helped me figure out I wasn't usin' my legs enough."

"Wow! You really know your stuff!"

"Not really. Besides, I still need to improve my body in a few ways. My quads could use some work, and I've been buildin' up my chest too much, so my balance is gettin' top heavy. Muscles are good and all, but not if they start fuckin' with your technique, capisce?"

Okay, I've heard enough.

I think it's about time I did what Papa Guacamole hired me for.

"But that ain't here or there," concluded Guac Jr. He held his hands out at Nabby. "You gonna give me my head back or what?"

"O-oh, right! Here you g—"

"*Yoink!*"

Without warning, Bosa snatched Guac Jr. from Nabby, sliding away from the group while making sure the dullahan couldn't see his own body. He wouldn't be able to move without a point of reference—leaving him powerless in Bosa's hands.

"B-Bosa, what are you doing?!" cried Nabby.

"Just our job—trust me. Sera, tie up boy-toy if he tries anything. I'll take you out drinking in exchange."

"Holy cow, a night out with Lilibosa?! Absolutely—he won't get anywhere near you!" Sera cracked her whip excitedly.

Bosa stopped once she was far enough from Guac Jr.'s body. Nabby had followed closely behind, but she didn't try to reclaim the dullahan's head. And from the sound of things, Guac Jr. was smart enough to stay put as well.

Though that didn't stop him from using his tongue.

"The fuck you think you're doin', itty-bitty?" he demanded. "I was just thinkin' I might be able to let all that shit you said earlier slide, but now you're pullin' *this stunt?*"

"Don't worry, Guacky, it'll all be clear in just a moment. Riddle me this: why do you think you've been stuck working with random, female adventurers recently?"

"The hell are you talkin' about? That's cuz my old man keeps fuckin' up our staff distribution." He paused. "...But now that you point it out, I guess I didn't notice they were *all* women."

"Of course you didn't. And I take it you also didn't think it was weird that your dad—the guy who's been running the business your entire life—was not only making such a stupid mistake, but doing it repeatedly over the past few weeks?"

"He... He's got a lot on his plate. Maybe he's just been feelin' overworked lately."

Bosa shook her head. "Wrong. He's feeling stressed, sure, but not enough to make any mistakes. The reason you've been saddled with adventurers was *intentional.*"

"What...?"

"The truth is that your dad is concerned about your love life—to the point he's been hiring women to flirt with you while pretending to help your family's business."

"Bosa! We were supposed to keep that a secret!" fretted Nabby.

"Don't worry about it. I don't think sneaking around is gonna solve the don's problem." Bosa looked back at Guac Jr. "Do you get it now? That's why Sera and those other girls were hitting on you. Your dad can't understand why you've never had a girlfriend, so he's been paying chicks to find out what you're into."

"Sonuva... So that's why you were askin' me all that crap about love." The dullahan's face flushed with embarrassment and rage. "That old bastard's gonna get his next time I see him. Can't believe he'd get so stupid over this shit."

"He did it because he's worried about you."

"Then I'll tell him to mind his own business. Thanks for lettin' me know; can I have my head back now?"

"Nope. We're not done yet."

"The fuck else is there to talk about?!"

"You're genuinely only attracted to yourself, aren't you?"

Guac Jr. twinged. "Th-this again?! Ain't you made fun of me enough already?!"

"Then why don't you show even the slightest interest in any of the women you've met?"

"M-maybe I'm just...into guys. Y-ya know?"

"I guess that's technically true. But while you're not into girls, you're not into *other guys* either," Bosa countered. "You don't need to hide it. You've already made it pretty obvious you're in love with yourself."

"Y-you're just makin' crap up now!"

"C'mon, dude. You practically shit yourself when I suggested you were a narcissist—you may as well have admitted it back then. But if you wanna play dumb, allow me to point out the other clues you've so generously provided." Bosa started a count with her fingers. "One, you're super fixated on your body and form. Two, you put a lot of effort into building a good reputation with the neighborhood but don't give a rat's ass about girls who hit on you. And three, *you carry a compact mirror.* You're cute, but not 'I primp my eyebrows while I'm out and about'-cute. All of that tells me you're concerned about your image, and if it was because of someone else, you'd be fucking them by now." She lowered her hand and grinned. "Am I wrong?"

"I— You don't— Er, I mean I... Uh…"

Guac Jr. fumbled for words. Evidently, he didn't consider how those habits of his made him look. Bosa would have loved to tease him some more while his guard was in shambles, but she knew better than to waste the opening.

Let's just drive the lesson home.

"Look, you need to be honest with yourself," she said. "I'm not gonna lie—being *that* in love with yourself is kinda unusual. But just because you're different doesn't mean you need to live in shame and denial."

"…"

"If someone doesn't like you for who you are, fuck 'em— they aren't worth your time. I can't even count the number of people I pissed off when I revealed I'm actually a rude bitch, but lo and behold—the world's still turning. Those dumbasses only wanted me to be their ditzy idol, so I'm glad they can't stand the real me."

"It's true. Bosa only cared about pleasing her fans when I met her," said Nabby. Finally understanding that this was all an effort to help Guac Jr. must have calmed her down. "I was really upset when I found out she was only pretending to be friendly, and I remember hoping I'd never have to see her again after she yelled at me. But then she turned out to be a genuinely nice person and helped me get where I am today! I'm happy I can call her my best friend!"

"Even though I leave all the cooking and cleaning to you?"

"Well... There's always room for improvement."

Bosa laughed. "There you have it. If an irredeemable asshole like me can still make a new friend, then I'm sure a hardcore narcissist can find a happy life—even if he likes sucking his own dick. I'd recommend investing in mouthwash, though."

That last remark was enough to drag Guac Jr. out of his doldrum. He grumbled something under his breath as he regained some of his composure.

"...Can't believe I let myself get played like this. You really are a bitch, you know that?"

"You say that like it's a bad thing."

"But...you ain't wrong," he sighed. "Fine. I'll spill my guts to you. Just let me do it from my own shoulders."

"Sure thing. Sorry about the abduction, by the way."

Bosa and Nabby turned and headed back to Guac Jr.'s body. Sera was still holding vigilance, but she relaxed when she saw Bosa hand the dullahan his head. He popped his noggin back on, looking away bashfully.

"...To be honest, I noticed there was somethin' different about me a long time ago," he said. "I ain't ever thought other people weren't good enough for me, but it's like... I just don't see the same appeal in them that I see in myself, ya know? And when I started trainin' with my head separated, I... I realized I wanted to be the best version of myself *for me*. But I just couldn't accept how wrong that was."

"Nobody's wrong for being what they are. Your dad hired us to figure out what you were interested in, not change your mind," said Bosa.

"I know. But it ain't easy to suddenly open up about somethin' as weird as this. Shit, my old man's gonna disown me when he hears this crap."

"I doubt it," said Sera. "Don Testa made it clear he didn't care what you were actually attracted to. He just wanted to know you weren't 'pretendin' to be somethin' you ain't'."

"He did?"

"But if anything *does* happen, you could always become an adventurer! You've definitely got the skills!" said Nabby.

"Nabs, he wants to inherit the family business. Joining Parti doesn't really fit into that plan."

"Oh. Right…"

Bosa looked back towards Guac Jr. "So, what are you gonna do? We're obligated to tell the don, but I think we can hold off a bit if you'd rather do it."

"Yeah. I wanna tell him myself. I'm tired of dodgin' his questions, and he's just gonna keep doin' stupid shit if I don't say nothin'. It ain't gonna feel good, but I guess it's somethin' I gotta do."

"Don't worry—we'll be there to back you up! And worst-case scenario, you can just blackmail him by threatening to tell the public he hired a bunch of women to sexually harass you!" Sera said cheerfully.

"That's a, uh, interestin' thought there. I'll…keep that in mind."

Guac Jr. buried his hands in his pockets and started walking. He sauntered past the fallen cockatrice and back onto the sidewalk.

"Are you going home?" Nabby asked.

"Hell no. Ward ain't gonna be ready for another nine hours. Still got patrollin' to do."

Bosa was impressed. Despite getting clawed by a cockatrice and dragged through what was basically an intervention, the young stud was ready to go back to his job like nothing had happened.

It was a real shame he'd never be interested in her.

"Well, good luck with that," said Bosa. She turned to her friends. "You got your pocket pyre, Nabby? After we burn up the cockatrice, I'm thinking we should—"

"Hey, your legs broken or somethin'?" Guac Jr. called from over his shoulder. "C'mon—time to get a move on."

Bosa cringed as her fears became reality.

"W-wait, aren't we done?" said Sera. "We figured out why you're not dating anyone, so isn't our job complete?"

"From what I heard, you were told to stick through the entire patrol. Or you gonna make me go alone now? I ain't got a problem with that, but my old man sure will."

The worst part was that he had a point.

Considering they were formally hired to aid in monster abatement, heading back now would technically be a forfeiture of their duties. Even though they had completed their under-the-table assignment, the don could turn around and say they failed to complete the job he had hired them for. And Parti would definitely have his back in such a situation.

But…there's no way we're actually gonna walk that much, right? Between my tentacles, Nabby's bird feet, and Sera's short legs, someone's not gonna make it.

"…Fuck."

The adventurers reluctantly followed after the vain dullahan while Bosa tried to gauge who was going to give out first.

6

The answer ended up being Bosa. Sera had to walk faster to keep up with everyone, but she managed to endure. Likewise, Nabby had built her boots for comfort, so marching long distances didn't affect her until the final hours.

But Bosa was basically barefoot. She was worn out after maybe two hours. The fact that she had finished the patrol was nothing short of a miracle.

Of course, the dullahan was unfazed. Even after they encountered a pack of monsters, even after it started raining, he just kept moving along like a train with a schedule. Bosa begged him to carry her after lunch—pointing out that it would be like a role reversal for when she had swiped his head—but he insisted on pushing them through the march.

I swear to god, you will pay for this, Guacky...

The group was now shuffling back onto the Testa Family's courtyard. Unsurprisingly, Papa Guacamole was waiting for them, acting like he just happened to be passing through. He greeted his son with a quick hug.

"Hey, welcome back. How'd the patrol go?"

"Usual shit. Turns out that cockatrice wasn't just a rumor, but we took it down no problem."

"Glad to hear it. What happened to your shirt?"

"Tch. I got careless and the fuckin' bird clawed me."

"Go get yourself changed. I'll take care of the debriefin'."

Guacamole then sidled up to Bosa. With as much subtlety as a guillotine, he leaned over and whispered to her.

"So—you learn anythin'?"

"We did, actually. We know exactly why he's not dating anyone."

"No shit? Well, don't keep me waitin'. What's goin' on?"

"About that..."

Bosa signaled her friends, and the three of them intercepted Guac Jr. before he could disappear into the mansion. Bosa and Nabby dragged him by the arms while Sera pushed from below.

"H-hey, what are you doin'?!" he yelped.

"Your dad's ready to hear you out. Get on with it," growled Bosa.

"I'll do it later! Let me change my shirt first!"

"No. It's late, I'm hungry, I'm tired, and I'm really fucking pissed you made me walk all day. You're doing this *now*."

"Alright, sheesh... Pushy bitch."

Guac Jr. shook the girls off and dragged his feet over to his father. Papa Guacamole watched him expectantly, even though the younger dullahan couldn't meet his eyes.

"W-well... You see, pops, I... I wanna say that I...had a good time today."

"Oh yeah? You like chattin' with those ladies?"

"Y...yeah. They're alright to talk to, and they really know their stuff. You should think about offerin' 'em jobs or—"

As exhausted as she was, Bosa still had enough energy to punch Guac Jr. in the back. His hard body absorbed the impact, but he got the message.

"...Hey, pops. I got somethin' I gotta come clean about."

"Okay. Then let's hear it. You're my son—you can tell me anythin'."

"I hope so..." Guac Jr. took a deep breath. "You see... The girls told me why you hired 'em—the real reason, I mean. I know you've been worryin' about me not datin' anyone."

"Oh?" The don eyed Bosa with suspicion. "Then I guess I oughta apologize. I just wanted to make sure you were livin' a happy life is all."

"I know, and I ain't mad about that. It's just... Shit, this really ain't easy for me to say."

"C'mon, you ain't got nothin' to worry about. If talkin' to 'em helped you figure out you were into scylla or even that bondage crap, then I'm happy for you."

"N-no, that ain't it..."

Guac Jr. looked back at the adventurers. It was surprising to see just how distressed he was. No matter how tough he acted, the dullahan was still just an awkward kid in front of his father.

It was enough to sap the last of Bosa's patience.

...Guess I'll take my revenge now.

"Your son isn't dating anyone because he's actually in love with himself," she said flatly.

Guac Jr. winced but didn't snap at her. He lacked the strength to get the words out himself, so having someone else tear off the bandage must have been a bitter relief.

However, his father just laughed.

"Ha! Good one! Don't I know how prideful my boy can be. You see that he even carries a mirror just to make sure he's lookin' good? No wonder he's always scarin' girls off!"

"...She ain't cracking a joke, pops. It's... It's the truth."

The don went silent, waiting for the next punchline. When it became apparent there wasn't one, his eyebrows shot up.

"...Wait. Really?"

"Yeah. For as long as I can remember, I ain't never felt anythin' about someone else the way I do when I look at myself," he said timidly. "I'm always tryin' to get stronger or be a better guy cuz I wanna make *me* happy. I never wanted to admit it, but after talkin' to Bosa and her pals, I feel like I can't hide this anymore."

"Giacomo..."

"I-I know I'm a freak. I broke so many goddamn girls' hearts just cuz I couldn't return their feelings. Hell, I even pissed off my pals cuz of this shit. They wanted to lend me a dirty movie once, but how was I supposed to tell 'em I only enjoy takin' my head off and—"

"Wait wait wait—*stop!*"

Nabby desperately yanked on his arm to interrupt him.

"Huh? What's the matter? I thought you wanted me to do this!"

"Y-yes, but not *that* part! That's too much!"

"You don't need to tell your dad *everything*," groused Bosa. "We wanted you to be open, not shameless."

"Oh. G-got it." Guac Jr. faced his father again. "Um, so…yeah. I guess the long and short of it is that I'm not lookin' to date anyone. S… Sorry, pops."

"…"

Guacamole's mouth was twisted in consternation. He didn't reply, and his son took that as a cue to continue excusing himself.

"B-but I'll make sure the business stays in good hands! I'll personally train my replacement, o-or maybe even adopt a kid of my own down the line—assumin' you still want me to inherit the business, that is. I…understand if you don't." Guac Jr. then bowed, placing a hand on his head to keep it in place. "But, more than anythin', I'm sorry for not tellin' you sooner. I didn't mean to make you worry."

"…"

The don, arms crossed, stared down at his son.

Bosa could feel the weight of that gaze. It left her wondering if pressuring Guac Jr. into speaking with his dad was the right call. Guacamole seemed like a decent man, but he also had a public image to uphold. It was entirely possible that finding out his son was a genuine narcissist would drive him over the edge.

Bosa knew all too well that a moment like this could ruin the relationship between a parent and their child.

"…Stand up, Giacomo."

Guac Jr. raised his head. The don watched him sternly, as though he were preparing to lay out the terms of his response.

But, instead, he simply wrapped his arms around his son and smiled.

"You really think I'm gonna hold somethin' like this against you? Have a little faith in me, eh? You're my son—I love you, no matter what you are."

Guacamole released the younger man and playfully clapped him on the shoulder.

"Y…you mean that, pops?"

"Course I do. I ain't gonna pretend I understand how you feel, but it's obvious it's been weighin' on you too. And let me tell you now: what you do with the business after I hand it over to you is your call. I was just thinkin' the whole nepotism thing is kinda outdated, so if you end up givin' to your top dog or whoever, you're doin' right by me."

Guac Jr.'s jaw dropped. For all his manly confidence, the dullahan clearly expected the worst out of this. He struggled to conjure a response.

"And if there's anyone who should be apologizin', it's me," said the don. "I didn't trust you to find your own happiness and got a lot of people involved where I shouldn't have. Rude don't begin to cover it." He bowed, mirroring his son's method of holding his head. "As your father, I beg for your forgiveness, Giacomo."

"H-hey, stop that, pops! You don't gotta apologize—you did it cuz you wanted to help me!"

"And it turns out I had nothin' to worry about. You could say…*it was all in my head!*"

The don then let go of his noggin and stood upright, catching his head midrise and presenting it like a prop. Guac Jr. looked at him in disbelief—before joining his father in laughter.

Even Bosa couldn't help but smile at the scene.

Guess we get the good ending after all.

Meanwhile, Nabby and Sera were holding one another as they bawled their eyes out. Bosa wasn't surprised to see the demon crying at the slightest hint of familial warmth, but she thought Sera was made of sterner stuff. At least the two of them were wiping their tears on each other and not her.

Once the tender feelings began to wane, Guacamole approached the adventurers while his son left to change his shirt. The old dullahan was grinning from ear to ear.

"I can't thank you three enough for the help," he said. "It ain't what I expected, but it's clear he's happy gettin' that off his chest. I'd give you six stars if I could."

"Happy to help! Sorry I couldn't seduce him," said Sera.

"I'm not sorry I didn't hit on him. Your asshole son made us patrol for *ten hours*," spat Bosa.

"That's what took you so long? The ward was up and runnin' back around noon. I'm guessin' my boy just wanted to make sure there weren't any more nasties crawlin' around the neighborhood, but you shoulda said somethin'."

"Are you fucking... Sorry, sir, but I'm gonna have to kill him now."

The don laughed. "Tell you what, you're all free to stay another night to make up for it. I'll even treat you to my favorite bistro tomorrow."

"Oh, unfortunately, I'll have to decline," said Sera. "I appreciate the offer, but I promised my sisters I'd be back home tonight. And considering how late it is, I'd better grab my stuff and head for the teleporter now."

"Yeah, same for us," said Bosa. "Nice as your place is, I'd rather sleep in my own bed tonight."

Nabby looked devastated. "B-but... What about the bistro...?"

"You'll live. We can get something on the way home, but I'm not gonna waste another day out here just for a fucking sandwich."

"Aww..."

"Well, that's a shame," said Guacamole. "Again, I deeply appreciate the help. Let me get you some money for your teleportin' before you go."

"Hey. You girls leavin' already?"

Guac Jr. returned, having swapped his dress shirt for a thin tank top. Bosa took a moment to appreciate his physique before reminding herself of the guy it belonged to.

"Ooo, good timin', Giacomo. You got any cash on you?" said the don.

"Yeah, like two hundred bucks. Why?"

"Hand it over. The ladies need teleportation fare, and I don't feel like walkin' back to my office."

"You serious, old man?" Despite his grumbling, Guac Jr. dug the money out of his wallet. His father then passed it to Bosa. "You're gonna pay me back, right?"

"I'll think about it. I also heard you ran 'em through the grinder on a ten-hour patrol, so how's about you drive 'em there too?"

"Oh, for fuck's sake... *Fine.* But I'm takin' your car."

The don didn't miss a beat in tossing his keys to his son. "Sounds good to me. Be sure to fill her up when you're done."

"Sure thing, pops..."

"Can we stop at Top 'N' Bottom along the way?" asked Nabby.

"We don't got those around here. Closest thing is Six Guys."

"Oh, that's good too! I've been meaning to give Six Guys a shot!"

"I wouldn't recommend it," said Bosa. "You need to use both hands, everything gets all greasy, and you're left feeling like shit the next day. Everyone always says it'll be great, but the mess really isn't worth it."

"Really? You've eaten there before?"

"...Oh. Whoops. You're talking about hamburgers. Nah, I hear Six Guys has good milkshakes, let's try it."

"..."

Nabby clearly didn't think that was funny. At least it got a laugh out of Sera.

After collecting their luggage, Guac Jr. then escorted them to his father's car. In a striking display of courteousness, he even opened the doors for them and loaded their suitcases into the trunk himself. Bosa didn't miss a beat in addressing him as their private chauffeur, earning a scowl from the young dullahan as he drove them away from the Testa Family estate.

But while she continued to pester him, Bosa was secretly proud of Guac Jr. Revealing such a personal part of yourself to your father couldn't have been easy, and to do it without losing your cool and starting a fight was truly commendable.

In fact, Bosa was *jealous*.

She hadn't spoken to her own father in over a year after all.

The last time they spoke resulted in an argument. After that, Bosa didn't visit for Christmas, and her dad didn't call on her birthday. Rather than ignore their differences and be a family, they continued to snub one another like prideful assholes.

And yet Bosa didn't hesitate to push Guac Jr. into exposing his shame to his father.

Looks like I'm just another hypocrite.

Sansei-san
Smoking A

Job Seven — Human Monk

1

"lmao u kno that demons possess like a 100 ppl evry year right???"

"Of course I do. But you can't judge an entire race by its worst individuals. Demons have consistently provided all manner of assistance to their summoners, yet we're still seen as menaces."

"cuz u r lol. theres a reason u guys are told to stay in hell lmao"

"Heaven's laws forbidding demons from extraplanar travel also haven't been altered in over eight centuries. I believe those laws and the image they cast on demonkind are in dire need of amendment."

"lol no. the govt should just exorcise u all"

"That's a very heartless thing to say. Demons are just as valuable to Rullian society as anyone else."

"yea???? show me ur proof. ill wait lmao"

Good gravy—what a huge jerk!

All Nabby wanted to do was post on her Squeaker profile about the merits of demonkind. Very few people acknowledged the great things demons have done for the world, so she thought she could help by spreading the word on social media.

But all her extolling did was attract some random bonehead who kept challenging everything she said. And even though she provided counterarguments, they just ignored her points and insisted that demons were awful people. Worst of all, they were apparently laughing at her throughout the discussion.

Nabby considered searching for the proof that jerk demanded but decided it wasn't worth the effort. They'd just ignore that too, so she instead closed Squeaker and huffed in annoyance.

Nabby was currently seated on the floor of her apartment, with her back against the sofa and Cerulean and Bergundy napping at her sides. Rusty was currently occupying the sofa's cushions with Bosa, enjoying a petting session as he laid across the scylla's stomach.

Today was supposed to be a relaxing day off but dealing with that jerk left Nabby feeling steamed. Thankfully, she had a friend who excelled at cooling her off.

"Why the heck are people so rude on Squeaker?" she asked Bosa.

"Anonymity. People will say whatever they want if they don't feel like it'll come back to bite them. Hell, some jackasses even make burner accounts just for that purpose."

"That's stupid. Why waste your time being mean for no reason? Isn't it easier to be nice?"

"Sure, but misery loves company," Bosa said as she flipped Rusty over for tummy rubs. "Some people aren't happy with their lives, so they take it out on others. Maybe it's a good thing they vent by shit talking strangers instead of getting violent or whatever, but that doesn't mean you should give them your attention."

"No kidding. It's fun talking with other adventurers, but some people make me want to chuck my phone out the window. I don't know how you put up with it while you were an idol."

"Heh. It's a helluva lot easier when you're getting paid to do it. Besides, I actually had the opposite problem where people were *too nice* to me."

"Really? What's wrong with that?"

"It was unbelievably awkward. I had to walk on eggshells because they were terrified of annoying me. There were also plenty of guys who just wanted to fuck me—literally *and* figuratively—so I was always on guard."

"No wonder you didn't try to go back."

"Even a little fame can fuck you up, Nabs," sighed Bosa. "You start doing stupid crap because you're afraid of losing your following and stop enjoying what got you it in the first place. A lot of people break under the pressure—and some don't ever recover. Makes me realize I'm goddamn lucky I had my meltdown before I did something *really* stupid."

"I don't think I'd ever want to be famous. It sounds like more trouble than it's worth."

"Aww, but what about getting immortalized as Rullia's big, badass demon healer? Don't you want legions of fans begging for autographed feet pics?"

"A-absolutely not! I wouldn't mind being recognized for my accomplishments, but why the heck would people want pictures of my feet?!"

"Oh, Nabby, you're so innocent I can't help but want to corrupt you. I'm sure a quick search on Squeaker will answer all your questions."

"No way. I'm double done with that stuff now." To emphasize her point, Nabby shoved her phone into her pocket.

Bosa smirked. "Smart move. You're better off saving your energy for tomorrow's job anyway."

"Right. It'll be my first real opportunity to see any improvements in my dark healing."

As part of her perspective training, Nabby had begun calling her techniques "dark healing". Doing so gave her a constant reminder of how to perceive her spells while simultaneously providing a straightforward description of her methodology to future party members—an elegant solution if she ever saw one. It seemed to be helping too, as she'd had few breakthroughs with her custom magic over the past week.

That's right—Internal Decay *is now ready to roll!*

After countless hours of trial and error, Nabby had finally managed to get the spell to stop rotting her targets and only affect pathogens. It wouldn't work on poisons or other ailments, but she now had a way of combating disease-based attacks—and she didn't even need a living monster to use it!

Best yet, Nabby had managed to keep it all a secret. If she got her wish, she'd be able to surprise Bosa with her new skill soon.

...N-not that I want *someone to get an infection, that is...*

"On that note, did you actually read about our job this time?" Bosa snarked.

"Of course I did. Knowing you, you'll probably call Sera and her sisters over next time I forget."

"Damn straight I will. So, why don't you tell me all about the gig before I dial up the pint-sized perverts?"

Nabby sighed. "It's a hunting job that takes place at Graham Canyon. We're going to be working with eight other adventurers to clear lesser wyverns out of the area and destroy their nest if possible."

"Not bad. What can you tell me about the Graham Canyon?"

"It's a national park in the neighboring state. It's known for being a tourist attraction and has a variety of unique wildlife living within it. The lesser wyverns are an invasive species so the park rangers want them removed before they disrupt the ecosystem."

"Shit, I guess you really did learn your lesson. You win this round, Nabs."

"Thanks? It's not like you gave me much of a choice."

"Gotta teach you somehow," said Bosa. "You don't sound all that excited about the job, though."

"Well, it doesn't sound like I'll have a lot of opportunities to practice my healing. A team of ten adventurers won't have any trouble against a few wyverns."

"True, but consider the terrain. Canyons aren't exactly known for open areas and big pathways. My gut says we'll most likely be working in smaller groups."

"Huh. That'd make things more interesting."

"Either way, it'll pay the bills. I'm just glad we won't be eating eldritch casserole again anytime soon."

"Me too. Being able to cook normal meals again is nice."

"How're your new dark healing spells coming along, by the way?"

Nabby twitched. "Oh, you know, I'm still working on them, ha ha..." she said capriciously. "I've been experimenting with turning *Defile Earth* into a mana-regeneration field as of late, but it's not going well."

"What's the problem?"

"It's actually too effective. I was successful in adjusting its corruption effect into a natural-to-dark mana conversion system, but it's so efficient that it overfills my reserves and gives me mana sickness almost immediately. I couldn't stand in it for more than a few seconds without barfing."

"Damn, that sucks. Any luck with *Internal Decay?*"

"Uh... K-kinda? Still got a few kinks to work out, y-you know?"

"...What are you hiding?"

"Nothing! I'm...just not sure how to react! You never really ask me about this kind of stuff—so I'm surprised!"

"Mmhm." Bosa looked at Rusty. "She's full of shit, isn't she?"

The little dog grunted affirmatively. The scylla hummed with greater suspicion.

Rusty, you're supposed to be on Team Naberius...

"A-anyway," Nabby segued, "taking today off was a good idea. After all the stress we had about making ends meet, getting to just sit back and relax for once feels great!"

"All work and no play makes Bosa a mean bitch. And having these puppies around makes me feel even nicer."

Nabby couldn't agree more. She stroked her dogs' fur, eliciting a massive stretch from Bergundy and a half-opened eye from Cerulean.

They spent the rest of their day in a similar manner, chatting as they whiled away the hours. Having found financial stability did wonders for their spirits, and the two even discussed what they'd buy with the cash their next job would bring. Bosa was interested in picking up a new hoodie for autumn, but Nabby had to pretend she was still deciding on the matter.

She didn't have the courage to tell Bosa she had already bought something.

It was a bit reckless, but they had just opened preorders for Sansei-san phone charms. So when Nabby saw they had a matched set that contained one Sansei-san charm and one of his rival, Fufuku-kun—and at a discounted price, no less!—she had to place an order immediately.

A pair of matching accessories would be perfect for her and Bosa after all. Nabby could hardly wait until they arrived.

2

Noon the next day, Bosa and Nabby had gathered with the other adventurers outside of a park ranger's cabin. The sun was shining through a cloudless sky, illuminating the beauty of Graham Canyon.

Nabby had seen plenty of spectacular sights since her arrival on Rullia, but Graham Canyon took the cake. Breathtaking waterfalls roared their cascades, and the red sediment of the canyon walls reminded her of Hell's most scenic wastelands. Charming cacti lined the pathways, the raptor cries echoed through the chasm, and the scents of the desert seasoned the air.

Man, no wonder people say traveling for work is awesome.

Presently, one of the park rangers was addressing the adventurers. He was going over the job again, restating that they wanted at least a dozen wyverns slain and how there was a bonus available should the adventurers take out the nest as well. But since Nabby had already researched the job thoroughly, she instead turned her attention towards her fellow adventurers.

For the most part, they seemed like average stock. Archers, warriors, mages—nobody appeared to have an unusual class. However, the presence of a druid and a cleric caught her eye.

Including Nabby, that meant healers made up nearly a third of the adventurers.

But, as if to dispel the demon's perplexity, the park ranger announced that they would like everyone to split into three teams—proving Bosa's assumption was correct. Wyverns were wary of large groups, and considering the canyon's paths weren't huge, small parties were required for this gig.

The adventurers were free to decide their own formations so long as each team contained a healer, and as the job's success would be determined by the sum of wyverns slain by all teams, no one complained about uneven groups. Bosa and

Nabby weren't going to split up, so that meant they just needed to find a fighter or two before the hunt began.

And in a way, they did. As soon as the park ranger stepped away, a bold voice made a declaration before discussion could even begin.

"Alright, everyone! I call dibs on the diva and the demon! Someone else can join us, but if you wanted them all to yourself, you're out of luck!"

Nabby was shocked someone would request her and Bosa immediately. She searched the group for the speaker—and spotted a man strutting right towards them.

He was a chubby human of average height. He had dark skin and black hair, and his eyes were hidden behind reflective sunglasses. Dressed in a yellow gi, Nabby would guess he was some sort of martial artist, but the business logos decorating his outfit made him seem more like a walking billboard than an adventurer. He grinned widely as he approached, shining brilliant teeth at his requested teammates.

Even more bizarre, there appeared to be a camera drone following him. It was made of stone like a common golem, but it was spherical in shape and levitated at head height. A red light was blinking near the lens as it focused on the man.

The other adventurers gave the loudmouth the stink-eye, but he showed no signs of noticing. He just strolled up to Bosa and Nabby like they should have been happy to see him.

"Nice to meet you," he said. "I'm Roman from Flinch.com, a C Rank Monk who'd love nothing more than to work with you two beauties. Would you do me the honor of teaming up?"

Bosa eyed him with skepticism. "Sure, I guess. Any fighter would be fine, though I doubt we're gonna get a fourth member after *that* stunt."

"Trust me, you won't need anyone else. I can take down a wyvern on my own easy, so all you gotta do is back me up and patch me up."

"Alright. It'll be your ass if you're lying."

"W-well, should we do introductions? My name's Nabby and—"

"Don't worry about it—I wouldn't have called dibs if I didn't know who you are. No way was I gonna pass on the opportunity to work with Lilibosa's support duo!"

"For fuck's sake, another one?" Bosa muttered. "Let's get one thing straight: I'm not the Seafoam Diva anymore. If you're expecting me to act like some airheaded bimbo, you're gonna be disappointed."

"Oh, no, I understand how things went down. But I'd still love to work with you!"

"Fine then. Just make sure you do your job."

"Consider it done!" Roman then turned around and smiled at his camera drone. "You hear that, guys? We're partying up with the legendary Lilibosa today! Make sure you've got some headphones ready for when she starts singing. Otherwise, you'll miss out on one helluva show!"

He continued to hype up their coming exploits to the camera, earning a loud groan from Bosa. Nabby leaned over and peered at the drone.

"Um, who are you talking to?" she asked Roman.

"My viewers, of course." He spoke like that was obvious but retracted when he saw the genuine curiosity on Nabby's face. "Oh, sorry about that. I'm guessing you've never seen my stream on Flinch?"

"No, I haven't. I've never heard of 'Flinch' either."

"Wow, time for a crash course then, huh? You see, Flinch is a website where people livestream themselves playing video games, making art, or doing any other hobby. But the platform isn't restricted to that kind of stuff, so you can also find some unique broadcasts—like mine, for example. I'm the site's biggest adventuring streamer!"

"You can stream Parti gigs?"

"Yup! It's for my series, *Do as Roman Does.* I wanna show people why adventuring is still one of the coolest jobs around and figured the best way to do that was to record myself while I punch a few monsters. This drone sends a live feed of everything I do, and these sunglasses let me read the stream's chat so I can talk to my viewers without missing a beat!"

"W-wait, we're being filmed right now?"

Nabby could suddenly feel countless eyes upon her. She nervously waved at the camera before double-checking that her outfit was in order.

Roman laughed. "You've got nothing to worry about—chat already loves you. Just be yourself so my viewers can see what an awesome healer you are!"

The piqued Nabby's interest. She didn't want to be famous herself, but if *someone else with a lot of fans* happened to record her on their show that spotlighted adventuring...

This could be my big chance to show the world how great my dark healing is!

However, Bosa wasn't half as excited. She looked at the drone with animosity.

"Whoa—if looks could kill!" Roman joked. He stepped between her and the camera. "Alright guys, be on your best behavior, okay? Make sure you only say nice things about these lovely ladies—as nice as the things I'd like to say about StewMiBrazo! Thanks for subscribing, buddy!"

Nabby tilted her head. "Subscribing?"

"If someone really likes my stream, they can support me by signing up for a monthly subscription. They get a few perks for doing so, but I like to call out their names to make sure they know they're appreciated."

"That's really cool! I bet that makes them feel special!"

"When you've got the best job in the world, you gotta show appreciation for the people who make it possible, right?" Roman said with a grin. "Anyway, what's our strategy? I'm a fist-fighter and know a little magic for buffing myself, so I'll take point. You two got anything special in mind?"

"Um, well, you already know I'm a healer. B-but to everyone watching, I can assure you that demons *can* be healers! Just wait until we find a wyvern—I'll show you the brilliance of my custom-made dark healing!"

Nabby pointed her determination right at the camera. Roman let out a friendly laugh. "Damn, you're really fired up!"

"Absolutely! I'm tired of people assuming I'm just pretending to be a healer because I'm a demon! Part of my dream is to prove to the world that demons are *just as valuable to Rullia as anyone else!*" Nabby made sure to emphasize her last statement—just in case that jerk from Squeaker was watching.

"You've got my support!" Roman then turned to Bosa. "Of course, we're all familiar with the peerless song magic of Lilibosa. I bet I don't even have to ask if you have a song that'll help us take down some wyverns!"

"I've got a bit of throat singing that will force them to stay on the ground. That good enough for you?"

"More than good enough! Fighting barehanded means my reach is kinda short, so knowing we can stick to a ground battle gets me hyped!"

"Whatever." Bosa faced Nabby. "Hey, I know you've been focused on your perspective, but our group's kinda limited with just the three of us. I'm not asking you to play battlemage, but would you mind helping out with combat if it comes down to that?"

"Sure. I can use *Chains of Punishment* to restrain a wyvern, or maybe just a normal *Drain* to help weaken it."

"Perfect. You're a superstar, Nabby."

"Sounds like we're all set then," said Roman. "Again, I really appreciate you teaming up with me—just like I appreciate the five-dollar donation from SuperDarkLord42069! He says, 'Best of luck, Roman! Looks like today's job will keep you busy. Hope you don't have too much trouble with that scylla whoorrr—hoo-hoo boy, we'll just skip the rest of *that!* Still, thanks for the donation, man!"

Bosa frowned even harder. Nabby could sense the growing friction between her and Roman—or specifically, his audience. The demon already had a feeling she'd have to act as intermediary at some point.

Not that she was surprised. Roman's stream-thingy must have reminded Bosa of the life she was trying to put behind her.

Hopefully that contempt wouldn't affect the job. While Nabby tried to judge people solely on their actions—excepting *priests,* of course—she knew Bosa wasn't so forbearing. But as the scylla had already agreed to work with Roman, she seemed resigned to their current arrangement.

Meaning it'll be up to me to make sure our teamwork…works.

Once their fifteen minutes were up, the park ranger addressed the adventurers again. Seeing that everyone was already in a group, he announced he was now going to escort them to where the wyverns were last seen. He walked towards the canyon pathway, waving for the adventurers to follow him.

"That's our cue. Let's go, Nabs."

Bosa didn't wait for a reply before sliding away. Nabby nodded and walked with her, but she paused momentarily to look back at Roman.

Still grinning like a showman, he stayed behind to speak to his camera.

"Alright, guys, looks like the real job's gonna start soon. We're gonna take a quick break and run some ads, but feel free to stay tuned until then. Otherwise, keep an eye out for the notification for when the stream resumes—just like how ElTortuga has been keeping an eye out for me, thanks for the four months! And if you guys get thirsty, be sure to pick up some Blue Lion energy drinks. Don't forget you can use promo code 'ROMAN15' and get fifteen percent off your first order!"

The monk continued to rail off advertisements and callouts, even as the rest of the adventurers descended into the canyon. Nabby was a bit worried for him, but she had to trust he knew what he was doing.

Roman claimed to be Flinch's top adventuring streamer. Surely he wasn't going to cause any trouble.

Right?

3

Considering the group was halfway to their destination before she saw Roman again, Nabby was already fearing the worst.

The monk sprinted at full speed to catch up. "Sorry I'm late!" he panted. "Had a lot of last-minute shoutouts that ended up taking longer than expected. Should be good now, thank goodness."

"It's okay. It looks like we still have a way to go," said Nabby. Conversely, Bosa barely acknowledged him, which was probably for the best.

Roman wiped the sweat off his brow and moved alongside them. After a couple minutes of walking, Nabby began to feel a small discomfort, and it took her a moment more to realize what was bothering her.

Roman was completely quiet.

He wasn't boisterously talking to his viewers. In fact, he wasn't even smiling. His sunglasses were now hanging from his gi, revealing the dark circles beneath his eyes, and his camera's light was no longer blinking.

Is he...not streaming right now?

"Um, Roman?" said Nabby.

"...Huh? Oh, hey. What's up?" It sounded like she had caught him off-guard—like he had already begun spacing out.

"Are you not filming your show right now?"

"Nah, I put the stream on break until we're done walking. The drone still follows me, but it's not recording anything. Sorry, I should have said something."

"Oh, it's okay."

"..."

"..."

"..."

"...Hey, Roman?"

"Yeah?"

"Are you okay? You seem kinda...down."

"Hmm. I guess I'm a little tired," he admitted. "I haven't had a day off in a while, so maybe it's starting to show."

"How long is a while?"

"Like two years, I think."

Nabby's jaw dropped. Not even her mom, a Marquis of Hell, would work that much. She couldn't begin to understand why Roman would put himself through such abuse.

But Bosa could.

"Hope it's worth it," she said dryly. "Your streaming persona is a real chucklefuck."

"Sorry about that. I know I can get obnoxious while I'm on camera, but it's what my viewers like to see. I really appreciate that you still agreed to team up with me."

"Feh. What kind of numbers are you pulling?"

"I've got almost a thousand subscribers and about as many concurrent viewers on average—just enough for me to do this full-time." He let out a heavy sigh. "Though…my numbers have been dipping lately. I'm thinking it's because my recent jobs haven't been that interesting, so I had to jump on the chance to fight wyverns with Lilibosa. I hope that doesn't upset you."

"It's your call. Just don't expect me to sugarcoat anything for your viewers."

Bosa sped up and put more distance between her and Roman. The monk wasn't ready to abandon the conversation, however.

"Um, I really meant it when I said it's an honor to work with you," he said as he matched Bosa's pace. "Back when I was a security guard, I thought that was all I'd ever amount to. But then I discovered your videos, and they made me feel like I could do more with my life. I ended becoming one of your top supporters on Batreon, though I was never lucky enough to join one of your gigs."

"Cool. What made you sell your soul to Flinch?"

"W-well, it's a little embarrassing, but since I was inspired by how you were the adventuring idol, I thought I could do something similar. I wanted to share my passion with others since you always made it seem so fun and exciting. I also wanted to be a teacher growing up, so maybe it's only natural I started *Do as Roman Does*, ha ha."

Nabby could sympathize. She was still bummed out that the job with Don Testa didn't involve showing kids how cool adventuring is.

"Hm." Bosa's expression softened, if only slightly. "You're not the first person to tell me I made an impact on their life. But I guess it's still nice to hear that."

"Oh, trust me—you helped lots of people!"

"But I'm not an idol *anymore*—so you shouldn't treat me like one. You saw *that* video, right?"

"...I did. And after all that awful stuff got posted on your Squeaker, I followed the crowd and told the world I wasn't your fan anymore," Roman said timidly. "But when I heard you were still adventuring—and with Nabby no less—I realized I didn't get the full story. Your apology video then confirmed my suspicions, so I'm really sorry for not believing in you."

"Relax. Even if the Squeaker shit wasn't actually me, I really did lose my cool at Nabby. Rolling with the masses was smart. Hell, I'd say you were a dumbass for eating up my idol persona in the first place."

"No, I can't agree with that. I jumped the gun and jumped on the bandwagon, not giving a second thought towards all the happiness your music brought me. And that's why I got so excited when I saw you were part of this job. I'd like to use this opportunity to repay you."

Bosa raised an eyebrow. "Repay me?"

"Yeah! By having you on my stream, I'll be able to show my viewers you're still an awesome idol! We can even set things up to make you look really good and help you get back on your feet!"

"Ah. Well, thanks, but no thanks."

Roman sputtered at Bosa's response. He must have assumed she was going to leap on such an opportunity—getting turned down never crossed his mind. He looked to Nabby for guidance, but the demon just shook her head.

It's a kind offer, but that's not what she wants.

Yet he refused to stop there.

"A-are you sure?" he asked Bosa. "My viewers won't mind! And my moderation team will make sure any hecklers get timed out ASAP!"

"I'm sure. The life of an idol just doesn't interest me anymore."

"B-but..."

"...Well. If you'd *really* like to help..."

She slid in front of Roman, putting herself deep in his personal space. Leaning against the monk, she walked her fingers up his chest.

"Maybe you can give my cam show a shoutout when your stream comes back on, *hmm?*" she purred.

"U-u-um... I... I can't. I just made partner on Flinch, so I can't promote adult content..."

He couldn't even maintain eye contact as he spoke. But—to Nabby's relief more than Roman's—Bosa backed off just as quickly.

"That's a bummer," she said indifferently. "Then just forget about repaying me or whatever. It's not like I did anything specifically for you anyway."

The scylla kept moving forward, waving off any further discussion.

Roman was rooted in place with shock. An adventurer from another team bumped his shoulder, but he was utterly focused on watching Bosa slide farther away from him. Even as he spoke to Nabby, he kept staring at the former idol.

"She's...nothing like she used to be, huh?"

"She might seem rough, but she means well," said Nabby. "She just doesn't want anything to do with her old life."

"Are you sure? It's hard to believe she's okay with losing her entire fanbase and becoming…*nobody*."

"She's had a lot of time to reflect. I know that if Bosa wanted to be an idol again, she'd find a way to do so."

Roman finally looked at Nabby. His brow was furrowed, and it was plain to see the gears were whirring behind his tired eyes.

Those mental cogs then churned out what he decided had to be the reason behind Bosa's new outlook.

"…No, she's gotta be putting up a front. There's no way she wasn't affected by that scandal. She's acting like she doesn't care because she doesn't want to show how sad she is."

"What? No!" Nabby couldn't begin to understand how he came to such a conclusion. "I spend every day with Bosa and can assure you she—"

"She's lying to you too. I watched Bosa for years, and she was never anything like this. She says I can't repay her, but it's obvious she needs my help. She did so much to inspire me—it's time I inspired her!" He slipped on his sunglasses, concealing his exhaustion once again. "I know she'll stop acting once I remind her of how fun it is to share your passion with the world!"

Roman then hurried after Bosa, darting away before Nabby could explain just how wrong he was. Even though those sunglasses only covered his eyes, they apparently blocked his ability to listen as well.

Oh no… I don't think I'll be able to intermediate this…

Nabby would have to warn Bosa as soon as possible. Roman may have spoken to her in confidence, but he was going to step on a landmine if Bosa wasn't expecting him to "remind" her.

It was a healer's job to mitigate pain, so Nabby would do what she could to dampen the inevitable explosion.

4

They were almost at the bottom of the canyon when the park ranger slowed to a halt. He then pointed out a nearby rest stop and told the adventurers to meet him back there in four hours before setting them loose.

Each group went a different direction, with Nabby's team electing to check out an alcove located off one of the trails. Bosa was confident they'd find a wyvern there since they liked to hide where prey couldn't see them, and seeing as no one had a better suggestion, they were now hiking back up the canyon walls.

As they walked, Roman rambled on to his audience. His camera was live again, broadcasting his explanation of the techniques he planned to use.

"When you get up close to a monster, you wanna start hitting them with a sequence they can't interrupt, so it's important to understand the strength of your attacks, okay? Using only strong attacks might sound good on paper, but then you gotta worry about leaving gaps in your offense or tiring yourself out. My personal favorite is to cycle through a light punch, a medium kick, a light kick, and then a heavy punch. Once you get a good rhythm going, you can just wail on them without any fear of a counterattack—just like how SteelDude wailed on me with the big sub! Thanks a ton, buddy!"

Nabby leaned towards Bosa. "Did that make any sense to you?"

"Nope."

"Thank goodness. I'm glad it's not just me."

"But when you gotta be more cautious, try rolling back instead of delaying your attacks," Roman continued. "You're less likely to mess up your defense that way and will have a smoother experience overall—as smooth as WifiWarlock, thanks for the eight months, man!"

Bosa growled. "God help me, I'm gonna rip out his vocal cords next time I hear a fucking shoutout…"

As expected, the tension within their group was only getting worse. Nabby was able to sneakily tell Bosa about Roman's scheme, but she didn't seem concerned at all. She just brushed off the idea, assuring Nabby that there was nothing Roman could do to affect her.

I mean, I don't think his plan would ever work, but he already made you mad. I was hoping we could stop things from boiling over…

But there wasn't much else Nabby could do to ease the situation. They only had four hours to take down as many wyverns as possible—she didn't have enough time to convince someone like Roman he had it all wrong.

She just had to hope whatever he had in mind wasn't too brash.

They crept carefully into the canyon alcove but didn't find any wyverns. There were signs that *something* had been there recently but sitting around and waiting for it to come back wasn't an option. They left the alcove—and were compensated for their time with a stroke of luck.

Perched on the guardrail set alongside the path's corner was their target: a blue-scaled wyvern.

Honestly, Nabby was a bit disappointed by the monster. As wyverns were cousins to dragons, she expected something imposing, but what she saw wasn't much bigger than Don Testa or his son, and it's long-necked body didn't look especially powerful. The job warned that the wyverns were capable of freezing breath attacks, but Nabby couldn't imagine such a dinky drake posing much of a challenge.

Regardless, their job was to take it down. The wyvern hadn't noticed them yet, so the adventurers ducked back into the alcove to decide their approach. Roman took the initiative and spoke first.

"Alright, no need for a plan here. I'll rush it down before it can escape, so I just need Bosa to keep it grounded with her song. Sound good?"

"Hell no, dumbass," growled Bosa. "Didn't you see where it's sitting? We don't know if it's got friends hanging around the corner. I don't give a shit how good you think you are—our team is two-thirds support classes. We can't take stupid risks."

"I agree," said Nabby. "I think we should check the area first. Bosa's song should work from a distance, so we can prevent the wyvern's escape once we know it's safe to attack."

"C'mon, we've got nothing to worry about. With you two backing me up, we can do a lot more to keep this job exciting. Nobody's gonna feel inspired from watching us take it slow!"

"I don't give a fuck what your viewers wanna see. *We* were hired to kill some wyverns, not entertain a bunch of man-children."

"Then you can leave the entertainment to me."

Roman then shot a thumbs-up at his camera—and sprinted towards the wyvern.

"*You motherfucker!*" Bosa hissed. She and Nabby tried to stop him, but he was already running up the path. "Goddammit! Nabby, make sure he doesn't get killed! And don't try jumping once I start singing—you'll hurt yourself!"

"G-got it!"

Bosa then put her headphones on, scowling as she selected her melody, while Nabby took off after Roman.

She only got a few strides away before Bosa's song started. It was a heavy dirge of throat singing, and its tone was unlike anything Nabby had ever heard. She couldn't even recognize the language of the lyrics, but that didn't spare her from its effect.

Nabby suddenly felt as though she were magnetized to the ground, to the point she couldn't even run anymore. Forget jumping—the most she could manage was a speed walk. It was like Bosa's song had tripled the gravity on everything in earshot.

But that wasn't enough to stop Roman. He somehow kept running, with only his camera bobbing as it adjusted to its greater weight.

The sudden commotion caught the wyvern's attention, and its beady eyes snapped onto the incoming monk. It then looked towards the open canyon and began beating its wings—only for the monster to realize it was unable to take off. It redoubled its flapping, desperate to avoid confrontation, yet it remained pinned to the guardrail.

Roman was almost at the wyvern by then. He pounded his fists together, sparking his magic. Flashes of electricity zapped along his arms, and he prepared to strike.

And he might have hit it—if something didn't trip him.

Roman let out a startled cry and fell flat on his face.

Nabby shuffled towards him as fast as she could. The wyvern was still struggling for lift off, but being the party's healer, Nabby prioritized checking on her teammate over pressing the attack.

Roman was still on the ground when she got to his side, and Nabby could finally see what had tripped him. Some breed of plant monster had wrapped its vines around his legs and was slowly creeping up his torso. Even with his magic buffs, the monk couldn't fight off the tendrils, leaving him struggling in the dirt.

Nabby winced. Roman was their only fighter, so it was imperative that she got him back on his feet. But there was no way Bosa was going to let this slide—especially since her song would have run its course before Nabby was done healing him. And as they still had no idea if there were other dangers lurking around, the demon had only one option.

She signaled for Bosa to stop her singing and let the wyvern go.

Bosa was obviously angered, but she evidently agreed that that was the best move. The songstress took off her headphones and meandered towards her teammates.

"Roman got tangled up by some weird plant!" Nabby shouted to her.

"Figures. This was exactly the kind of shit we wanted to avoid," Bosa said, shaking her head. "Does it look like a bunch of vines coming out of an asshole?"

Nabby looked back at the plant, following its tendrils to their source. Sure enough, while she wouldn't have used the word "asshole", the main body did resemble some sort of…*sphincter.*

"Yeah, it does!"

"It's probably a nobunga scrub then. It's a carnivorous plant monster that eats armadillos and other dumb animals. Be careful with the thorns—they carry neurotoxic bacteria."

"What?! Oh, crap!"

Roman redoubled his efforts to pull the vines off himself, still to no avail. Bosa appeared ready to snap as she looked down at the constricted man.

"Where did you learn that?" Nabby asked.

"The park ranger warned about them in the briefing," said Bosa. "…Don't tell me you weren't paying attention again."

"Um…"

"For the love of… If there wasn't someone else pissing me off, I'd have your ass right now. Whatever—we need to burn the main body in we're gonna free Romulus. You got any spells for that?"

"*Hellfire* normally makes a big explosion, but I think I can keep it contained."

"Good enough. Let me get out of range first."

Bosa retreated beyond the maximum blast zone as Nabby readied her spell. The demon then pulled up the hem of her skirt, raised a foot, and stepped on the plant.

"*Hellfire.*"

Normally the ground would have erupted with the flames of the underworld, but in this minimized state, the spell merely resulted in turning the underside of Nabby's boot into a furnace. Still, that was all she needed to set the nobunga scrub on fire.

The plant's body quickly shriveled and burned, though the severed vines persisted in ensnaring their prey. They still had enough strength to resist Roman, so Bosa reached under her hoodie and tossed the monk one of her daggers. He cut himself free, happily shaking the tendrils off his body.

"Whew... Thanks for the save, girls!"

Roman went to climb onto his feet—and fell over again.

"Dumbass. You're full of that bacteria now. Sit your ass down and wait until Nabby's done with you," said Bosa.

"R-right..."

Nabby knelt next to the monk and looked over his injuries. The thorns had left surprisingly deep abrasions on his legs, particularly around his ankles. It was unlikely he'd have serious trouble walking like that, but fighting was another story.

The bigger concern was the bacteria—or it would have been just one week prior. If Nabby still had to rely on *Contaminate*, she'd have left the scrub alive just so she could send the infection back into it. But now—

"Alright! It's time I busted out my new spell!"

"Huh? You learned a new spell?" Bosa seemed impressed.

"Sort of. I actually figured out how to make *Internal Decay* work last week. I wanted to surprise you with it."

"Ah, so that's why you were acting weird yesterday. Good work, Nabs."

"Thank you! I even gave it a new name to celebrate!"

Nabby gathered her mana and chanted her spell. A moment later, she pointed her palms at Roman, releasing slithers of dark energy into his body.

"*Antagonistic Microbial Eradication!*"

Bosa looked at her with disbelief. "*That's* what you named it? That's stupid as hell and way too long."

"But *Internal Decay* sounds kinda sinister. I wanted to make it obvious that this spell only helps people."

"Then just call it *Disinfect*. You're a healer, not a fucking video game character."

"Oh... That does sound a lot better..."

"When did you practice that, anyway? I haven't smelled any rotten cheese lately."

"I still practiced on food. I just used it to clean the chicken meat and veggies I'd cook instead of washing them."

"What the fuck? Why didn't you say something?!"

"I wanted to see if you thought it tasted different! You might have given me a false positive if I told you!"

"Um... So when did you first try it out on a person?" Roman asked from the ground.

"Just now, actually. I was worried it might not work on a living body so I'm really glad to see it's not melting your organs or anything!"

"Y-yay for me..."

A few moments more and Nabby could sense that *Disinfect* had annihilated the bacteria. Roman sat up straight and tested his arms, working to restore feeling in his limbs while Nabby considered how to treat his injuries.

Without a monster nearby, Nabby had nothing to sap vitality from. She could have left the nobunga scrub alive, but considering it was actively attacking Roman, it was better that she destroyed it before it caused more harm.

So that left Nabby with two options: she could give him a healing potion, or she could cast *Drain* on herself. Considering the latter was a last resort—and one that would invite Bosa's ire like nothing else—Nabby dug a bottle out of her coat and handed it to Roman.

Though I doubt she'll be happy about me using an emergency potion either.

Roman thanked Nabby before gulping it down. Seconds later, his wounds knit themselves shut, and the monk looked no worse for wear.

"Wow, that's some good stuff!" he said. "Where'd you get this?"

"My hero, an alchemist named Reese, left a few of those with me. I don't have that many left so please be more careful."

"Don't worry about it. You guys were right—I shouldn't have rushed in. But, hey, learning from your mistakes is part of what makes adventuring fun, right?" He smiled widely at his camera. "You see all that, guys? I looked like a real cheeseball, didn't I? That's why it's important to talk to your party members and make sure you're all on the same page. This is one of the few times you *shouldn't* do as Roman does!"

Roman then hopped back onto his feet. He continued to pass advice off to his viewers, talking as though his impulsive actions were just a simple goof before reading off the names of the people who subscribed while he had been tied up.

Meanwhile, Nabby could see Bosa was doing everything she could to keep her white-knuckled fists from flying into Roman's jaw.

Once he was done appeasing his supporters, Roman faced his teammates again. "Alright, where'd the baddie fly off to? It couldn't have gotten too far, so if we—"

"You have got to be the dumbest fuck on Rullia."

While she succeeded in stopping herself from decking the monk, Bosa couldn't keep her mouth in check any longer.

"You are so goddamn lucky I'm not the healer. If it were up to me, I'd have left your ass paralyzed so you wouldn't shit the bed again," she seethed. "We could have taken that wyvern down no problem, you just had to run in. My only consolation is the fact that all your viewers got to see you eat dirt."

"Y-yeah, that was my bad. I thought for sure it'd be fine, but I can see I messed up."

"Is that all you have to say for yourself? *Whoopsie-daisy, guess I made a stinky, ha ha!* The wyvern got away, we had to waste time healing you, *and* you made Nabby use one of her potions! That was a gift from her hero—*she can't replace it.* But I guess that doesn't matter to you since you only care about what your fans want to see."

"..."

"You know what? It's no wonder your viewership is dropping. You're not funny, you're not cool—*you're just a fucking idiot.* Try listening to your own advice and pull your head out of your ass before you get someone killed."

Bosa then put her back to Roman and slid down the canyon path.

"C'mon, Nabby—the wyvern went this way. It didn't look particularly scared—probably because it doesn't see our team as a threat—so let's find it before someone else does."

"Coming."

Nabby took a last glance at Roman. She wasn't happy about what he had done, but she could also see he was under a lot of pressure from his stream. Part of her wanted to mollify him and say it would be alright, but...

The way he's still smiling tells me he didn't listen to Bosa at all.

And as if to cement Nabby's consternation, he went right back to speaking to his fans.

"Heh. Well, I guess that's the new Seafoam Diva for you—right, guys? Doesn't hold anything back!"

At least he didn't stop to read more shoutouts. Roman dusted himself off and swaggered ahead, putting himself a few steps in front of Bosa. Neither of them acknowledged the other, and they moved without a hint of solidarity.

Despite Bosa's merciless tongue-lashing, nothing had changed. The tension was higher than ever for their party.

But Nabby did notice something in Roman's gait. It might have been her imagination, or perhaps a lingering effect from the scrub's bacteria, but she swore there was something different about the way he carried himself.

Somehow, the man looked a little smaller.

5

Of all the people Bosa had ever worked with, no one had ever pissed her off as much as Romulus.

She didn't even get that mad during her first job with Nabby. Maybe that was because Bosa felt she was untouchable back then, but her pride was also out of control. The fact that Romulus had managed to draw so much contempt out of her current, more-relaxed attitude would have been impressive if she weren't the one feeling so irritated.

Can't believe this asshat's a C Rank. How the hell did Parti let him hit the same level as me?

Bosa knew from the beginning she wasn't going to *like* Romulus, but holy hell, she didn't expect him to actually cause any trouble. And while his insistence on blindly rushing in grated on her, it wasn't until the dumbass forced a potion out of Nabby that Bosa decided to snap. Partially because those were a precious commodity—especially with how effective Reese's were—but more so because *it made Nabby look bad.*

The demon didn't realize it, but Romulus' fans had to have been confused when they saw the team's healer hand over a potion instead of casting a spell. They were likely about to question the validity of Nabby's dark healing, maybe even push Romulus into harassing her, when Bosa chewed him out.

It was about time I gave them what they came for anyway.

Even if she wasn't an idol anymore, Lilibosa was still an expert at taking center stage. Those halfwits probably forgot all about Nabby's bizarreness the moment Bosa started barking at their precious streamer.

Frankly, Romulus should have thanked her. He was so desperate to entertain his viewers—what better show could he provide than *The Seafoam Diva is a Colossal Bitch?*

Still, Bosa would be lying if she said she didn't understand why that desire dominated his life. She had been so deep in that rabbit hole she could have called herself queen of the warren.

But that was also why Romulus frustrated her: she was all too familiar with how fame narrowed your mind. He wanted to generate excitement for his stream, and that hunger left him deaf to the people he was working with. It was like he was off in his own little world.

Or maybe his own theatre—where thousands of eyes watched him dance like the puppet he was.

At this rate, they'd have to pray the other teams held more competent fighters. Considering their payment hinged on the sum work of *all groups*, there'd be a lot more pissed-off adventurers if Romulus caused everyone to miss the quota.

The three moved along a cliffside trail. The park had set up several plaques sharing information on the local ecology, and Nabby stopped to read a few while Bosa searched for traces of the wyvern. But beyond some birds taking flight a few levels below, the canyon was as still as ever.

It would have been positively picturesque if it weren't for Romulus' blathering.

"Man, I still can't believe the skills of these ladies," he said to his audience. "It might've been hard to see, but there was no way that wyvern was gonna take off while Bosa was singing! And Nabby's dark healing? Top tier stuff—I've never seen someone remove an infection that quick!"

Nabby blushed slightly. Bosa ignored the empty praise and told them to keep walking.

They descended to where she saw the birds but found nary a wyvern. Bosa was about to suggest they search elsewhere when she spotted one of the other teams approaching.

Their group consisted of a lizardman druid, a human carrying a huge club, and a gorgon mage whose eyes were hidden behind her snaky bangs. They didn't seem to have any business with Bosa's team and were simply passing through, but the human greeted them, nonetheless.

"Why, hello there! I take it your hunt is going well?" he said enthusiastically.

Bosa was quick to speak before Romulus had a chance. "Unfortunately not. We found a wyvern but lost it due to a 'mistake'."

"Ah, my sympathies. But fear not—our luck has been grand so far! We were able to corner a trio of the beasts, and they were so turgid with fear that not one of them escaped! I'm sure your own fortunes shall rise soon enough!"

"I hope so. I'd like it if our team didn't turn out to be dead weight in this gig."

She made sure to point those words at Romulus. But for whatever reason, he took that as his cue to start talking.

"Man, I'm jealous. All we've done is walk around—I'd love to find some monsters! Hard to help people get into adventuring when you can't even get into a battle, right?"

"Ho-ho—indeed! But I'm sure your allies are happy to have a fighter with such a turgid fighting spirit at their side!"

"Y-yeah! Of course!" Romulus' smile wavered slightly. "By the way, you didn't happen to see a wyvern flying around here, would you?"

"We did—just a few moments ago, in fact. It flew towards that waterfall." The club-wielder pointed at a cascade ending in a pool at the canyon's bottom. "We considered pursuing it, but ultimately agreed that a break was in order. If that is your once-lost target, then you may rest knowing that we shall leave it to your discretion."

"Really? Awesome!"

"Thanks," said Bosa. "Hopefully we won't lose it again."

"I'm sure it shall not escape your grasp twice. Good hunting, and stay safe!"

The other team then continued up the path. But just before they were out of earshot, Bosa heard the human murmur to his teammates.

"Quite the turgid atmosphere amongst that trio, eh?"

You have no idea, buddy.

Bosa turned back around. "Nice people."

Nabby nodded. "That lamia lady's hair was really pretty too. The way it moved was almost hypnotic."

"...That was a gorgon, Nabs. Do you really not know the difference?"

"I thought you said gorgons had special eyes that could petrify you. I was able to look at her just fine."

"You couldn't even see her eyes—they were covered by her fucking bangs. Look, if it's their bottom half that's a snake, it's a lamia; if it's their hair, it's a gorgon. Really not that complicated."

"This is why Hell is so much easier to understand. Demons come in a variety of shapes and sizes, yet we all identify as a single race. Why can't Rullians do the same?"

"Because a lamia and a gorgon are separate *species*. We're not gonna simplify our taxology just because you're too dumb to learn the differences." Bosa shook her head. "Forget it. Let's just get down to that waterfall before the wyvern moves on."

"You two are a regular comedy duo, you know that?" chuckled Romulus. "You see, guys? Nothing beats having a good friend at your side while you're on a job! You'll have a lot more fun *and* you've got someone to watch your back. Just like you always told us—right, Bosa?"

The only response he got out of her was a pair of middle fingers.

"Whoa there! I wanted our luck to flip, not those birds! Hey, nobody clip that, alright?"

He tried to laugh it off, as if he weren't worried about how Bosa's conduct was affecting his stream. Between her foul mouth and crude gestures, Romulus was probably feeling hard-pressed to continue recording, but like Nabby said, he wanted to use his show as a way of reigniting Bosa's idol career—even at the risk of damaging his own brand.

She'd find it endearing if it weren't so petty. Romulus was so convinced he was enjoying his own fame that he couldn't understand why Bosa let hers fall to the wayside. The thought of her finding happiness in an average life must have flabbergasted the dumbass.

But if Romulus wanted to waste his time and energy trying to change her mind, he was free to do so. Bosa only had to put up with him for another three hours.

The group silently hurried along the cliffs. Once they reached the canyon's bottom, they made a beeline for the waterfall, weaving around the increasingly lush flora.

And against all odds, they found the wyvern idling at the water's edge.

It was alone and unalarmed, occasionally dipping its head down for a drink. The nearby vultures were unbothered by the wyvern's presence, and a couple smaller birds were resting on its scaled back. The scene was tranquil—and ripe for an ambush.

Assuming someone *doesn't fuck it up again.*

The adventurers slipped behind a nearby boulder. Bosa then squatted down for a huddle, gesturing for the other two to join her.

"Alright, first things first, *you* will do exactly as I say," she said to Romulus. "If you rush in again, I'm gonna turn your nutsack into a coin purse. Do I make myself clear?"

He smirked. "Crystal."

"Tch. Nabby, can you use your chainy spell on the wyvern?"

"I can try, but I'm not sure if *Chains of Punishment* will work if it takes off."

"Don't worry—I'll keep it grounded until you're ready. We just need something that'll keep the monster in place until it's dead since I can't sing forever."

"Got it."

"And where do you want me?" asked Romulus.

"Somewhere else, but since that's not an option, just be ready to attack as soon as Nabby chains the asshole. You're still the only fighter in our group."

"You don't wanna check the area first?"

"We already got a good look and saw there aren't any other monsters around—including nobunga scrubs. You and Nabby just need to sneak as close to the wyvern as possible before I start singing. It's a simple plan—I doubt even you can fuck this up."

"Hey, I know I messed up, but cut me some slack, alright? I'm still a C Rank—I've got plenty of good reviews under my belt. My sponsors would have dropped me if I didn't have the skills to back up my lessons."

Bosa sneered. "Oh yeah? All I've gotten to see is a dipshit who tripped on a goddamn plant. As far as I can tell, someone paid Parti to get you your rank."

"C'mon, you know that's not possible."

"Whatever. You're damn lucky we kept you around after that stunt."

"And you're just as lucky I'm putting up with how rude you're being."

Still smiling, Romulus tilted his sunglasses down to show the seriousness in his eyes.

"Like you said, I'm the only fighter here," he said calmly. "I could have walked off after you yelled at me and left you two high and dry, but I'm made of better stuff than that. I stuck around because *we all* want to complete this job. It's fine if you don't like me, but could you please stop acting like I'm some problem you need to work around?"

Bosa was surprised. She never expected him to show any spine, let alone talk back to the idol he adored. She assumed he'd just bottle up any frustration and vent it at his viewers later.

But Romulus spoke to her not as a fan, but as a person. Rather than kiss up to her, he chose to appeal to Bosa's sensibilities. He even did so while his camera was rolling.

For just a moment, he let his viewers see something besides his streaming act.

...Hm.

Maybe he's not a lost cause.

"Fine then," said Bosa. "Show me you're not utter dogshit. Do that, and I'll lay off you for the rest of the gig."

Romulus grinned. "Heh, you'll see why they call me Godfist Roman in twelve seconds or less. Trust me—I'll take care of everything."

"Sure."

She tried to remain flippant, but Bosa couldn't overlook the determination in Romulus' tone. It sounded as if he actually wanted to make up for his mistake. He might have already gone back to his showboating, but for a moment, he sounded like a real adventurer.

With respect to that, Bosa allowed herself to place the tiniest bit of trust in him.

And immediately regretted it.

"—Just like how Barneycrust is taking care of me with the big one-hundred-dollar donation! Holy shit—thanks a ton, man! Let me know if that was an accident, alright?"

Romulus very literally shouted out his latest patron. His voice echoed through the chasm, alerting the wyvern.

Its head swiveled towards the boulder. The monster didn't hesitate before raising its wings.

"You stupid shitbag!"

6

Bosa struggled to get her music going as the team sprinted towards the wyvern. She was cursing up a storm while Romulus spewed excuses.

"Sorry, sorry! I've never gotten a donation that big before—I couldn't help myself! It caught me off-guard and I was so excited that... R-really, I'm sorry!"

She shot him a furious glare. Nabby glanced anxiously at her teammates as she readied *Chains of Punishment*.

Bosa gave up on finding the melody and instead belted out the tune raw. Throat-singing without any background music was awkward, but it was imperative that she kept the wyvern from taking off.

She just barely managed to get the effect going in time. The wyvern flapped its wings futilely.

Romulus then closed in on the monster. With lightning sparking along his limbs, he swung at the wyvern with a roundhouse kick.

A loud crack resounded as his foot connected with its jaw, and the wyvern was staggered by the electricity, leaving it wide open. The monk then spun on his back foot and followed up with a punch before finishing with a flying knee to the wyvern's chin.

The beast let out a furious cry and counterattacked with a swipe of its wing, but it was too slow to hit Romulus. He deftly hopped back and punished the swing with a kick, and the wyvern hissed as it retracted the wounded limb.

An impressive display by Romulus. But considering Bosa's standards for him had been driven into the dirt, that wasn't much of a compliment.

He continued to square off against the wyvern as Nabby finished chanting her spell. At her intonation, molten-hot chains erupted from beneath the monster and wrapped themselves around it. It managed to stay upright, but the chains made any hope it had of escaping.

With the wyvern secured, Bosa then faded out her throat singing and switched to death metal. Now that they had managed to overcome Romulus nearly ruining the job again, she just needed to do everything she could to get the monster killed as quickly as possible. Death metal was just as much a pain in the ass to sing without a background song, but Bosa didn't feel like bothering with her headphones now—getting Romulus the strength buff was all that mattered.

In hindsight, she should have bothered. Leaving her ears uncovered was practically an invitation for Emperor Dumbass to continue throwing out his worthless apologies.

"Really—I'm super sorry about that!" he said as he landed an uppercut. "Most donations I get are like five or ten dollars, so seeing such a big amount made me forget where I was! I didn't mean to yell like that! Y-you understand—right, Bosa?"

She couldn't even tell him to fuck off, though she considered breaking her song to do just that.

"But, I mean, it all worked out in the end, right? You still stopped the wyvern from flying—and now Nabby's got it tied down! Maybe I messed up our sneak attack, but now it's just a matter of time until I've beaten it! S-so maybe you don't need to yell at me again…?"

Oh, don't worry. I'm not gonna yell at you.

I'm gonna do something worse.

What would suit a shithead like Romulus? Bosa could hijack his stream and take her top off, but that would just make his viewers happy. It would be better if she used her lullaby on him since Flinch had a policy against people sleeping on the job, though that presented the issue of Bosa and Nabby losing their only fighter. In which case, she could always do it *after* they finished the job, and she could even leave him in a compromising pose while she was at it.

Decisions, decisions. Bosa could hardly contain herself as she conceived of her revenge.

Romulus pounded away at the wyvern. Constricted as it was, it had no choice but to take the brunt of each attack, and the lightning effect was eating at the monster's strength. While bare hands might have seemed poorly suited for fighting a scaled beast, the magic within each strike went right through the wyvern's natural armor. It would need a strategy if it wanted to survive much longer.

And unfortunately, wyverns were intelligent enough for simple strategies.

It endured a few more blows from Romulus, waiting for its chance. He then drew his leg back for another kick, and the wyvern retracted its head accordingly. In response, the monk hopped a step forward to compensate for the new distance.

Giving the wyvern exactly what it wanted.

Now that he had overextended, it immediately struck with a vicious headbutt.

Romulus didn't have a chance to bring up his guard. He was knocked hard to the ground, giving the monster ample time to draw breath.

The wyvern then blew an icy gale on its chains. They were cooled to brittleness, and it only took a spread of its wings to shatter them. Some of the shards flew at Nabby, and she stumbled onto her ass as the wyvern roared in triumph.

Son of a bitch… Of course the monster would be smarter than him.

Bosa dropped her song. There was no reason to buff Romulus' strength right now, not while they needed to scramble a new plan. She pulled Nabby back up while Romulus dashed towards the wyvern.

The monster wasn't even trying to take flight now. It was either too injured or had decided offense was its best hope. But even in its wounded state, the unchained wyvern was able to dodge Romulus' attacks and send back strikes of its own.

Slashes from its claws, lunging bites, and a few icy breaths—it did whatever it could to keep Romulus at bay. The monk recognized the battle wasn't one-sided anymore and focused on evasion, limiting his successful hits to mere glancing blows, but until Nabby had it restrained again, he couldn't risk getting hit. Accordingly, he ducked when he saw the wyvern swing its tail at him.

The attack missed him completely—and instead spiked his camera drone out of the air.

It crashed into the canyon wall and sputtered as its levitation stones failed, letting out a woeful beep before its recording came to an end.

Romulus spun around and gaped at the fallen drone. "Aw crap, not the camera! My stream's—"

"Who gives a shit?!" shouted Bosa. "Pay attention to the fucker in front of you!"

But Romulus didn't listen. He stared at the dead machine for a heartbeat too long before facing the wyvern again. Nabby was rushing to summon another batch of chains, but it wasn't quick enough to stop the monster from blowing another breath of ice.

The freezing gale washed over Romulus. He tried to dodge midway through, but his moment of idiocy sealed his fate.

His left arm and leg were encased in ice.

He threw out a kick with his free leg. The desperate strike clapped the wyvern's jaw shut, but the effort cost Romulus his balance. He hit the ground hard, struggling on his back like a frosty turtle.

Nabby's second round of *Chains of Punishment* was finally ready by then. Once more, hot steel bound itself around the wyvern, but anyone could see it hadn't forgotten how to escape. The monster was already drawing in air while Nabby ran to Romulus' aid.

Alone and unprotected.

Bosa watched in horror as their team's healer put herself in harm's way—a sitting duck in front of a monster more than twice her size.

"What the hell are you doing?! Get your ass back here!"

"I-I have to help!" Nabby yelled over her shoulder. "The wyvern's gonna kill him!"

"Dumbass! You can just revive him if he dies, but if you get killed, it's all over!"

"But—!"

Nabby wouldn't budge. Even though she didn't have an easy way to unfreeze Romulus, even though he was too heavy for her to quickly drag away, she refused to abandon her ally. She didn't have the heart to leave him there nor the prescience to turn around and attack the wyvern instead.

She just fumbled for time, not even fleeing after the wyvern shattered its chains once again.

Of all the times for you to be so fucking stubborn…!

Lullaby wouldn't work in time—assuming it didn't get drowned out by the wyvern's screeching. Same with her confusion-inducing rap. Buffing Nabby wouldn't help either, and increasing gravity was pointless now.

Bosa didn't know a single song that could save her friend. But if she didn't do *something*, Nabby would be seriously hurt. And the chances of another healer coming by before it was too late were slim at best.

Meaning Bosa had no choice but to do *the most desperate something* she knew.

She took a deep breath, gathering as much mana as she could into her lungs. As soon as she was at capacity, she focused her mind and unleashed the only offensive spell she knew.

Sonic Boom!

With a shriek, Bosa's voice manifested as a blast of condensed energy. It shot towards the wyvern, nailing it right in the head and stunning it. The beast wobbled from side to side, struggling to maintain its balance with ruptured eardrums.

Bosa could hardly believe she actually hit it. That was the first time she had used *Sonic Boom* in years, and she was reeling from its effect almost as much as the wyvern. The spell used way more mana than any of her songs and felt like it almost ripped her throat apart, leaving her holding her neck in pain. Doubtless she was going to be hoarse later.

But she'd worry about that then. They weren't out of the woods yet.

Bosa knew *Sonic Boom* wouldn't be enough to kill it. She was hoping it would buy enough time for Romulus to get unfrozen, but since the wyvern was already steadying itself, that ship wasn't going to sail. She ran between Nabby and the monster, looking for her next move.

She found it quickly.

The wyvern had lowered its head in a bid to ease its vertigo. Doing so stopped it from stumbling—but also left it vulnerable.

Wide open for an attack.

Bosa swallowed hard. She knew what she had to do, but that didn't make it any easier. If it weren't to save Nabby, she wouldn't have even considered it. But since the demon wouldn't abandon a teammate, neither could Bosa.

So, with no other options, Bosa darted forward and leapt onto the wyvern's neck.

The monster screeched again and tried to buck her off, but she quickly wrapped her tentacles around it. Terrified and hanging on for dear life, Bosa screams joined the wyvern's as she did everything she could to keep its attention off Nabby.

Now she just had to not die in the process.

"Bosa!"

Nabby cried out from Romulus' side. Bosa could only bark an order back.

"I'm fine! Get the fuck out of here!"

Nabby shouted a response, but the wyvern's tantrum drowned her out. As Bosa was more than a little preoccupied, she just needed some sort of confirmation that Nabby was moving to safety.

A split-second glance showed her that the healer was moving back towards the boulder—dragging Romulus behind her.

...*Good enough.*

At least Bosa only had to worry about her own ass now. Her heart was pounding her chest as she clung to the wyvern. Even though she had been on hundreds of gigs, Bosa had never fought a monster directly. She wanted to just let go and run away, but that would risk endangering Nabby again. Bosa desperately held on as she wracked her brain for a way out of this.

The wyvern's balance was still shot. It was wobbling back and forth near the waterfall, though it refrained from thrashing too hard and falling over. It was wounded and had to be running on fumes after all this struggling, meaning it wouldn't be able to take much more.

The dots were quick to connect in Bosa's mind. She had her solution.

With a grimace, she wriggled herself up the wyvern's neck and towards its head.

The monster noticed her movements and intensified its efforts to shake her off. It stumbled a couple times from the effort, but it wasn't enough to dislodge the scylla. Once it became apparent to the wyvern that it was only hurting itself, it tried to bat her off with its wings.

Bosa yelped as she dodged left and right, the flexibility of her tentacles letting her evade in ways the wyvern couldn't follow. She even swung herself in a full loop around its neck while avoiding an attack.

But while exhausting, such maneuvers let her reach the wyvern's head unscathed. With adrenaline threatening to make her head pop, Bosa's rearmost tentacles reached under her hoodie and drew a pair of daggers. She passed the blades to her hands before clinging to the monster harder than ever.

And without allowing herself the slightest moment of hesitation, Bosa plunged the daggers into the wyvern's eyes.

Its screeching tore through the canyon, matched only by Bosa's own wailing. Blood spilled onto her hands as she pressed harder onto her daggers, and the wyvern's struggles grew fiercer in kind. It gave up on keeping its balance and fell onto its side in the hopes of whipping the scylla off its head.

It managed to succeed in that regard. Between the blood and her terror, Bosa lost her grip on the wyvern. She was sent flying from the monster and—by some miracle—splashed into the pool beneath the waterfall.

The wyvern continued to toss and turn on the ground, kicking up dust as ichor flowed freely from its wounds. Soon, its roaring grew more pitiful than intimidating, and its thrashing weakened into desperate throes. It then let out a mournful cry—a final warning to its kin—before slumping to the ground.

Silent. Unmoving.

Dead.

Bosa had slain her first monster.

7

After getting tossed into the pool, Bosa hid in the water for a time. Even if it was unlikely that a blind wyvern would be able to find her at the bottom of a pond, Bosa wasn't about to skimp on precautions.

She could breathe underwater for god's sake. She might as well stay safe while she waited for her heart to slow down. *Besides, Romulus should be thawed out by now. That motherfucker can take over.*

Once the monster's shrieking stopped, Bosa slowly paddled back to the surface. Poking her head out, she saw the wyvern lying on its side—with no sign of Romulus nearby. But between the daggers sitting in its skull and the amount of blood spreading beneath it, Bosa could comfortably assume the wyvern was dead.

Shit... I actually killed it, huh...

How fucking miserable.

She dragged herself back onto land and plopped onto the shore. Bosa was in the middle of wringing water out of her hair when Nabby came running up behind her.

"Oh my goodness—are you okay?!" The demon didn't wait for an answer before checking her friend for injuries.

"Yeah, I'm fine. Somehow. I managed to get by without a scratch, in fact."

But while Bosa was genuinely amazed by her own fortune, it did nothing to keep her anger from resurfacing. It was great that she wasn't hurt, but she shouldn't have been in any danger in the first place.

A certain monk had promised he'd do all the fighting for her.

"What? Really?! That's incredible, Bosa! I thought you said you didn't know how to fight!"

"I don't. I just panicked and did the first thing that came to me."

"Huh? B-but you did that awesome boomy thing and all!"

"That was the only attack spell I know—and my last resort." Bosa rubbed her throat again. "I never would have thought I'd end up stabbing the damn thing. Fuck, I can't believe that actually worked, too."

"Wow… Um, but you did look super cool while you did it! You were like a hero, zooming in there and jumping on the wyvern before it could get me!"

"Thanks, but I really shouldn't have had to do that. You and I—the healer and the support—aren't supposed to fight, remember?"

"Y…yeah." Nabby looked away. "…I'm sorry I didn't run away. I knew it was dangerous, but I just… I couldn't bring myself to leave Roman like that."

"You should have," Bosa said gruffly. "But I know that's not the kind of girl you are. Just try to think it through a little more next time. If that wyvern hadn't already been beat to shit, you'd be resurrecting freeze-dried calamari right now."

"Urgh…"

"On that note, where's Romulus?"

"I left him behind the boulder. I thought I should back you up before helping him, since I didn't think you'd be able to beat the wyvern on your own."

"Go thaw him out. I've got a bone to pick with him, but I need to catch my breath first."

"A-are you sure?"

"I can't feel good about beating his ass if he's got hypothermia. Besides, you're the healer. Go heal."

Nabby frowned a little but nodded. "Got it. Just…try not to be too mean? We still have the rest of the gig to go through."

"No promises."

Nabby climbed to her feet and hurried back to the frozen monk. Bosa stared at the waterfall, listening to its cascade before turning her eyes towards her belongings.

Her clothes were soaked, but that wasn't really a problem. While her top was supposed to be machine-wash only, getting dunked in a canyon pond wouldn't ruin it. Her daggers might end up rusting, but they were cheap garbage anyway—she could just buy a new set. Bosa's real concerns were her electronics.

She was always happy to have splurged on the extra features for her headphones but seeing the water-resistance at work told Bosa just how good of an investment that was. The battery light came on and the noise-cancellation was still working, confirming her babies were just fine. The cups were soggy, but a little time in the sun would fix that.

Unfortunately, her phone didn't fare as well. No matter what she tried, the screen wouldn't turn on.

Are you fucking kidding me? This shit again?

Bosa groaned. After the incident with *that priest*, she had sprung for a high-end case, but she was going to have to demand a refund now. It was supposed to safeguard her phone from impacts, water damage, and more—proudly advertised as "the adventurer's choice in phone protection"—but apparently that was a load of bullshit.

It couldn't even survive five minutes in the water. What goddamn adventurers chose this crap?

As for Bosa's phone itself, she'd stick it in a tub of rice when she got home. She was pretty sure that trick didn't work, but that's why she regularly backed up her data on the cloud network. She'd be fine as soon as she replaced her phone.

And as luck would have it, I know who's gonna pay for it.

It was about time Bosa paid him a visit too. She just had one stop beforehand.

She slid over to the wyvern. It somehow looked bigger as a corpse, leaving Bosa in utter disbelief of what she had done. She watched the monster closely for any sign that it might be playing possum, but it wasn't until after she hit it in the head with a rock that she felt comfortable enough to retrieve her daggers.

It took an unsettling amount of effort to dislodge them, but Bosa soon had the blood-soaked weapons back in her hands. She then washed them off in the water before placing them back in the sheath.

Bosa normally wouldn't have bothered. She carried eight of the frigging things—losing two wouldn't matter much. But if this battle were any indicator, she might need them again before the day was done.

The fact that she might end up with even more kills to her name stirred Bosa's anger anew. She stomped off towards the boulder, itching to have her chat with Romulus.

As she approached, Bosa could see Nabby tending to Romulus' frozen half. Rather than use *Hellfire*, Nabby had summoned her dogs so Bergundy could wreathe himself in flame and melt the ice. Romulus' leg was already free, and the hellhound seemed as happy as ever to help his master.

Bosa wouldn't have had a problem tearing Romulus a new one before he was thawed out, but she could hear them talking. Neither he nor Nabby had noticed Bosa, so she decided to slide behind the boulder for a little pre-tearing eavesdropping.

"—which is gonna be a big problem. Those kinds of drones are really expensive," said Romulus. "I'm really hoping my buddy can fix it. I won't be making any money until it's repaired—not to mention how I'm probably gonna lose subscribers during all this downtime."

Bosa wasn't surprised to hear it, but some stupid part of her had hoped he'd have more on this mind than his stream. Yet he wasn't even back on his feet before he started bitching about lost revenue.

He hasn't learned a goddamn thing.

"Well, at least Bosa avenged it," Nabby offered. "She managed to finish off the wyvern on her own, by the way. She didn't even get hurt doing it."

"Dang. She's really something, isn't she? I thought she was a delicate flower, but it turns out she's a fatal power, huh?

Who'd have thought such a cutie could take down a wyvern—and with song magic to boot."

"Actually, she climbed on its head and stabbed it in the eyes. It was kinda gruesome, to be honest."

"Crap and a half. I never would have guessed she'd try something like that. Wish I could have gotten that on film." He sighed. "Man, she's gonna be super pissed when she sees me."

"Well... Yeah. I asked her to go easy on you, but...you know."

"Yeah, I know. No way I'm getting out of this unscathed, right?"

"Right."

"Guess I'd better brace myself then."

Romulus' flippant tone was wearing on Bosa. She moved to reveal herself—

"I just really wanted to see her smile like she used to."

—but paused as he continued speaking.

"I know all that smiling was just part of her schtick, but Bosa always looked like she was having fun while adventuring. I really admired that about her. She was the whole reason I started streaming, so it hurt to see her give up on her old fans—and switch to *porn* of all things."

"I understand, but that was her decision to make," said Nabby. "Bosa doesn't want to be an idol anymore, and you shouldn't try to force her to think otherwise. Maybe she doesn't smile like she used to, but now her smiles are genuine. Even if she's moved to...*inappropriate ventures,* at least she's happy doing them."

"Yeah. You're absolutely right. I wanted to get her excited just by showing all the support my fans gave me, but I ended up just pissing her off. I was hoping it'd inspire her to go back on camera again."

"I wish I could say I didn't warn you."

"You wanna know the worst part? That hundred-dollar donation wasn't even real—I asked one of my mods to do it.

I thought hearing me get a big donation would impress Bosa, but then we messed up the timing and made everything worse. Guess I really do have my head up my ass!" Romulus let off a self-deriding laugh. "Well, no way she's gonna talk to me after this mess. If she was mad before, I can only imagine what awaits me now. I guess it's a good thing my fans won't be able to see what happens, huh?"

"It'll be okay. Bosa can be mean, but she's not unreasonable. I'm sure she'll forgive you if you're sincere with your apology."

...You think too highly of me.

"You think so? Well, it's worth a shot. All I've got to lose is my pride anyway."

"I'm surprised you still have your pride..."

Something popped behind the boulder, and judging from Romulus' relieved sigh, Bosa would assume it was the ice around his arm.

"Ah—I'm free! Thanks again, Nabby."

"You're welcome, but Bergundy's the one you should be thanking."

"Good point. Thanks, Bergundy—you're a good boy!"

The hellhound woofed back. Nabby then sent her familiars home as Romulus tried to knock feeling back into his arm.

"Bosa's still not back?" he asked.

"She said she wanted to take a break by the waterfall before talking to you. She was pretty tired from the fight."

"Ah. Well, I'll save her the effort and go to her. I'd also like to see the wyvern and—"

"Don't bother."

Bosa stepped around the boulder, staring daggers at the monk.

He was startled by her sudden appearance but quickly put on his showman's smile as he tried to stand. However, his leg was still numb from the ice and couldn't bear his weight. He began to fire off his apology before he was even eye level with her.

"Okay, Bosa, I'm really sorry about what happened. I was being stupid and got so excited about that big donation that I wasn't really thinking. And, uh, funny thing about that donation, I was just telling Nabby that—"

Before he could spit out the rest of his excuse, Bosa slapped him as hard as she could.

8

Romulus fell back onto the ground, wide-eyed and holding his cheek.

Nabby gasped. "Bosa?! What the heck are you doing?!"

"You've got your pocket pyre, right? Go burn the wyvern so we can prove we killed it," she growled without looking away from Romulus. "I've got business with this asshole, so stay out of my way."

"What?! I can't leave! You just hit him!"

Bosa ignored her friend as she towered over Romulus. Nabby gaped at her but remained off to the side, ready to step in if Bosa got physical again.

Don't worry—I only wanted one good hit. I'll keep it verbal from here.

"I overheard everything," said Bosa. "I was already gonna skin your ass over that donation shit, but now you're telling me *it was fake?* Man, between that and how you looked away from the wyvern mid-fight, you're reaching levels of dumbfuckery I didn't think were possible. I don't care if you wanted to 'inspire' me or whatever—you almost got Nabby and me killed today."

"H-hey, now hold on. You guys weren't in danger when that happened, so I—"

"If the next words out of your mouth aren't 'but I was still a stupid bastard', I'm gonna spin your head again."

"..."

Pathetic.

"God, did your fucking brain fall out your ears or something? I bet you didn't even think about how scylla are weak to the cold, huh? If it weren't for Nabby, I'd have left your ass on the canyon floor and had someone revive you after the job. But instead, I had to fight—for the first time in my goddamn career, by the way. Even though you promised all we'd have to do is back you up, I had to bloody my hands *as a songstress.*"

"…"

"Fighting that wyvern broke my phone too, and seeing as it's your fault, *you're* gonna replace it. I heard you bitching about getting your camera drone fixed, but I don't care if you have to live on bologna sandwiches for a year—*you will pay for it.*" Bosa crossed her arms and looked down at the pitiful man. "Well? Got anything to say for yourself? I can't wait to hear what you'll pull out of your ass next."

"…"

Romulus remained silent. Without his sunglasses, Bosa could see the shame in his averted eyes. He seemed to be deciding what to say next, but it was hard to tell with someone like him.

Seconds passed without a word. Bosa was about to rip into Romulus again—when he started to laugh.

At himself.

"You know what? I was trying to think of a way to turn this around, but I give up. What can I say—I fucked up, big time."

Bosa furrowed her brow. "You're finally realizing that?"

"No. To be honest, I knew I wasn't in my right mind before this gig even started," he admitted. "I mentioned back at the beginning that my numbers have been dipping, right? That's been really eating at me—enough that I've been doing stupid crap to try and make my streams more exciting. Today wasn't the first time I ignored my teammates and did something reckless."

"You've gotta be kidding me."

"That's awful!" said Nabby. "Adventurers are supposed to work together! You even said so to your fans!"

"I know, but nobody's going to listen to advice like that if everything else I do is boring. Hell, part of the reason I wanted to work with you and Bosa was because I knew it'd make a good stream. Inspiring her to become an idol again or having her yell at me—either way, plenty of people would tune in."

"But that's—"

"Disgusting? Absolutely. But I can't risk losing what success I have. Not a lot of people can live off streaming, so I have to do what I can to grow my channel."

Romulus shook his head. Being cornered by the people he endangered must have finally brought him a moment of clarity, allowing him to see what a selfish idiot he'd become.

But even if he acknowledged his actions, the reasoning behind them killed any chance of Bosa forgiving him.

"You undermined this job... *over your fucking sub count?!*"

Romulus recoiled. If he thought voicing his worries would pardon him, he had another thing coming.

"Finding out you were doing stupid shit because you wanted me to be an idol again was annoying, but this is beyond the pale. You're not just an idiot—you're a goddamn catastrophe waiting to happen."

"I-I know. And I'm really sorry for everything. I've just been so stressed that—"

"Shut up—I don't give a fuck. I'm reporting you to Parti as soon as I get the chance."

The color drained from his face. "W-w-wait, you're gonna *report* me?!"

"You put us in danger because your camera got murked and just admitted to wrecking your past jobs. If that doesn't deserve Parti's attention, I don't know what does."

"But I...! I only did that because—"

"Because you were worried about your fans? Those dickheads are safe at home while we're out here fighting *very real monsters.* It was your choice to cater to them, so don't cry victim now that you've realized that shit will get you banned."

"I... I didn't think..."

"No shit you didn't think. Too bad it took you this long to notice."

"..."

"...Hey, Bosa? Isn't getting him banned a little harsh?" said Nabby.

"You heard what he said—we're not even the first ones he's fucked over. He's not gonna stop unless we get Parti involved."

"Well, maybe, but—"

"No—she's right."

They both looked at Romulus. The man was still seated on the ground, but his cowering had been replaced with a solemn grimace.

"All I've done lately is ruin gigs and piss off the person I idolized most, just so I could *maybe* get a few more subscribers. Karma was bound to catch up to me at some point, so I might as well go out after finally getting to work with Lilibosa."

"Don't try to be a martyr. You're not gonna change my mind," scoffed Bosa.

"Don't worry—I'm done making excuses," he said firmly. "I haven't been able to sleep lately because I've been so fixated on those goddamn subs. I wanted to make a living doing something I love, but it's not worth it if I have to keep putting myself and others in danger. Everything that happened today was my fault, and all I can say is that I'm sorry."

"And why should I care that you feel bad *now?* Are you gonna admit to Parti that you've been disrupting gigs for your viewers? You gonna go find every other adventurer you screwed over and bow and scrape before them too?"

"What would you want me to do?"

"I want you to buy me a new phone before getting the fuck out of my sight. And the only way I can make sure that happens is to tell Parti what you've done."

"Then, please, report me." Romulus carefully rose to his feet. "If that's what it takes to make up for this, then I'll do it. I'm not gonna run away or pretend that's overkill. Frankly, I'm just tired of lying."

"Really. You'll give it all up—just like that?"

"Yeah. I'm clearly not cut out for streaming. If Parti doesn't ban me, I'll switch to full-time adventuring like you did. And if they do, I'll go back to being a security guard. I just can't keep going on like this—I know I'll end up making a mistake I won't be able to fix. I really did love showing all my fans just how much fun adventuring could be, but I've gotta reap what I sow, right?" He paused. "Hey—Bosa?"

"Yeah?"

"Thanks for not pulling any punches. I... I think I needed this."

He smiled widely, beaming with sincere gratitude.

Bosa had to resist the urge to smack that smile off his face.

"...Tch."

It was good that Romulus had finally come clean. Today proved it would take someone dying for the bastard to realize just how much of a menace he'd become, and Bosa didn't feel a lick of sympathy for him.

But, in some wretched sense, she could understand where he was coming from.

She used to be like that too, after all.

For years, Bosa slaved away for the sake of her fans. Her fame transformed her into a two-faced idol that was addicted to the fortunes her singing brought—destroying herself for the sake of a happiness she didn't feel. Soon, all she had left was contempt for herself and others, culminating in the outburst that ruined her career and saved her soul.

A blessing in disguise if I've ever seen one.

But unfortunately for Romulus, he didn't wrong a kind-hearted demon—not solely anyway. He had forced Bosa into a situation that endangered her life and put a stain on her once kill-free record, and she wasn't half as forgiving as Nabby.

Furthermore, while Bosa's scandal didn't directly impact Parti's business, Romulus' attempts at making his gigs "exciting" certainly had. People got hurt, hunting targets had been lost, and who knows how many hours were wasted cleaning up after his antics. Once Parti learned he'd done all that and more for the sake of his Flinch channel, getting banned would be the least of his worries.

But that was the bed he made. It was time for him to sleep in it.

Regardless of what happened to him, the world would keep turning.

"Alright then," said Bosa. "Give me your phone. I'm gonna call Parti right now and let them know what happened."

Romulus chuckled. "Not gonna waste even a second, huh?"

"If I wait until after the job, there's no guarantee you won't delete the recording of today's stream or your previous gigs. As far as I know, you're just trying to bluff your way through this. But if you're telling the truth, it shouldn't matter if I report you now or later."

"Fair enough. Here."

He dug his phone out of his pocket, unlocked the screen, and handed it to Bosa. A photo of Romulus and an elderly woman—probably his grandma—decorated the background. Bosa put it out of sight as she began dialing the number for Parti's help line.

She got six digits in before a gloved hand grabbed her wrist.

"Bosa. You don't actually want to do this, do you?"

Nabby was looking at her with deep concern. But it wasn't out of fear for Romulus or the future of his career.

It was like she was worried about *Bosa*.

"The hell are you saying? Of course I do," said the songstress. "This jackass made me kill a monster—getting him taken down is very much in my interest."

"Maybe, but doesn't it seem like you're rushing things? Why can't we wait until the end of the job to call Parti?"

"What? I just said why. If I don't, he'll erase the evidence of all the shit he's been pulling."

Nabby shook her head. "That's not true anymore. He willingly gave you his phone—*he can't call anyone for help, and he can't stop you from notifying Parti.* That basically guarantees he's telling the truth, so, like you said, it won't matter when you report him."

What the fuck's gotten into you? Why are you trying to buy him time?

"Then what do you care if I do it now? We can't exactly finish the job with him."

"Yes, we can. It wouldn't make sense for him to do anything crazy at this point. His fans aren't watching and disrupting the job again would only incriminate him further. I'd back up everything you'd tell Parti, so if anything, he'd want to do a good job in the hopes we'd go easy on him."

"Sure, but again—*what's your fucking point?* Do you really want to keep working with him?"

"Not particularly, no. I'm not oblivious to how much danger he put us both in. But I'm worried you'll regret this if I let you go through with it. I think you're only pushing to report him right away because you haven't thought this through."

Bosa narrowed her eyes. "Nabby, I love you and all that jazz, but what the hell are you talking about? My mind's made up—there's no way I'd regret getting this shithead axed."

"You don't think there's *the slightest possibility* he can learn from what he's done and become a better person?"

"No. I don't."

"Then why did you ask me to give you a second chance after my first job?"

A knee-jerk retort came to Bosa, but her mouth failed to verbalize it. She lowered Romulus' phone as she was stunned into silence.

"Back then, you said awful things to me. You even intimidated me so I wouldn't say anything to your fans."

Nabby remained composed, but her voice was tight with sadness. "But I forgave you because I could tell that wasn't who you really are. You were stressed, and I just happened to push you over the edge. I had every right to walk away and never speak to you again, but I didn't because I felt you deserved the opportunity to prove you were actually a nice person."

"Well, y-yeah, but that… That was different."

"Not really. The only difference is that *you* were the one asking for forgiveness back then. You're just on the other side of things this time."

"…Are you trying to say that I'm just as bad as him?"

"In a sense. You can't deny how similar the situations are. But despite how Roman admitted to everything, you're set on condemning him right away. You're not giving him a chance to show he can be better than this."

Having Nabby defend him was frustrating enough but being likened to Romulus broke Bosa's temper.

"Why should I?!" she angrily snapped. "Why should I give a fuck about whether or not he can be more than a pile of dogshit?!"

"Because the Bosa I know wouldn't do that. She'd give him a hard time—definitely get back at him somehow—but there's no way she'd be so heartless."

"Then I guess you don't actually know me!"

"I do, and I think that's why you're only doing this because some part of you wants him to go through the same pain you did. Even though I forgave you, your fans didn't, so you want him to lose it all too. You want him to feel what it's like for his fame to cause his downfall."

Bosa winced.

"And if I do?!"

"That's why I'm asking you to think this over! I know you'll regret it if you ruin his life for such a selfish reason!"

Nabby's calm exterior finally crumbled, revealing her for the distressed demon she was. Hands held against her chest, tears began to roll down her cheeks as she pleaded to her friend.

"*You're not a hypocrite, Bosa!* You believe in second chances—you know that people can grow past their mistakes! That's why you're always helping me improve, even when I keep messing up!" she bleated. "But if you truly think Roman shouldn't be allowed to prove he can be better, then that's the same as saying I was wrong for forgiving you and that your fans were right to not even try to hear your side of things!"

Her case made, Nabby broke into sobbing. Just like always, she couldn't bear the weight of her emotions, leaving her a soppy, hiccupping mess.

Across from her, Romulus stood dumbfounded, unsure if he should say something or stay out of it. He was prepared to accept his punishment moments ago, so hearing someone else defend him so late in the argument must have fried his brain.

And as for Bosa, she was speechless after learning how Nabby saw her.

Not as merely a roommate, a friend, or a gutter-minded bitch who can't clean up after herself.

But as someone who empathized with those in need of a fresh start.

"Is that…?"

Is that really me…?

Bosa knew she came off as rude and distasteful to most. And she didn't particularly care. If anything, she enjoyed seeing her behavior filter out those who wouldn't want to know her.

But she couldn't deny that she never tried to be cruel—at least not since she'd stopped being an idol. While she never spared a biting remark, Bosa knew better than to pass judgment like some unfeeling twat. Surface impressions rarely told the whole story and digging a little deeper usually revealed a sensible reason behind any errant behavior.

Yet even though she understood Romulus' situation better than anyone, she still sought to crush him and his career—and for the worst possible reason. She told herself it was because the monk was a danger, but somehow Nabby saw right through her.

More than his misguided efforts to retain his platform, Bosa hated Romulus *because he still had fans that adored him.* So, like a jealous child, she leapt on the chance to take that away from him, not once considering the repercussions.

She didn't think things through at all.

...I really am just as bad as him. Maybe worse.

And that gave Bosa all the more reason to be thankful someone had stopped her.

"...Nabby."

The demon sniveled and wiped her face. "Yeah?"

"Stop crying—you've made your point. I hear you loud and clear."

"Y-you do?"

"You just said you know me. Like hell I'm gonna ignore you after you put on your ugly face."

"Then...does that mean...?"

"Yeah."

Bosa then turned to Romulus. He stiffened up as she glared at him, more afraid of her now than when she had slapped him.

"First things first: this conversation never happened. Understood?"

"I-I don't—"

"*Understood?*"

"...Understood."

"Good." She held his phone up, waving it around. "Let's make one thing clear—*I hate your fucking guts.* You're a piece of shit who's *extremely* lucky Nabby was here."

"..."

"You oughta kiss her feet, you know. She's right—under normal circumstances, I'd have given you a chance to redeem yourself after bitching you out. But everything about you pissed me off so much I jumped straight to the conclusion you'd only get worse from here."

"Well… Maybe that's true," Romulus said dismally. "I put you—*Lilibosa of all people*—in a bad spot for the sake of my stream. That made me realize just how low I'd sunk."

"I hope so. I deserve a helluva lot better than this shitshow."

"So then why—"

"Because that's not the person I want to be." Bosa already knew what he was going to ask. "Nabby's right: I hate being a hypocrite. I said some really nasty shit to her, but she somehow turned the other cheek. I'm not gonna disappoint her and get you banned just to satisfy some petty whim of mine."

Romulus' jaw dropped. He had already consigned himself to Bosa's anger, yet the path to a better future had appeared before him. He looked as if he were about to join Nabby in the blubbering club.

Too bad this miracle has some strings attached.

"But," Bosa continued, "you're not off the hook. You still fucked us over just to boost your clout. All I'm doing is giving you a *chance* to show you're not a lost cause, got it?"

"O-of course! If it'll prove that I'll focus on my gigs and not my sub count, I'll do whatever you think is best!"

"Tch. Well, we'll start by finishing this job."

Romulus was flabbergasted all over again. "I-it's that simple?!"

"Don't act like it's in the bag. We still need to kill three more wyverns, and we've wasted a lot of time here. Besides, just completing the gig isn't going to save you."

"Ah—got it. What are the conditions then?"

"If we manage to meet our piece of the quota without you causing any more problems *and* you reimburse me for my phone, then—and only then—will Nabby and I give you bad reviews for your dumbass behavior instead of reporting you."

"*Just* bad reviews?"

"Yeah. That'll put a nice, permanent scar on your record, but it shouldn't cost you your job or your stream. You can then go back on your word and ruin your next gig for all I care—just stay the fuck away from me."

"I'll do it!" Romulus said without hesitation. "I want nothing more than to continue showing people just how great adventuring is—without lying to my viewers or messing with my gigs! I'll be the best damn monk you've ever worked with if that's what it'll take for you to forgive me."

"Don't get it twisted—I'm never going to forgive you. I'm just giving you a second chance because *I* don't want to feel like shit down the road."

"R-right. Still, thank you, Bosa!"

His arms raised like he was about to hug her, but he managed to correct himself and instead shook her hand. She immediately pulled it back.

"Don't touch me. Go watch over Nabby while she burns the wyvern's corpse."

The demon perked up. "Oh—right! I still need to do that!"

"Yeah, cuz you don't listen to me." Bosa looked at the phone in her hand. "By the way, I'm holding onto this. I wanna be able to call Parti the moment you fuck up again."

"Sure thing, that's fine by me," said Romulus.

"Then tell me your unlock code."

"Oh, it's… Zero six zero eight…"

She tapped it in and was greeted with the photo of him and his grandma again. "Yeah, that worked. What is that, your weight or something?"

"…It's your birthday…"

Bosa's thumb froze in place. A chill ran up her spine.

"…God, you're a creepy motherfucker. Get the hell out of here."

Romulus didn't argue. Red-faced, he shuffled off towards the fallen wyvern.

But Nabby didn't go with him. She waited until Romulus left, then smiled at Bosa with still-wet eyes.

"Thank you," she said.

"I oughta be the one thanking you. How'd you figure out why I was trying to get him canned before I did?"

"You're not the only one with gut feelings. We've worked with some weird people who have done dumb things, but you've never been that hostile before. I'm also pretty sure you wouldn't have said anything to him if you genuinely felt he needed to be fired immediately. I have a phone too, after all, so I realized you only took his because you wanted him to really feel the consequences."

"Jesus, and here I thought I was Sherlock. Seems my dear Watson showed me up this time."

"Hee-hee. My family does specialize in rhetoric, you know!"

"I'm sure Mommy Naberius will be very proud." Bosa then looked at her friend more seriously. "But really, Nabs, *thank you.* I know damn well I wouldn't have been happy taking Romulus down like that. I'm glad you made me second-guess myself."

"You're welcome. And…I'm sorry I brought up some bad memories. I just couldn't think of another way to get my point across…"

"Don't worry about it. Sometimes, we all just need a kick in the ass."

"Right. I know you'd do the same for me."

"Damn straight. What else are partners for?"

Bosa felt herself finally relax. It put her in a playful mood. She held a fist up to Nabby. The demon looked at it curiously for a moment before getting the message. She raised a fist of her own and the two reaffirmed their camaraderie by bumping knuckles.

Grinning from ear to ear, Bosa and Nabby left to finish the gig. They had wyverns to fight and a dumbass monk to support.

9

Unfortunately, they never found another wyvern.

The adventurers spent the rest of their time searching high and low for any signs of their targets, but the wyverns were as scarce as rivers in a desert. Nabby even summoned her dogs again so they could try tracking one down, but time ran out before they got even a whiff of ice breath. The three of them then had to return to the meeting spot with one measly kill.

And, boy, were our buddies peeved.

The other groups had had much better luck. Not only did they manage to take down eleven wyverns—allowing everyone to just meet the job's quota—but one of the teams even found and destroyed the nest. The park rangers were thrilled to be able to hand out their bonus, but the other groups made it clear they weren't going to share it with Bosa's team.

Not that they had any room to argue. They knew they looked like dead weight. Hell, if Bosa pointed out that she was the one who made their single kill, the other groups probably would have assumed her team just happened across a dead wyvern.

But at least they'd get the basic paycheck. The job was finally over and adventurers were leaving the canyon—with the sole exception of Bosa's team.

They still had to figure out what to do with Romulus.

Even Bosa had to admit he took the rest of their job more seriously than anyone else. He was diligent in keeping an eye out for trouble, he was the one who suggested Nabby bring out her dogs, and when they ran into some stray kobolds, he took them down quickly and cleanly. He even pinned one down just so their healer could drain it and mend the single injury he had suffered.

But none of that changed the fact that Romulus had technically failed his second chance. The stipulation was that they needed to fulfill their part of the hunting quota—returning with a single dead wyvern left them woefully short.

"Well, at least I tried, right?" he said with a weak smile. "Guess it just wasn't my destiny to stay an adventurer, ha-ha… Still, thanks for not giving up on me."

Shit. I can't feel good about ending things like this. But…

How the hell was Bosa supposed to justify going back on her conditions without looking like a pussy?

It wasn't his fault they couldn't meet the quota—the wyverns just happened to be elsewhere. And now that he wasn't fixating on his stream, Romulus was able to prove there really was a competent adventurer beneath his idiocy. It didn't feel right to still kick him to the curb, but letting him get away with just bad reviews felt like it'd defeat the whole point of their agreement.

Could I just pretend I'm so mad about missing the quota that I don't feel like reporting him now? Or should I wait and see if he starts begging? Nabby would probably take his side, so then I could act like she convinced me again, though that still seems kinda limp-dicked…

Maybe I'll say I'll only let him off the hook if he changes his phone's code?

The three of them stood in silence as they pondered Romulus' fate. Thankfully, Nabby came to rescue once again.

"Um… We can all agree that it was just bad luck that we didn't find any more wyverns, right?" she said apprehensively.

"Right. If even your dogs couldn't find one, then we must have been in the worst part of the canyon," said Bosa. Romulus didn't object either.

"Then I'm not alone in thinking it would be unfair to still report him?"

"Yup."

"But it also seems kinda wrong for us to not do anything because we might have actually found more wyverns if we didn't have to waste so much time on the first one, correct?"

"Right on the money, Nabs."

"Then…what if we just add another penalty alongside the bad reviews and stuff?"

"Oh, wow! That's a great suggestion!" Bosa acted as though she hadn't considered anything like that. "In fact, why don't we add three more—one for each lost wyvern! How's that sound?"

Romulus rubbed the back of his neck. "Uh… Well, I feel like we're just doing whatever we want now, but since I want to improve my show and can only do that by keeping my job, I'm fine with changing things."

"Perfect! Then my first new condition is that you have to change your phone's unlock code."

"D-does that really bug you that much…?"

"It's better than you using measurements, but not by much."

"Alright… Then what else?"

"Um… Shit. You decide, Nabby."

"Me?!"

"Yeah. Just pretend you're making a wish with a genie."

"*Ugh*…" The demon furrowed her brow in thought. "Uh… M-maybe Roman has to give us both five-star reviews? A-and he has to cite what a good healer I am!"

"Oh, c'mon—that's weak as hell."

"But that's all I've got!"

"Well, I was gonna do that anyway, to be honest," said Romulus. "What's my third punishment?"

Bosa paused in thought for a moment. "…How about you foot the bill for Nabby and I's trip to Stummelschwanz tonight?"

"Huh? I didn't know we were getting dinner there," said Nabby.

"That's because we weren't until just now."

"Y-you want me to spend more money?" Romulus looked at the broken drone in his arms. "But I'm already buying you a new phone, and my drone needs to be fixed so…"

"You either give up some more cash or give up your income entirely. I don't think I need to guess which one you'll pick."

"…Okay, I'll do it. But is it alright if I come along? I might as well get a bite to eat while I'm treating everyone."

"Fine. But you're not allowed to talk or sit next to me. Deal?"

"Deal."

Bosa took out Romulus' phone and pulled up Stummelschwanz's address. She then tossed it back to him.

"We'll be there at seven. Be sure to have the money for my phone ready by then too."

"Will do. Thanks, Bosa."

"Whatever."

"You don't need to worry, Roman; Stummelschwanz is pretty cheap. Bosa just likes the atmosphere there," said Nabby.

"Oh. That's a relief."

"Dumbass." Bosa bonked the demon on the head. "You're supposed to make him sweat. We're already letting him off easy for some borderline illegal shit—don't give him any reason to think he's less than fucked."

"Ow…"

"It's fine, I'll be feeling today's costs for a while. But you're right—I'd rather buy everyone a drink than watch my platform sink. Money's meant to be spent anyway, right?"

"You're almost tolerable when your head's not up your ass. Make sure I don't regret listening to Nabby." Bosa spun around, putting her back to Romulus. "We're out of here. See you at the 'Schwanz."

"Count on it. Later."

With his drone tucked under his arm, Romulus took out his phone and made a call. From what Bosa could hear, he was simultaneously asking a friend to come pick him up while informing them of why his stream went down earlier. It was entirely possible their conversation would lead into a scheme on how to remove any incriminating footage of Romulus' misdeeds, but Bosa was comfortable in walking away and assuming it was just going to be benign chatter.

He was desperate to prove he was serious about mending his ways. I suppose I can trust him to not fuck up right before the finish line.

Bosa and Nabby headed towards the local teleport station. It was in a small shopping center about a mile away from the park ranger's cabin, but Bosa didn't mind the walk. Now that Romulus was gone, she could finally unwind.

And stop straining her voice.

"Mother of fuck, I'm tired," she rasped in a terrible, gravelly tone. "This was supposed to be a simple job, not a lesson in patience."

It took Nabby a moment to realize who was speaking. "What the…? What happened to your voice?!"

"Side effect of *Sonic Boom*. Shit blows out my vocal cords. I didn't want Romulus to hear me like this, so I've been forcing myself to sound normal."

"You should have said something! I could have healed that!"

"It's not a big deal—nothing a few cold drinks can't fix. Though it's half the reason I said he's not allowed to talk to me at Stummelschwanz."

"What's the other half?"

"I just don't wanna talk to him. I've had enough of his shit to last a lifetime."

"Hm. It was pretty cute to see how big of a fan of yours he was though. He still had your birthday as his phone's code."

"Don't remind me." Bosa made an act of shivering. "I mean, it was kinda sweet to hear how I inspired him to start streaming, but I wish he didn't also happen to be a complete tool."

"At least you helped him turn it around before it was too late."

"Don't act like it's not your fault he's still employed."

"Maybe, but you could have ignored me. Are you sure you don't have a soft spot for your old fans?"

It was unusual to hear Nabby tease anyone, but she'd have to try a lot harder if she wanted to catch Bosa off guard. A weak strike like that wouldn't make her bat an eye.

"My *soft spots* are available for viewing during my nightly cam shows. Though I guess I'll have to cancel tonight's stream since I'll be too drunk and hoarse to properly fuck myself."

"I-I didn't mean *those* soft spots…"

"Speaking of fucking, can you text Sera and see if she wants to join us tonight? I still owe her a night of drinking, so I may as well settle all my debts at once."

"I thought you said you didn't want anyone to hear your voice right now."

"I don't want *Romulus* to hear it. Sera's alright."

"Okay. But what about Roman? It'll be kind of rude to add one more to the group without telling him."

"Do I sound like I give a fuck?"

"No, you sound like a baphomet."

That earned a laugh out of Bosa. "Not bad. But don't worry about Romulus. He's not gonna give half a shit about the bill after he sees what I've got in store for him."

"'What you've got in store'? After today, that's kinda scary…"

"Oh, it'll get a rise out of him, that's for damn sure."

"You're not gonna squeeze him for even more money, are you?"

"Nah, I can see when the sponge is dry. You'll find out what I've planned soon enough, so don't bother trying to figure it out."

"You sure do like your mysteries…"

"I *was* an entertainer, you know. Still am, in some respects." Bosa rubbed her throat. "Shit, why the hell am I still talking? I'm not gonna be able to sing for a week at this rate."

"Let me know if it still hurts tomorrow. We'll find a monster so I can heal you."

"Sounds good. But I don't wanna walk in silence—so how about you explain why you didn't tell me you were casting dark magic on our food?"

"I-it wasn't just 'dark magic'! It's dark *healing!*"

"Same difference. Confess your sins, Marquis of Hell."

"*Nngh…*"

Bosa spoke as little as possible while Nabby tried to justify experimenting on their meals. As expected, her rationale was beyond any mortal's understanding, and Bosa had no trouble poking holes in her friend's logic at every turn.

It was the perfect way to punctuate the end of today's nonsense.

Bosa truly was flattered to see just how much she had inspired Romulus. Her idol persona compelled him to leave his day job and become Flinch's number one streaming adventurer, and that was no small accomplishment. He transformed himself from a nobody into a name people would recognize—all because he believed in the joy Bosa brought her fans.

She could respect that.

But she couldn't respect how he fell into the same pitfalls she did.

Recalling how much he doted on his fans—especially all those damn shout-outs—made her blood boil. It was all too reminiscent of how she let managing her fame infect every part of her life, and it drove her to try and bring him down to her level.

But, ironically, the fact that his camera had been smashed may have also saved him. While its destruction was a key factor in forcing Bosa's hand, it also kept his admission of wrongdoing out of the public eye. If Romulus didn't go back on his word, he'd be able to leave all his stupidity in the past.

A kindness Bosa was never offered.

Hopefully letting him keep his secrets will help him maintain his platform longer than I did mine. Last thing I need is to be responsible for the downfall of another internet personality.

It was hard to say if Romulus would really stick to his promises. He didn't have a demonic partner to help keep him in line after all. No matter how much he claimed to have learned his lesson, anyone could fall off the wagon.

So… Maybe Bosa would check in on him at some point in the future.

It would be a delight to see his asshole pucker when she showed up unannounced, and she'd probably have a good time regardless of if he improved. If Romulus managed to stay on the straight and narrow, she could convince him to buy her something as thanks. And if he'd gone back to his old ways, she could guilt trip his ass before blackmailing something expensive out of him.

It certainly wouldn't be an excuse to help him succeed where she had failed.

No way. No how.

Don't even think it for a second.

That just wasn't something the Seafoam Diva would ever do.

Sansei-san
Smoking B

Epilogue — Orc Proprietress

Stummelschwanz is always open.

Not that we operate twenty-four hours a day or something like that. What I mean is that, in all the ten-odd years we've been in business, we haven't had our doors closed for a single night. I work my ass off to make sure we pass every health inspection, and between all our staff, someone's always manning the bar—even on holidays.

Sure, sometimes we don't have *all* our amenities available. Can't run the kitchen if the only body is working the bar, right?

But part of my vision for Stummelschwanz is that its patrons will always feel welcome. We're not the busiest place in Ambarino, so I gotta make sure the people we pull in feel special. Besides, not everyone has somewhere to go on Christmas—why not offer a better alternative to drinking by yourself at home?

Eh, but that's neither here nor there. My point is that you shouldn't be surprised that I'm the only one on staff right now. It might just be another Tuesday, but my guys need days off too, you know. I've only got one group of customers anyways, and they didn't mind me stepping away to cook their meals. And now that everyone's full, I can just relax and mix drinks.

Shit—I haven't even introduced myself. Sorry about that.

The name's Frauke, and I'm the owner of Stummelschwanz. I'm a thirty-seven-year-old orc lady who's taken on a little extra weight ever since I quit adventuring, and while I'm not as spiffy as Felix, you'd be lying if you said I don't look cute as hell in my uniform. Plenty of customers have said they love the way I tie my hair, and I'm so good at my job that I wouldn't fault you for thinking I still had both my arms.

Before you ask: yes, I quit adventuring because of that. A fire elemental killed my party's healer before incinerating my sword arm and half my face. I got a prosthetic, but since the damn thing never felt right, I retired. Always wanted to open a pub, and I think scars look charming on a bartender.

Ah, but I know you're not here for my life's story. Let me set the scene for you before I get on with this narrator bullshit.

Like I said, Stummelschwanz is almost empty right now. The sofa in the back is unoccupied, most of the tables are still shining from last night's cleanup, and nobody's gawking at all the art I hang around here. The radio's playing some rock ballad, but hell if I know who the band is.

That means the only points of interest right now are the four people I'm serving tonight. Despite coming in as a group, half of them sat at the stools while the other half took the table closest to the bar. I only recognized the young scylla, Mikayla, but I've had enough time to learn who the other three are—and get an idea as to why they're split up.

From what I gathered, Mr. Roman Annuler did some dumb shit, so Mikayla blackmailed him into treating everyone to dinner. Ms. Naberius was with her when it happened, but Ms. Sera Sullivan was invited last minute. Normally I'd have some reservations about serving a group under such circumstances, but since nobody looked like they were gonna cause a scene, I let it slide.

Besides, this is Mikayla we're talking about. That little minx went through her own fiasco not too long ago, so I can trust she's got a good reason for this crap.

Speaking of my favorite cephalopod, she's being unusually quiet. Nabby whispered to me it's because Mikayla ruined her voice, but I was surprised she didn't even say hello. She just let Sera do the talking for both of them, and now those two were midway through some kind of drinking game at the table.

That left just Roman and Nabby for me to play with at the bar. The former's sipping on a rum and ginger ale while the latter just started her second beer. Nabby requested that I not serve water alongside her drinks for some reason, but since that's not normal procedure, I had no problem keeping another glass clean.

Now, these two didn't seem particularly close—they left an empty stool between them for god's sake—though I did get the feeling that Nabby was the sort of soft heart that didn't want to leave Roman feeling ostracized. But since I'm getting a little tired seeing all the fun happen behind them, I decided I'd prompt some conversation myself.

I mean, *c'mon.* This epilogue is gonna be pretty shit if no one talks.

"So, what kind of job did you three do today?" I asked as I leaned on the counter.

Roman jumped a little in his seat. I guess he was already accustomed to the silence. "Oh, it was a pretty basic hunting gig at the Graham Canyon. We worked with seven other adventurers to slay a dozen blue wyverns. But…things didn't go smoothly for us."

"What happened?"

"We ended up finding only a single wyvern," said Nabby. "The idea was that each group had to take down four, but we had to waste a lot of time taking down our first one, and then we never found another."

"Well, at least you didn't go back empty-handed, right? Must have been a helluva thing seeing you punch the shit out of a wyvern anyhow."

"About that… I might have attacked it first, but Bosa was the one who actually killed it."

Oh. No wonder she refused to sit next to him.

"She was really unhappy about that too. I knew she wasn't much of a fighter, but I had no idea that was the first time she'd killed a monster," said Nabby.

Roman nodded. "Personally, I was surprised to find out she was carrying daggers. I watched her videos every day, but I never realized she had goodies under her hoodie."

"I feel like she'd make a dirty joke if she heard that. But now that I think about it, wasn't it kinda weird that she asked me to help out with the fighting?"

"What do you mean?"

"She wanted me to bind the wyvern, and I ended up burning that nobunga scrub. In fact, we had a job last month where she made me confront monsters as a means of sharpening my mindset as a healer. Bosa never does any fighting, but she didn't have a problem asking me to do just that."

"Hmm. I heard Bosa use *Sonic Boom,* but does she know any other offensive spells?"

"No, she said that's her only one."

"And you know a ton of dark magic, right?"

"Yeah...?"

"Then, while I see your point, I don't think she was being unreasonable." Roman fiddled with his drink. "She only asked you to do all that out of necessity, since I was our only fighter. I don't understand why she made you fight the monsters in that other job, but you just mentioned it was meant to help you. It sounds like she didn't offer to do any fighting herself because she really doesn't have the skills for it."

"True... She does make a point of never practicing with her daggers. And she was really surprised she actually beat the wyvern."

"Sorry, Nabby, but I think she made the right call given the tools at hand. I wish I could have just done a good enough job so you wouldn't have had to help, though."

"O-oh, it's okay. I'm just peeved that I won't have a good comeback next time Bosa tries to make me battle a monster." Okay, this was a good start. There was still plenty of frost at the bar, but the ice had been broken. This subject was a little iffy, though, so it'd be best if I shifted things.

"Hey, Nabby," I said.

"Yes, Boss?"

"'Boss'?"

"Isn't that what everyone calls you?"

"No, only Mikayla calls me that. I prefer 'Frauke', but she's a smartass."

"Oh. Then what is it, Frauke?"

"What the hell are you?"

"Huh?"

"Pardon my bluntness, but you don't look like any demon I've ever seen," I clarified. "Your ID says you're a displacement from Hell, but I'm just not seeing it."

"Oh... I don't know why, but I wasn't born with a lot of demonic traits." She lifted her bangs. "My horns aren't exceptionally large, and neither are my fangs. I've got the red eyes, but I don't think most people would guess 'demon' unless they saw my legs."

"What's up with your legs?"

"They're all birdy like a crow's."

"Neat. Guess that's why your boots are so big."

"I think I read somewhere that demons' appearances are influenced by the beliefs of mortals," said Roman. "But I have no idea how that'd make you look so human."

"Me neither. Everyone else my age has a bunch of traits that make it obvious they're demons, so I guess I'm just a weirdo..."

"Don't say that. I think your unique appearance among demons *is* your defining trait."

"It is?"

"Yeah. You're also a lot nicer than I expected someone from Hell to be so I'd say you've done a good job distinguishing yourself."

"…Hold on, are you hitting on me?"

Roman nearly spat out his drink. "What?! Of course not! Why would you say that?"

"Bosa warned me that you might try to 'get fresh' with me if I sat near you. I thought that was only a joke, but it's starting to look like she was right."

"Jesus… She really doesn't like me at all, does she?"

"Nope."

"Damn. Well, to be clear, I'm not hitting on you. I've never talked to a demon before, so I just had a few assumptions that you debunked."

"Got it." Nabby's tone made it clear she still had her suspicions, but she didn't kill the conversation. "You know, I hear Lord Lucifer's appearance has changed the most over the years. Even his name has changed. He used to go by Satan and even Hades in the past."

"Really? I thought those were…separate entities, I guess."

"It's kinda tricky. Like you said, a lot of what goes on in Hell is based on what mortals believe. When your stories change over time or adapt for different cultures, it can affect things. For example, if it was generally accepted that Satan and Lucifer were distinct entities, then there would be two demons. But since everyone just uses those names interchangeably, Lord Lucifer is Lord Lucifer."

That sounded like a pain in the ass to me. That would be like having so many people spread a rumor that it gets misinterpreted as the truth.

Demons must have it rough down there.

"My grandad says there was a time when people mixed my family up as the gatekeepers of Hell too," continued Nabby. "It never really went anywhere, but we almost got stuck with guard duty."

"Oof. You've got sympathies for that."

"That's right—you mentioned you used to work as a security guard. Normal jobs seem really boring to me, so I think becoming an adventurer was the right call."

"Hey." I pointed at myself. "Normal job-haver right here."

"Oops! Sorry, Frauke…"

I smirked. "Nah, I'm just giving you a hard time. I'd still be adventuring myself if I hadn't lost my arm." I jabbed my chin at Roman. "Tell us about your old beat while I get everyone another round."

"Ah—I'm okay. I don't mind if they get refills, but I'll stop here."

It would take more than one cocktail to get a man his size tipsy. He must be trying to keep his bill as low as possible.

"Eh, yours are on the house. You're sipping on cheap shit while everyone else is going to town, so I don't mind saving you a few bucks."

"R-really?!" He looked at me like I was an angel. "Then, yes—please! I'd love another!"

Man, just how strong was the vice Mikayla had his balls in?

I slid a fresh mug over to Nabby before topping Roman off. I then grabbed a few more bottles and brought them to Mikayla and Sera's table while Roman recounted his days as an average joe.

"Let's see… I worked grave shift, so I tended to run into weird stuff from time to time. First thing that comes to mind is when I found a CPR dummy in the middle of an empty warehouse. I nearly crapped my pants over that one."

"Really? What's so scary about that?"

Nabby smugly asked her question as she drank from her third beer. Unlike Roman, I could smell her for the featherweight she was. Per Mikayla, I was giving her our lightest stuff, but her cheeks were already a little pink.

It was fascinating to think I might have to cut her off already.

"You know 'grave shift' means overnight work, right? It was like four in the morning and the lights were off in the warehouse," said Roman. "I was just scanning the interior with my flashlight and my snap reaction was that it was a dead body. It was a huge relief to see it was just a dummy, but that passing glance almost gave me a heart attack."

"Hm. I guess that does sound a little spooky."

"Almost as spooky as the time my boss had me check the fields behind our site for a real dead body."

"What?! You're kidding!"

"Wish I wasn't. We got notified that a suspected murderer may have dumped a body nearby, so my boss and I were ordered to go look for it. We didn't find anything, thankfully, but I still wonder what became of that whole shindig."

"No wonder you wanted to quit that job."

"It was alright. Other than dragging me into the dead body search, my boss was a pretty cool guy. He didn't mind if I messed around on my phone during down time, and we had *a lot* of down time on grave shift. The business' receptionist always had candy at his desk too, so that was nice."

"You got any funny stories?"

I asked my question as I plopped down on the open stool between Roman and Nabby. Some people might think it's inappropriate for the bartender to sit with her customers, but not me, and especially not when business was this slow. It's not like I couldn't just circle around and get them more drinks anyways.

Roman seemed a little perplexed by my seating choice but still answered. "Hmm... Only funny thing is when I got called about a snake near the end of my shift. They made it sound dangerous, like it might have even been a monster, but it turned out to just be a little garden snake slithering near the cafeteria. The dumb part is that I would have gotten written up for 'safety violations' if I touched it, so I had to call animal control."

"What they'd say?"

"They told me not to waste their time and hung up."

I laughed. "Figures. What'd you do with the snake?"

"I told the guy who called me that I was gonna keep an eye on it until animal control showed up. The snake then left on its own and I clocked out."

"That's better than I would have done. Good job."

"Thanks, I guess."

"After you quit that job, did you start streaming or adventuring first?" asked Nabby.

Streaming? Didn't Mikayla do something like that before her fiasco?

Another clue towards the mystery of why she was giving a silly boy like Roman the coldest shoulder in history.

"Adventuring," said Roman. "I learned martial arts back when I was in high school, but I had to test if those skills were actually good for fighting monsters before I committed to streaming my gigs. I had to take an online course for basic magic to get certified as a monk, though."

"What made you want to do streaming? I know Bosa was your main inspiration, but I thought she just posted videos instead of doing anything live."

"No one else was streaming adventuring work back then so I thought it was worth a shot. It's still not a popular category on Flinch since it's basically just watching someone do their job, but it's caught on enough that I've got a few competitors now. But I think I'm the only one who can make a living off it."

"Were your fans upset about your stream getting interrupted today?"

"Actually, they were really cool about it. A lot of them were worried and sent me nice messages when I explained what happened on my Squeaker. It was a good reminder of why I work so hard…even if I've been going *too hard* recently."

"You didn't…delete any videos, did you?"

"No, I kept everything from today. I'm sure there are some people who are excited to pass around that footage of Bosa yelling at me, but I know it'd piss her off if I removed it." He paused. "Hey, Nabby? Do you mind if I ask you a question about Bosa?"

"Go ahead."

"Do you know if her new 'ventures' have been working out at all?"

Nabby frowned. "I try not to listen when she talks about that stuff, but I heard it hasn't been going well. She apparently gets more people talking smack in her chat than actually watching her…*show*."

"Damn, that's a shame. I figured as much since she only has one other subscriber, but I still wanted to ask."

My ears perked up. Bullying my customers wasn't really my thing, but Roman's little slip of the tongue was too good to pass up.

I grinned sadistically at the poor fool.

"'One other subscriber'?" I asked. "So she's only got two?"

"Yeah. You'd think Lilibosa's name alone would pull in more, but I guess it's a hard business out there."

"Who's her first subscriber?"

"Huh?"

"You just said *'one other'*. That tells me you know who it is. Spill the beans—I wanna know what ugly bastard is drooling over the sight of my precious Mikayla demeaning herself."

Roman looked like someone just reamed him with a broomstick. "U-u-um… I mean… I-I don't *really*—"

"Yeah, you do. Tell me or I'm charging double for all this."

"W-wait! Um…it's… It's Nabby!"

The demon nearly dropped her beer. "What?! Hell no! I would never waste my money on something so gross!"

"She's right. Why would she pay for a subscription when she can just open Mikayla's door and watch for free?"

"That's not what I mean!"

"U-um…" Roman was sweating harder than ever. "Oh! I think you m-misheard me! I said she 'got another subscriber'! I knew she had one, so it made me happy to hear her side business was growing!"

"Uh huh. And how'd you find that out?"

"I, uh…checked her page?"

"You were just popping into her cam show to check her subscriber count?"

"Y-yes."

"Not at all because you're still horny for some idol you fawned over?"

"Y…yes…?"

Jesus, this guy was one good tap from cracking like an egg. I thought Mikayla had put some real pressure on him, but he probably would have buckled under a passing glare. It was hard to believe such a milquetoast was able to drum up his own fanbase, but, then again, maybe that was his appeal.

Either way, I'd had my fun. I decided to pretend like he had pulled to wool over my eyes.

"Alright then. You must have been a pretty dedicated fan to check on her like that. You should consider vouching for her sometime."

"A-ah, I can't," he said. "My advertisers want me to avoid explicit content as much as possible."

"Do they pay you or something?" asked Nabby.

"Yeah. It's not a stretch to say they're the main reason I can support myself now."

"Just adventuring earns enough money for me and Bosa. You can't do the same?"

"I live alone, so I need to supplement my income somehow. I had to borrow money from my parents to get my streaming equipment when I started, and I only finished paying them back a couple months ago."

"Why not get a roommate?"

"No space. My apartment only has one bedroom."

"So does ours. I just sleep on the couch."

"Nabby, I hope you're not paying half the rent for just that…"

"I'm not. Bosa lets me cook and clean to keep my costs down."

"I don't think that's any better…"

"Well, I'm a pretty good cook, so I think it's great that I can save a little money by making tasty food."

I nodded in agreement. "Hell yeah—nothing makes me happier than filling bellies with good food. What's your favorite dish, Chef Nabby?"

"To eat or cook?"

"Both."

"Hamburgers are my favorite to eat by far, but I like making things like ravioli and gnocchi the best. It's a lot of fun to make the pasta, and I have my own signature recipes for sauce and meatballs too!"

"Goddamn, you go the whole nine yards. Let me know if you ever wanna make some extra cash cooking for Stummelschwanz."

"I'll keep that in mind next time Bosa and I can't seem to find a job. I don't really want to work as anything besides a healer, but I'd rather do that then resort to making another eldritch casserole because we can't afford groceries."

"What the hell is an 'eldritch casserole'?"

"It was something I made from sauce packets and old hot dog buns. Bosa gave it a mean name, but it didn't taste that bad."

"I'm simultaneously fascinated and horrified. Be sure to call me if things ever get that bad again."

"Will do." Nabby took another pull from her beer. "Could I get another one, please?"

"Sorry, sweety, but I'm cutting you off."

"What? But I feel fine!"

"You're as rosy as a sunrise and rocking like a ship on the sea. Besides, think of poor Roman's wallet."

"But I'm not drunk…"

"Nabby, I'm here to help people relax, not get wasted. I've owned this place long enough to know when someone's at their limit and you're one bottle away from letting Mikayla do whatever she wants to you. I'm impressed by how much of a lightweight you are, but the most you're getting out of me is a diet cola."

"Aww…"

I turned to Roman. "How about you? Care for another?"

"No, thank you. I've got work tomorrow so I can't drink too much."

"Smart man." That piqued my memory. "Oh yeah—here. Mikayla told me to give this to you if I decided you were alright."

I pulled an unmarked envelope out of my vest and handed it to him. He looked at it curiously.

"Bosa said that?"

"Well, to be specific, Sera did since Mikayla's not talking for whatever reason. But as she didn't shoot the messenger, I figured Sera didn't just make that up."

"Hmm…"

"Well, what are you waiting for? Open it."

"I'm not sure I want to. It's probably a harsh letter. Or maybe some kind of prank."

"I doubt it. If that were the case, wouldn't she have asked me to give it to you in case you were an asshat?"

"True. Still…"

"Tell you what: if it *is* something mean, I'll give Mikayla an earful. How's that sound?"

"I think that'd just put me in even hotter water. But… Fine. Let's see what Bosa's got for me…"

Roman slipped a finger under the fold and tore the envelope open. He then pulled out its contents—a single photograph.

From how wide his eyes went, it must have been one hell of a picture.

"This is…! This is one of the photos from Bosa's last shoot—back when she was still the Seafoam Diva! Sh-she even autographed it for me!"

"No shit? Let me see."

He was reluctant to hand it off so soon, but I plucked the photo out of Roman's hand.

It showed Mikayla in a bikini, lounging in the surf on a scenic beach. She was smiling coyly at the camera, and a couple of her tentacles were bent into the shape of a heart. There was a special message for Roman written in black marker across the sky.

"To Roman:
Don't ever forget why you still have a job.
XOXO,
Lilibosa"

Not exactly the sweet poetry I expected, but its recipient seemed touched enough. I passed the photograph to Nabby and went to ask Roman about the message, but he had spun around to look at Mikayla.

The scylla side-eyed him for a moment before irritably looking back. Without the slightest change in her expression, she flipped Roman off before returning to her game with Sera.

To his credit, Roman just laughed before leaning on the bar again.

"You know, I guess I don't mind treating everyone now," he said.

"You're kidding me. One pin-up shot and you're okay with footing the bill? You really are a horny bastard."

"Wait, I didn't mean it like— N-Nabby! Please be careful with that!"

Nabby's face was contorting with the beginnings of tears, and she held the photo in a trembling hand. Roman quickly snatched it back before she caused any damage.

"Bosa's so nice… I'm really, *really* lucky to have her as a friend…" the demon blubbered. "E-even now, she still cares about her fans so much!"

I raised an eyebrow. "I'm not sure about that one. It looked more like a thinly veiled threat to me."

"No, it's a good message. It really means a lot to me."

Now Roman was gushing about the autograph too. I thought he just liked the picture, but I guess whatever happened between him and Mikayla must have had more weight than I thought.

Whatever—I give up. Those kids can keep their drama.

I was more concerned with getting Nabby to shut up. I never liked hearing anyone cry, and her tiddly ass seemed about ready to bust open the dams. I'd have to go back on my word a bit, but I had a good idea on how to keep her from wailing.

"Hey, Nabby? Can demons die?"

Mid-sniffle, she looked at me with confusion. "Huh? Why do you ask?"

"Aren't you guys immortal? I was just thinking that having an invincible healer is actually really clever."

"Oh, well, it's not like that. We're immortal, but not invulnerable. I can get hurt and die, and I'll end up back in Hell if that happens."

"Wait, you just go back to Hell? No other repercussions?"

"Oh, there's plenty—especially for members of the Goetia. It's considered a massive embarrassment to die in the mortal realm, and the imps are always eager to spread the news when someone shames their house."

"Ah. No wonder you didn't just bite it so you could go home."

"Yeah. I don't think I'd ever hear the end of it from my mom…"

"What happens if you die in Hell?"

"Same thing. You just end up in the inferno with all the dead mortals."

"No Super Hell waiting beneath the Underworld?"

"Not that I'm aware of."

"Hm. Maybe only the real demons know about Super Hell."

Nabby scowled. "Hey! I'm a real demon!"

"You sure? You definitely don't look like one, and there's no way you'd cry so easily if you were."

"I am *so* a demon! And I don't have to prove it to you!"

"Fair enough. But I'll let you have another beer if you *do* prove it."

That got the gears in her head turning. Nabby sneered at me with confidence.

"Deal! I want a little slice of lime with it too!"

"I'll give you two. But you're not getting anything until I see some bird feet."

"Then look and be amazed! Behold the truth of my form as a member of the Goetia!"

Hopefully Mikayla could forgive me for pushing her friend over the edge. One more light beer probably wouldn't get Nabby *too* drunk, but who knows what she'd do after they left.

On second thought, scratch that. Maybe I should be praying for Nabby's forgiveness. Who knows what *Mikayla* would do once she noticed the demon was schnockered...

Nabby fumbled a bit with her laces but soon had one of her boots tugged off. She then tossed it aside like a theater prop before rolling up her leggings and pulling her sock off.

Sure enough, her legs looked just like a crow's. Nabby proudly held up her foot, wiggling her trimmed talons.

"There!" she barked. "Now you can't deny I'm a demon!"

I chuckled. "Guess not. Orrr...maybe you're just a wingless harpy."

"No way! All members of House Naberius have crow-like features! You can look that up on the internet!"

"Oh yeah? Then what's the difference between a demon's birdy feet and a harpy's?"

"Allow me to explain!"

I smiled wider as Mikayla's best bud drunkenly educated me on what made her different. I didn't give two shits about the nuances, but it was better than hearing her cry.

She forgot all about getting that extra beer by the end anyhow.

And I think that's where we'll stop. I'm getting a little tired of this whole narrator schtick, and since my customers will be on their way out soon, we might as well close here.

What is it Felix says right about now? "I'm grateful for your patronage" or some crap? I mean, don't get me wrong, I really am thankful you chose to join us tonight. I'm just not as stuffy as my husband.

…Huh? You didn't know Felix and I are married? I guess I forgot to mention it, but I can't believe that jerk never said anything. We've been together longer than Stummelschwanz has been open, and you'd think he'd take every opportunity to brag about having a wife as cute as me.

Ah well. That's the guy I love, you know? I wouldn't trade him for anyone in the world.

Anyways, I hope you'll stop by again. Like I said, we're always open, and if you're lucky, I'll be working the bar again. If not, then you can enjoy Felix, or maybe even my lovely protégé, Casimir. He's a hoot too.

Until then, take care. I'll see you around.

Thank you
for reading!!

Afterword

For a long time, I couldn't beat Marathon Mode in Tetris DS. I'd get to the higher levels, then make some mistake that would domino into failure. But thanks to being a fourteen-year-old who couldn't afford more than three video games a year, I kept at it—hungry to see whatever sort of prize was waiting for me. Eventually, I learned how to endure those high speeds, and I remember roaring with exhilaration as I finally got to see those goddamn credits.

But what I found most interesting about that victory was that I never failed to clear Marathon Mode ever again. It was like I had evolved as a creature, and the fast-paced line-clearing that once thwarted me became a walk in the park. My thumbs were swift warriors where matters of block arrangement were concerned, with some burgeoning lobe of my brain acting as their diligent coordinator. My spirit had ascended, and I spent months witnessing the infamous Tetris effect as the reptilian part of my mind tirelessly arranged every square shape in sight into perfect columns long after I had stopped playing. And even now—years after I felt that Tetris fever—I'm still able to stack combos at max speed without any trouble. I even got first place in my first game of Tetris 99, and the fact that I did so in front of a friend after we powered on the game to "see what it's like" has cemented that moment as the coolest I will ever be in life.

So, why am I bragging about this shit—especially when there are Tetris gods out there who can squash me before I clear a single line? Well, first off, I'm not trying to brag (maybe a little), I just wanted to illustrate how far I've come with that silly puzzle game. More to the point, isn't it interesting how someone can fail to realize they're improving until they reach some arbitrary goalpost? If you asked me to chart my skill's progress, I would have given you a flat line—

it wasn't until after I beat Marathon Mode that was I able to perceive my own growth. But once that dragon was slain, I could finally see all the little breakthroughs I had made along the way. Better setups, improved pattern recognition, the ability to think a few pieces ahead—those were all things I learned on the path to overcoming Marathon Mode.

What I'm trying to say is that it's important to appreciate the little lessons you'll learn on the path to mastering anything. During my first novel, I didn't know what the fuck an em dash was (it's this little guy here, "—") or have a real understanding of when it was appropriate to slip in some exposition, but in making those mistakes and reflecting on them, I feel I have been able to better gauge my improvements. Same with my recent dances with fighting games: I'm still a panicky klutz but giving myself a little pat on the back whenever I successfully anti-air my opponent— even if it's then followed up by me dying to a raw Super move—helps me see the experience I'm gaining, not just the level-ups.

Basically, if you feel like you're stagnating, try to focus on everything you're doing right instead of the hurdles you're failing to surmount. It's entirely possible it's your perspective that's keeping you from your goals.

Thank you very much for reading *Demon Healer Naberius: Volume Two*. Honestly, I didn't plan to release this so soon after *Volume One*, but I just had so much fun writing Nabby and Bosa's antics that I couldn't help myself. I tried to play around more with the characters and themes in this volume, and it's my hope that you had a good time as well. The kind reception the first volume received has put a flame in my heart, and it is my sincerest wish that you'll join me for our girls' next round of adventures.

Once again, a hearty shoutout to my man Thanaphon Kaewmuangmun (aka @Tos_tantan on Twitter) for the beautiful art. He continues to blow my mind, as it feels less like I'm commissioning an artist and more like I've hired a mystical brain wizard to show me the best versions of characters I can just faintly imagine. I can't thank him enough for the wonderful designs (my favorite being Roman's), and it continues to be a pleasure to work with him. Please consider him for your own artistic needs.

If you'd like to hear more from me or see photos of my dogs, you can follow my Twitter, @varnicrast, or check out my equally creatively named website, varnicrast.com. The latter isn't half as active since I ran out of chapters from my first novel to post, but you can still hit it up for irregular content updates or my old articles.

Thanks again, dear reader. As of this writing, the world is still under the wet blanket of a global pandemic, so I hope my story has brought you some joy. Treat yourself with dignity and affection, and I'll see you next time.

Love,
Peter Varnicrast

About the Author

Peter Varnicrast is the luckiest human alive. A twenty-eight-year-old Californian who thought his love for writing was just a passing fancy, he now seeks to fill the world with his oddball stories. Focusing on traditional and light novels, he enjoys writing fantasy settings flavored with comedy and mythology.

Varnicrast enjoys the fine life of an aspirant, writing freely in his spare time. He is surrounded by a family of weirdos who treat the writer far better than he deserves and shares a room with two lovely dogs. Rumor has it he had his heart broken by the poor online infrastructure of his favorite fighting game, but you didn't hear it from me.

Made in the USA
Las Vegas, NV
20 July 2021

26746045R10144